JOURNEY INTO SLAVERY

by

JULIETTE NEVILLE

Published by **CHIMERA**

ISBN 9781780806648

CHAPTER 1
A Lesson in Obedience

Elizabeth Ashton, standing stiffly to attention in front of the wooden desk, was trying, unsuccessfully, to control the delicious trembling in her limbs. The large, airy room was quiet, although the muted drone of insects and faint sounds from the market filtered through the woven blinds. Despite the tiled floor and white painted walls, the heat of the West African sun made the atmosphere heavy and sticky, even this late in the afternoon. She didn't move because Sir Roger had forbidden it and she knew better than to disobey.

Keeping her eyes firmly on the wall behind the desk, Elizabeth was only too aware of the other people in the room. As usual, Leila and Mebele were standing quietly by the tall double doors leading back into the main courtyard of the villa. She shivered again as she remembered the maidservants' clever fingers working on her body, only too aware of the thrilling combination of pain and pleasure that the two expert tormentors would be wringing from her body in a few short minutes.

Sir Roger looked up and smiled grimly. 'Well, my dear, quite a catalogue of errors it seems. Lateness, rudeness, your abrupt and noisy departure from the governor's reception last night... what explanation do you wish to offer me this time?' He stared across the desk at the slim, fair-haired young woman standing before him. His eyes feasted on the golden skin of her bare shoulders, before moving to dwell on the proud upper swell of her breasts. The low-cut gown Elizabeth was wearing revealed her upper body boldly to his gaze. Her long blonde hair was swept back from her face with a jewelled clasp before cascading straight down her back, almost to her waist.

The rest of Elizabeth's well-formed figure was decently concealed from his gaze by the white, floor-length gown. Beneath its soft folds, he could just see the toes of her silk shoes peeping out.

Sir Roger Stanley brushed his tongue over suddenly dry lips. Only two days ago he had been studying his young ward... but in very different circumstances. On that occasion, as so often in the past three months, she had been naked and bent, spread-legged, over a polished mahogany bar, writhing and moaning in ecstasy as he lashed her buttocks with a thin, whippy cane. Sir Roger could feel his erection hardening within the tight confines of his britches as images of those sessions pounded in his imagination.

'I'm sorry if I have offended you, sir.'

'I am afraid that sorrow is not enough, my dear. I fear you will have to atone for your transgressions in the usual way.' Sir Roger stood, a hot, cruel excitement thickening his voice. 'You know only too well what awaits you. Do you have anything further to say to me?' Elizabeth watched his tongue slowly moistening his lips once again as their shared excitement grew.

'Have mercy, sir, have mercy! I did not mean to offend you again.' The plea was not even half-hearted, but Elizabeth felt compelled to play the charade out to its inevitable conclusion.

After a number of less than discreet affairs, and glad to flee the stifling constraints of 1830s London, Elizabeth had revelled in the hazards of sea travel and the grand adventure of travelling to join her guardian's household in this remote trading centre of the so-called 'Gold Coast', some six months before. Elizabeth knew nothing of Africa, or the dark trade in human lives that had establish the settlements along the hot, fever-ridden coast. All she knew was that the crowded and damp streets of London had been replaced by the smells and sounds of a wonderful and strange land. For the first month she was prostrate with the heat and effects of the strange food. But gradually she learned the gentler, easier rhythms of colonial life. The midday rest, numerous silent servants to fetch and carry at a whim, the sounds, colours and smells of the teeming noisy streets outside the walls of Sir Roger's villa, soon became routine. Elizabeth Ashton began to enjoy her new life as a lady of ease and leisure.

Accra vied with Lagos, some three hundred miles along the coast on the Niger delta as the centre of the gold and slave trade. From there white men could travel inland, using the great rivers to make trading links with the vast unexplored lands of the interior. Jewels, gold and ivory provided rich pickings for those willing to brave the heat, disease and the every present threat of tribal violence. The human trade flourished too, one aspect of Sir Roger's business that he carefully concealed from his ward's inquisitive gaze.

Cosseted in the luxury of their wealth and power, beneath the rigid social round of the colonists ran another darker strand of sexual intrigue and perverse pleasures. Aware of Elizabeth's passionate nature, her guardian had wasted no time in drawing her carefully and delicately into that darker world, a world that Sir Roger and his friends enjoyed in secret behind their oh-so-respectable façade.

Firm discipline and insistence on physical punishment for even the most minor offences was very much what Elizabeth expected. A wilful child, she was well used to being beaten for her various lapses, particularly sexual, when her parents had been alive. But it was the way in which Sir Roger used the combination of punishment and sexual stimulation that had acted like a drug on her body. Each time, he and his friends had drawn her deeper into their web, each time she ended up welcoming the experiences they forced upon her.

The small, mixed European community kept within their own area of the expanding settlement. When Arab merchants and slavers had been driven out in a short and bloody struggle some years before, one or two bolder spirits, such as Sir Roger, had taken over the ancient stone buildings that had been part of their old slaving quarter. Here, all the houses and villas were walled and fortified against possible native unrest, each one looking inward and offering only blank walls to the narrow maze of streets. Inside, the closed courtyards and airy rooms were copied from the Moorish houses of North Africa. Safe and powerful within their small community and with an abundant supply of young native girls to add to the limited numbers of white women, Sir Roger and his friends enjoyed the pleasures of the flesh to the full.

Elizabeth shivered, goose bumps prickling her arms, remembering the useless struggles when he and his friends had first involved other women in those punishment sessions. Restrained, and under the fiery attentions of a bamboo cane, she learned quickly about the peaks of pleasure one woman could arouse in another. She knew, with a further shiver of delicious anticipation, that both Leila and Mebele would once again take their part in whatever Sir Roger planned for her on this occasion.

Elizabeth's reverie was broken as Sir Roger lifted his hand, holding her chin still as he looked into her clear, blue eyes. 'This is not the place for what must soon befall you,' he said softly, lifting her head. 'Leila and Mebele will prepare you...'

He beckoned the two maidservants forward. Mebele was local, tall and muscular, her black skin polished and gleaming against her thin cotton robes. Leila was an Arab, brought up in the household of a Portuguese trader; she had joined Sir Roger's staff only a few months ago. Dark-haired with a smooth, olive skin, her figure was full and voluptuous. To visitors they seemed demure and shy, the perfect servants. But Elizabeth knew the truth behind those modest robes and lowered eyes. Naked beneath their thin cotton robes, both would be wet and eager with anticipation already. 'Take her to the Punishment Room and prepare her,' he ordered quietly. 'Use the bar... but do not begin until I arrive.'

Elizabeth stumbled slightly as the two maids gripped her arms from behind, hurrying to carry out their master's bidding. She was about to add something when Sir Roger raised his hand, able to stop her speaking with a gesture. 'Silence now, go with them as I have ordered.'

The two maids led her, unresisting, along the tiled hallway, across the paved courtyard with its heavy scents of lemon and sweet herbs and down a short flight of marble stairs. At the end of the corridor, beyond another pair of slatted double doors, lay the Punishment Room. In the doorway Leila lifted one hand, delicately stroking Elizabeth's shoulder, before running her fingers downwards across the swell of her left breast. Mebele smiled, watching Elizabeth shiver and turn away from the deliberately intimate caress.

The room was quite plain. White walls, large grilled openings high up along two sides and a floor of polished wood. To one side sat the squat, black whipping frame, with its curved leather top and footrests, laced with a network of straps and buckles. Long ropes dangled from the beamed roof, most now held back against the wall, but each one ending in its own padded cuff.

Elizabeth's eyes were drawn to the centre of the room. Her heart began racing as she took in the familiar sight of the strong, adjustable uprights bridged by the three-foot long, polished mahogany bar. She winced as she felt the strong fingers of the two maids digging into her arms, forcing her further into the room.

The two servants began to strip her naked. Elizabeth shuddered, despite her determination not to reveal her secret enjoyment in being forced to obey Sir Roger's demands in this way. She could feel their fingers, like ants creeping over her body, untying and loosening the laces of her gown. Taking every opportunity to probe and fondle her body, the maids removed her drawers to leave her clad only in white silk stockings, and the shaped and boned corset that nipped her waist and cupped the fullness of her breasts.

Leila reached forward, stroking the blonde fur peeping below the lower point of the corset. Stripped of her garments, there was little to conceal the plump lips of her labia and the deep split of her sex from the maid's knowing touch. Elizabeth tried clenching her legs together, but she knew that Leila could feel her wetness, the moisture of her arousal gleaming on those busy fingers. Shivering in delight at Leila's touch Elizabeth gave up pretending to resist. She let her knees part slightly so the fingers could move down and inwards, stroking the sensitive lips and delicately easing into the moist heat

4

between them.

Not to be left out, Mebele caressed the curves held outwards so firmly by Elizabeth's corset. Lifting each breast in turn, she eased them in the stiff cups, uncovering the wide pink aureoles and nipples for her attentions. Only then did she concentrate on stroking and rolling the two sensitive pleasure peaks between finger and thumb, pressing more firmly as each one swelled and hardened.

Elizabeth closed her eyes, face upturned as though denying her body's clear responses to the double stimulation she was feeling. Giggling at the success of their ministrations, the maids hurried to complete their work, untying the ribbons holding her stockings before rolling them down to reveal long, shapely legs and trim ankles.

Together, they untied the laces holding their young mistress's corset in place. Elizabeth gasped in sudden relief as they removed the boned fabric, wriggling in sudden freedom as she stood before the two maids, her smooth, golden skin contrasting with the maids' darker colouring.

Elizabeth was breathing fast and hard, panting from a mixture of stimulation and fear. She knew the maids were enjoying the signs of her obvious arousal; the rigid peaks of her nipples and the dew of moisture gleaming on the tops of her thighs providing them with clear evidence of her own excitement.

'Across the bar... please, mistress,' Leila said, her hand resting on the thick, polished rod. As Elizabeth stepped forward and the two maids pressed her against the wooden bar, pushing her hips hard against its smooth surface. 'Astride please, missy, you been here plenty times now so you know how you must stand...' Mebele scolded. Reluctantly, Elizabeth moved her legs apart, pushing her feet across the boards until each was braced hard against a wooden side pillar. The wide splay of her thighs lowered her body slightly so she could feel the bar running across the top of her hips, an insistent pressure just above the firm thrust of her mound.

With her legs apart, the two maids lost no time in buckling leather cuffs tightly round each ankle, securing them to the base of each upright. As the cuffs were cinched tight, Elizabeth automatically tugged and pulled at her restraints. Just as she remembered, however she struggled, she was now powerless to bring her legs together or shield the tender fork of her body from their attentions. She dropped her hands but, before she could take a balancing grip on the crossbar, the girls seized a wrist apiece to fasten another soft leather cuff round each one.

Securely cuffed, the maids released her hands. Elizabeth seized the bar, grateful for the extra support, even for a few more moments. Her breasts jiggled as she panted, excited and aroused by what was still to come.

Sir Roger walked quietly into the chamber. Now clad only in an unbuttoned pair of tight doeskin britches, his muscular torso matted with dark hair. He had removed his formal wig to reveal a scalp covered in short, black hair. The mass of pink scars, and the puckered lines of inexpertly mended tissue on his chest and arms, bore witness to his earlier career as a soldier, not to mention the many fights and duels he had come through, more or less successfully, in the course of a turbulent and violent life.

He studied his ward's figure, enjoying the straddled pose, erotic curve of her back and the delightful swell of her bottom as she held herself against the bar. He thought for a few moments. 'Apart this time, I think,' came the quiet command.

The maids each tied a rope to one of Elizabeth's wrist cuffs before leading it back to a brass ring set in the white painted stone wall. Elizabeth, who was craning round at the sound of her guardian's voice, gasped in surprise as her hands were jerked off the bar, her arms pulled remorselessly forward. Soon her upper body was being bent down over the wooden bar, her arms reaching forward as though trying to touch the wall. Eventually the maids stopped pulling, leaving Elizabeth's arms outstretched, her torso held taut and parallel with the floor.

'A few inches more, if you please,' came the quiet command. Both maids hauled the ropes again. Elizabeth gave a low, wailing groan as her whole torso was stretched even further by their unrelenting pull. Sir Roger nodded in satisfaction, watching carefully as the ropes were made fast. Now only Elizabeth's head, and the hanging globes of her breasts, were free to move.

'Good day, Elizabeth, God, what an attractive picture you make!'

She started wildly, heaving at the binding ropes in sudden frenzy at the familiar voice from behind her. Her eyes widened in shame and horror as her latest lover, Richard Elford, strolled up to her and gently began to stroke the soft curve of her raised and exposed buttocks.

'Well, my dear, since I was due to discuss a business matter with Sir Roger anyway... He thought it might prove amusing if I joined him to play a part in your chastisement...'

CHAPTER 2
Gentlemen's Pleasures

'A revealing sight, my friend,' Richard continued as he studied the splayed figure bent over the mahogany bar. 'When we had our little dalliances over these past weeks, I had absolutely no idea of dear Elizabeth's other talents.'

'You monster!' wailed Elizabeth, the hurt of rejection and betrayal creating more anguish than any caning ever could. 'How dare you betray me in such fashion? I thought you felt something for me, sir.'

'Oh I do, believe me. I felt for you most deeply. You helped to pass the long and tedious afternoons most admirably.' He reached beneath her body and teased a gently swaying globe. 'These pretty titties gave us both so much enjoyment. I'm pleased to find them still as hard and welcoming as when first we met at that party at the governor's house.' He laughed, giving her nipple a hard twist. Elizabeth cried out at the sudden stab of pain. 'She is unmarked, I see. Am I in time for her punishment then, Sir Roger?'

'You are very punctual, Richard.' He turned back to the maids. 'Leila, please fetch me a suitable cane, one of the thinner bamboo's, I think, on this occasion... oh yes, and bring that little toy you like so much. Mebele, attend to our guest and see that he is... satisfied.'

Sir Roger raised a finger. 'Before you begin,' he paused, 'I'm sure neither of you will wish to be hindered by those garments of yours as you attend to your duties.' Sir Roger's comment was an order, not a request.

They immediately stripped off their concealing dresses. As Elizabeth had known, neither of them was wearing anything beneath the cheap white cotton. Leila's body was the more voluptuous, with strong curves and large breasts whilst her ample hips and buttocks swelled invitingly from a trim waist. Unlike Mebele, the deep cleft of her sex was only too obvious, smooth and completely free of hair, an enterprising brothel keeper having plucked her sex bare.

In contrast, Mebele was tall with a hard-muscled, lithe figure and long legs. Her skin was a lustrous black apart from the startling pink of her palms, the soles of her feet and the soft folds of her sex. Her breasts stood out as firm, sharp cones, topped with nipples that jutted outwards as long, hard stubs. The mound of her sex was covered with a thicket of curly black hair.

Mebele fetched a small padded stool and placed it next to Richard Elford as he continued teasing Elizabeth's breasts. 'May I assist you to be more comfortable, sir?' Accepting his nod as unspoken agreement, she knelt, unlacing the fastening of his doeskin britches and pulling his shirt free as she did so. Within a few moments she had bared him to the waist and was stroking his lean, muscled torso. 'May I assist you with your boots now, sir?'

Richard nodded to the naked maidservant once again, this time sitting back on the stool and allowing Mebele to try and heave the first of his tight-fitting riding boots free. Declining to offer any assistance, both men enjoyed the sight of Mebele's breasts swinging wildly with the force of her exertions. Finally, just as the young rake had planned, Mebele was forced to straddle his leg, facing his foot, to get the leverage she needed. He delayed matters further by slipping his hand between her thighs, his fingers probing into the wetness of her sex so that she shuddered in excitement.

Tiring of this he leant back, hands holding the sides of the stool. 'Come on, how long does it take to remove a boot, damn you?' With that he raised his other leg, planting the leather sole squarely on Mebele's bottom. 'Now haul, my hot little bitch!' His thrust catapulted Mebele, and the boot, into a flailing heap on the floor.

The two men roared with laughter as Mebele scrambled back to her feet, the dusty imprint of his sole clearly visible against her gleaming black skin. 'Come on, come on, blast your eyes! That's only one. Expect me to fuck you with one boot on, eh?' Mebele joined the horseplay, deliberately widened her stance as she straddled the other leg, waiting for him to fondle her again.

This time she jerked, almost losing her grip on the boot, as he wriggled his stockinged foot between the cheeks of her bottom, making her jump as the harsh fabric scraped across her sensitive skin. Then, as before, he lifted his foot, pressing hard and shooting the maid across the polished floorboards. Eager to complete her task, Mebele hurried back to remove the rest of Lord Richard's clothes.

Leila handed her master a long thin cane. The one she'd chosen was deep yellow in colour, highly polished from long use and with a series of prominent ridges along its length. Grinning at Mebele's efforts, Leila moved to Elizabeth's side, her left hand holding the small ivory dildo he had called her 'toy'. Very soon it would be time to use the gently pointed cylinder to tease her mistress.

Enjoying the thought of what was still to come, Sir Roger ran the cane through his hand, feeling the way the ridges bumped across his fingers, relishing that wonderful noise of the stinging impact on unprotected flesh.

After flexing the cane between his hands for a few moments Sir Roger made the whippy rod whistle through the air, sweeping it back and forwards. Elizabeth, unable to see what was happening behind her, shivered as she heard the familiar noise.

Richard Elford, now completely naked, was again seated on the stool but this time, as well as fingering Elizabeth's breast, his other hand was stroking Mebele's wiry hair as she crouched between his parted legs. Her left hand rested on the young trader's thigh whilst the right steadily stroked up and down the slim shaft of his manhood. The stroking motion was almost automatic since she was really concentrating on tonguing the smooth helmet of his penis as she brought him to full arousal.

Richard Elford breathed more deeply, trying to remain still as Mebele continued to run her lips across the wet shiny dome, her tongue probing into the tiny slit before flicking against the nerve centre underneath. Mebele giggled as she felt his shaft jerking at her expert touch, knowing he was nearly ready for her to ride him.

Elizabeth, head hanging between her outstretched arms, stared at them with a mixture of anger and excitement as her onetime lover smiled mockingly back at her, so obviously enjoying the maid's expert attentions.

Sir Roger walked to Elizabeth's side, lifting her head by simply pulling a handful of hair. 'Now, my dear, we may begin. I'm not an unfair man so, to give you pain and pleasure in equal measure, Leila is going to tickle your cunny, whilst I lay on with this rod. You, my lady, will keep count of the strokes. But be warned, forget and the stroke gets added as an extra one!' Releasing her hair with that dire threat, Sir Roger took up his position.

Elizabeth's restraint meant that her buttocks were held in a taut curve over the bar. Not only could she not move to ease the pain of each stroke, worse still, the soft skin at the top of her legs was exposed, as were the tender lips of her sex that peeped like a split fig from between her straddled thighs.

Leila, seeing that her master was ready to begin, eased herself quickly onto her back under Elizabeth's belly. Now she could reach up and finger her young mistress's dangling breasts, but more importantly she was able to apply the little dildo to the parted cleft of Elizabeth's sex.

Leila licked the ivory rod. There was a long expectant pause, everyone's eyes fixed on Leila as she started probing the sensitive core of Elizabeth's body.

Suddenly the blonde head flicked up and a sharply indrawn breath broke the silence. Elizabeth's neat white teeth bit into her lower lip, muscles tensing against the straps so that the leather creaked with the strain.

The collective sigh of satisfaction and squirming adjustments of positions revealed everyone understood; knew that the smooth ivory tip was now turning and twisting very delicately under the fleshy hood and against the tender nub of Elizabeth's clitoris.

Well aware of the Arab maid's skill and sure that Elizabeth was concentrating on the delicious feelings now spreading through her body, Sir Roger raised the cane. 'The count, my dear, don't forget the count,' he warned.

With that, Sir Roger swung the cane back before whipping the first stroke in to sear a line across the firm mounds of Elizabeth's bottom. He watched entranced as the fiery welt appeared, the tethered cheeks surging and bucking at the scalding pain.

'One,' came Elizabeth's quavering voice. 'Aaah! It hurts, it hurts, sir! Yes... ah, ah... go on, yes, yes...' Elizabeth was desperately trying to cope with a storm of conflicting signals. With the first stroke Leila had immediately jiggled the little ivory rod a bit harder, creating that awful mixture of pain and pleasure that Sir Roger had promised.

The beating, and the steady masturbation, continued for long minutes, Elizabeth's cries and entreaties becoming more heartfelt and confused with every new cut. By the time her tremulous count had reached twenty she was barely in control of her senses at all. Sir Roger paused, resting his arm whilst allowing his ward to recover, at least a little, before the next stage where, as planned, he and Richard Elford intended to take their own pleasures.

Watching the erotic display from the stool, Richard was now thrusting his hips forward, trying to increase the deep suction of Mebele's mouth as she brought him, aided by the sight of Elizabeth's violent reactions, towards a peak. But Sir Roger was intent on ensuring that it was Elizabeth who provided the fulfilment for both of them that evening.

He dragged Mebele away, sending her sprawling once more. 'Richard, why not find out how accomplished my ward can be at that game? I kept her arms apart so that you had room.' Mebele, aware of what Sir Roger had in mind, sat back on her heels as Lord Richard got to his feet, smiling cruelly at his friend's offer. He ducked under the rope holding Elizabeth's left hand to stand facing the curtain of blonde hair, the shiny wet shaft of his cock curving upwards towards his belly.

Sir Roger once again pulled Elizabeth's hair to raise her head. 'Now is your chance to show your ability, my lady. You were the one who spoke so eloquently about the joys of young Richard's body, as Leila tells me. Now is your chance to show your devotion. Go to it my lady, go to it, or it will be the worse for you.'

Richard moved forward, letting Elizabeth feel the slick moist crown of his penis against her lips, making her realise she had no choice. He jerked as she opened her lips, the hot length of his shaft filling her mouth. She gagged a little, feeling the bulb of his gland butting into her throat as her false lover renewed the slow thrusting stimulation he had been enjoying with Mebele a few minutes before.

With his ward fully engaged in her task, Sir Roger moved to where her parted thighs revealed the split purse of her sex. Placing the bulging crown of his own manhood against her, he slowly pushed forward, sighing in satisfaction as he felt the sliding warmth sheathing him. Now both of them thrust more vigorously, spurred on by Elizabeth's muffled cries and her muscle spasms as the double penetration filled her body. Sir Roger's own pleasure mounted, stimulated by the sight of watching the vigorous younger man enjoying the talents of Elizabeth's mouth and tongue as they rocked her tethered body between them.

Elizabeth's tormented concentration on her double impalement was broken as the maids added their attentions to her body once again. Mebele, kneeling beside her, reached up to finger the rigid nipples as they jiggled wildly with Elizabeth's frantic movements. Leila used one hand to part the young blonde's labia, before once again twirling the dildo's rounded point under the hood and against the little nerve bundle at the top of her cleft.

The overload was too much; Elizabeth, quivering and shaking in frenzy, was quite unable to prevent her orgasm, her body bucking and twisting madly as she came. Mebele's earlier stimulation, and the hot depths of Elizabeth's mouth, proved too much. Despite his best efforts to prolong matters, Richard Elford thrust his hips even harder, jerking wildly in his release as hot streams of fluid jetted into Elizabeth's throat.

Gasping frantically he gripped her blonde mane, enjoying the long moment of satisfaction before drawing the softening length of his cock free and sinking back onto the footstool. He looked up just in time to watch Sir Roger reaching his own climax, thrusting deep between his ward's buttocks in that final jerking fury of release.

9

Elizabeth was now free to wail in her own wild excitement. She needed to because the busy fingers of the two maids had not relented at her first orgasm. Like the practiced tormentors they were, they had redoubled their efforts as they watched those first jerking spasms overtake their mistress's body, their fingers driving her to reach a second peak of ecstasy.

'P-please don't stop! Go on harder, harder, squeeze my nipples, please, harder. Yes, I'm there... *I'm there... Aaaaah*!'

Elizabeth gabbled mindlessly, twisting and shuddering in her bonds. Driven onwards by the maddening stimulation, sweating like a fever victim, she stormed and raved to her second orgasm of the evening, finally slumping against her bonds and desperately trying to bring her breathing back to normal.

The two maids, still roused from their masturbation of Elizabeth, were sitting together. Leila, the little dildo held lightly between her fingers, was using it to trace lines across the sharp curves of Mebele's breasts.

Mebele, feeling somewhat left out of the last session, but enjoying the attention, had braced her arms back on the floor so she could push her chest out against her friend's caresses.

Their master, more relaxed after fucking his ward so satisfyingly, looked at their growing preoccupation. It was clear where that little scene was heading, he thought, but not just yet awhile.

'Leila! Mebele! Wine, wine for our guest and myself! Stir yourselves, quickly, if you please.' He laughed aloud, enjoying the sudden scramble as they leapt up, scurrying to do his bidding. Sir Roger looked across to where his friend was resting on the padded stool. 'Well, Richard, did you find her satisfactory?'

'A masterly performance, Sir Roger, but only what I'd expected.' He reached across to the bar, tweaking Elizabeth's nipple playfully and extracting a jerk and a surprised squeak of pain as he did so. 'This young lady has obvious qualities I would wish to explore further, but another time, perhaps?'

Sir Roger looked at the sweating figure still stretched painfully over the bar and laughed. 'Sooner than you think, I suspect. I am due to go up river for a week or so but Helene Birencourt has asked to meet her tomorrow. She's been away for six months or so, and hasn't had a chance to get to know Elizabeth yet.' He paused and smiled at his companion. 'Since you two are close you will know her tastes better than I... but I am given to understand that she enjoys taking high spirited and rebellious young women to task.' The men looked up as the two naked maids returned with a decanter of claret and two glasses.

'Oh yes indeed, dear Helene and I have enjoyed a number of pleasurable encounters. So, Elizabeth will be staying with her while you are away?'

'It seems safer. Besides, there is so much for her still to learn. And after all, as a companion to a respectable and prominent lady of quality any untoward gossip is immediately silenced.' Sir Roger chuckled. 'Nothing to stop you paying the odd social visit, though.'

He turned to Leila as Mebele poured a glass of the deep red wine. 'Release your mistress and take her to her room. See that you apply some salve to her stripes before you leave. And Leila, ensure you do not forget to lock the door behind you.'

The maid nodded in understanding, but before she could move away Sir Roger caught her arm, turning her back so he could reach up and fondle one breast. 'Be quick with your duties, my dear.' He breathed heavily. 'I know you and Mebele have not yet reached your own pleasure. Besides, Mr Elford and myself desire some further entertainment and we do not wish to be delayed. My room will be more comfortable for our next romp, I feel, so be quick about your duties and join us there with all speed.'

Smiling to herself, Leila knelt beside the frame, undoing the buckles and freeing Elizabeth from where she hung, still breathing heavily, over the bar. With Mebele's help she led Elizabeth gently away to her room.

Once inside Elizabeth collapsed, facedown on the wide bed, while the two women fetched a creamy salve from the dressing room. Working with care and firmness they ignored Elizabeth's half-hearted protests, smoothing the cold ointment into the network of crisscross welts left by Sir Roger's cane. Leila, still aroused by the scenes in which she'd so recently been involved, slyly slipped her oily fingers down between Elizabeth's buttocks, bringing another protesting groan from the girl as she made sure the soothing cream was applied deep into her body as well.

Their work finished, the maids rolled Elizabeth onto her back. Mebele took a moment smoothing a strand of hair away from the flushed face of the girl. 'Sleep well, missy, Sir Roger will want you ready and dressed by ten tomorrow. We will return to attend you before then.' With that they left, locking the door as ordered.

Elizabeth was completely drained; although the salve had taken most of the sting out of the caning her body still tingled from the sexual excitement of the evening. Finally, the events of the past few hours overwhelmed her and, despite the clinging heat, Elizabeth Ashton fell into a deep, exhausted sleep.

CHAPTER 3
In the Hands of a Lady

She woke to a blaze of light, the bright shafts of the morning sun beaming through the blinds to create patterns on the white walls of her room. Stretching against the crumpled linen, she was pleased to find that almost all traces of last night's session had disappeared. She was both well and uninjured.

The lock clicked back and the maids came in. Leila carried a shift of thin white cotton. 'Sir Roger's orders, missy, you're to wear this and nothing else save your slippers.' Looking at them, Elizabeth knew she had no choice. Mebele helped her into the loose robe then combed her long blonde hair so that she once again looked every inch the beautiful young woman she was.

Leila then ordered, 'You are to join Sir Roger in the drawing room as soon as possible, missy.'

Elizabeth lifted her chin and led the way along the veranda to the large reception room.

'Ah, welcome Elizabeth, you slept well, I trust?' Sir Roger was at his most polite and charming as he greeted his young ward and led her across the room to where open archways faced a central courtyard. Elizabeth looked out with curiosity at a figure seated quietly on a woven rattan chair.

'Madame Birencourt, may I have the honour of introducing my ward, Elizabeth Ashton?' Sir Roger performed the introductions as Elizabeth stepped forward to take the soft hand of his guest.

'I am pleased to meet you, Madame...' she said, then stopped, tongue-tied, staring at the beautiful woman before her. Helene Birencourt's perfect skin seemed to have a dusky matte glow to it. Her hair fell to her waist, black and gleaming in the morning light. The proud swell of her gown and the deep cleavage between her breasts hinted that her figure was even more voluptuous than Elizabeth's.

Helene Birencourt calmly returned Elizabeth's stare, her dark eyes making a quiet appraisal of the attractive young blonde standing awkwardly before her. She smiled knowingly at the girl's sudden high colour and the quick heaving of her bosom. Sir Roger was right as usual, she thought, this one could be made to enjoy the darkest pleasures. 'I'm delighted to make your acquaintance, Elizabeth. Sir Roger has told me all about you.'

Elizabeth wasn't sure, but she thought she detected a suggestive tone in the woman's voice, and the thought of what Sir Roger might have divulged made her blush even deeper and she realised that her sudden flush of colour had not been lost on the commanding figure before her.

'Tell me,' one slim hand caressed the swell of Elizabeth's breast, making the girl gasp with shock and rousing the nipple so that the hard peak was clearly outlined against the soft fabric, 'do you enjoy the games you play with Sir Roger?'

Elizabeth stared at the floor, her face blazing red with embarrassment. 'I - I don't, I mean I didn't...' She couldn't go on, and shivered with excitement as the possessive fingers continued stroking her breast.

'Look at me, Elizabeth... look at me.' The command was soft but insistent, and Elizabeth looked into Helene Birencourt's dark brown eyes. 'That's better. Ah, you like that, don't you?' Elizabeth could only mew wordlessly as her seductress lifted her other hand, cupping the firm weight of each breast and allowing her thumbs to graze across the rigid peaks in a tormenting caress. 'Charming, Sir Roger, she's quite charming,' the woman purred, 'and you say she responds well to the rod, too?'

'Delightfully, Helene, quite delightfully,' he confirmed. 'She's very responsive and she pleads so enjoyably each time you bring her off. Richard Elford and I took her last night, and I know she spent twice at the maids' hands. Isn't that right, my dear?'

Elizabeth nodded wordlessly, her cheeks on fire as her guardian and this dazzling woman discussed the terrible and intimate details of last night's punishment.

'I told you to look at me.' The woman's voice was still soft, but with the hint of steely authority in it as well. 'You must learn obedience, I fear. Come closer.'

As Elizabeth obeyed, Helene looked up and a mischievous smile played across her lips. 'Sir Roger, the shoulder ties if you'd be so kind.'

Elizabeth trembled as she felt her guardian's hands tugging at the bows holding her shift in place.

'Ah, please...' Elizabeth gasped as the soft cotton fell away, and instinctively she clutched it against the swell of her breasts to prevent the garment falling to the floor.

'Silly child,' Helene's hands gently touched Elizabeth's, opening her fingers so the shift tumbled in a circle round her feet. 'I want to look at you. How can I do that when you're all covered up?' She studied the beautiful girl standing naked before her; shapely legs, taut stomach and proud, pink-tipped breasts. One finger ruffled the golden curls at Elizabeth's groin. 'We'll have to do something about this fur,' the woman said. 'Now, just hold her for me, Sir Roger, very gently.'

Elizabeth jerked as she felt her guardian's hands clasping her upper arms, no real pressure, just a restraining grip that held her in position for whatever was to come. 'The... the servants, m-might see me, sir...' the young blonde pleaded as Helene eased her legs apart, the soft swell of her sex pouting openly as she stood astride.

'I don't think Leila and Mebele will mind very much, do you? After all, they've both diddled you with that ivory toy of theirs.' Sir Roger's indifferent words cut her. His grip tightened as he watched the Frenchwoman fondle the full lips of Elizabeth's cunt.

'Oh, my dear girl, you're wet already,' the woman whispered enthusiastically. 'Let's see just how excited I can make you, shall we?' The fingers slipped back between Elizabeth's thighs, stroking up between the soft lips, coating her sex with the wetness of her own arousal. Helene smiled as she saw the rapid heaving of her young victim's ribcage, the gently instinctive movements of her pelvis, and how she shuffled her feet, widening her stance so as to ride the artful masturbation of her. 'That's nice, isn't it my darling. So nice. Shall I use just this finger to find that little spot to bring you off?' Her hand moved again, the finger probing at the top of Elizabeth's sex.

'Oooh, please my lady,' Elizabeth sighed, her cheeks flushed, her eyes misty. 'I... I... I'm going to come. Please, don't stop, please... oooh, yes there, yeeeeesss!' Elizabeth squealed in delight as Helene Birencourt vibrated one finger rapidly against the swollen bulb of her clitoris. 'Oh yes, p-please. Oh, oh, aaaaah!'

After a few moments Elizabeth realised she was free of her guardians grasp, and collapsed wearily across Helene's knees panting as though she'd just run a race. 'My lady, I'm sorry, I-I don't... it's... your fingers, my lady, such pleasure...' Elizabeth buried her face in the soft silk of Helene Birencourt's dress, embarrassment and her orgasm combining to reduce her to incoherence.

'You were quite correct, Sir Roger, most interesting,' the woman adjudged. 'I shall be delighted to take this young lady's education forward a little.' She lifted Elizabeth's head. 'Your guardian has suggested that I take over your care for a little while, whilst he is away. Would you like to come and stay with me for a few weeks, my dear?'

In the afterglow of her climax, Elizabeth shivered at the thrilling promise offered by this exciting, dominating woman. She knew she wanted more, to explore the darker fantasies she had started to enjoy in her guardian's salon. There was no doubt in her voice as she replied. 'Oh yes, Madame Birencourt, I'd like that very much.'

'In that case, my darling, I think you'd better call me Helene.'

In the soft dusk of early evening Elizabeth, accompanied by Mebele and an escort of other servants, made her way through the teeming streets to the edge of the old town.

Torches and lanterns flared and bobbed in the breeze and the noise of the frogs and insects provided a continual buzzing backdrop. Like most of the important buildings, Helene Birencourt's villa was invisible behind its high walls. Once inside the heavy wooden gates spacious courtyards and deep overhanging roofs provided some relief from the pitiless glare and heat of the day.

Helene, surrounded by servants holding lanterns, stepped forward, arms wide in welcome. She held Elizabeth lightly by the shoulders so she could brush her lips to each of the girl's cheeks in turn. 'Welcome, my dear, welcome.' Grasping Elizabeth's hand, she led her along a wide veranda into a large open room with sofas, and other beautiful furniture around the walls. Dismissing the servants, except Mebele, she led Elizabeth across to a couch heaped with covers and soft cushions.

Elizabeth looked at a pretty native girl standing beside the couch, noticing the bold smiles she exchanged with Mebele as they entered. Then the smile widened as Helene turned to her. 'This is my own special maid, Jenni,' she told Elizabeth. 'Like Mebele and Leila, she also enjoys bringing pleasure to young ladies, as you will discover shortly. Now, my dear, just to complete your welcome, Jenni and Mebele will help you to disrobe.'

Elizabeth stood motionless, bewildered as the two maids hurried forward to busy themselves with her silk day dress. 'But, I thought... I mean, I expected that I would...'

'Have time to settle in?' The woman finished for her. 'Why ever should you need that? Besides, if you are to understand the kind of pleasure discipline I expect we might as well start immediately. Now, less chatter and lift your arms so they can get all those things out of the way.'

Elizabeth, still in the thrall of Helene's brisk commands, obeyed, feeling the coolness as first her dress and then the rest of her garments and her stockings were removed so that she was again naked in front of her new mistress.

'Turn around, my darling, let me look at that sweet little bottom of yours.' Elizabeth winced as Helene ran her nails across the marks left by last night's caning. 'Still a little tender, are we? Jenni, the chair... and then help Miss Ashton into the position, please.'

Elizabeth was led to where a plain upright chair, its back and seat padded with dark blue leather, stood on its own on the polished floorboards. Curiously, the chair was facing the wall, its back towards the room. The girls pressed her against it, and she realised that the chair was not there to be used as a seat at all.

'Hands down flat on the seat, Miss Elizabeth,' Jenni's voice whispered in her ear as she pushed her forward over the wooden top. Her long blonde hair cascading down as she was bent over the chair back, its polished rigidity digging into her tummy, suddenly curtained Elizabeth's world. She felt the girl's hands on her neck and fingers busy on her breasts, teasing fingers that sent delightful swirls of sensation through her body.

'Are you ready, my dear?' Helene's voice seemed to come from a distance. 'Just ten for now, to welcome you to your new home, as it were.' Elizabeth heard the familiar *swish* and a sharp *thwick* as a line of fire lanced across her upraised buttocks.

'Aaah...' she gasped, trying to surge upward against the restraining hands.

Thwick!

The whippy rod cut a second line across the taut curves of her bottom, dragging another outraged squeal from the young blonde.

Five more strokes fell in slow, deliberate succession, stoking the fiery torment until Jenni was using all her strength to hold the twisting and crying girl in place.

'Take a grip, both of you; you know how she'll wriggle with these last few strokes,' Helene warned. 'Let her loose and I promise, neither of you will sit down for a week.' Her voice was still soft, but filled with controlled authority as she talked.

'Now, my dear,' she returned her attention to the bent, snivelling girl, 'the last three will be lower, across the tops of your thighs. Just be good and hold the position and it'll all be over. If not...' Helene didn't finish, leaving her blonde victim to imagine her own punishment for disobedience.

Thwick!

This time the sound was slightly deeper as Helene let the cane whip accurately into the soft crease dividing Elizabeth's taut buttocks and thighs.

'Oh noooo!' The young blonde writhed desperately in the maid's hold, fingers digging into the leather seat as she fought the fresh agony.

'Oh please, stop!' she begged, then yelped as the next stroke blazed another thin stripe just below the last.

'I can't, no more, please no more,' she wailed, but still the hands pressed hard into her neck and shoulders.

Thwack!

The last stroke was delivered with extra force, so that the blazing line kissed the split purse of Elizabeth's sex, peeping between her thighs.

'Arrggh!' Elizabeth shot upright as Helene signalled her release. 'Oh, oh, that h-hurts... Oh Helene, it stings so much...'

The three observers enjoyed Elizabeth's pain-filled writhing for a few moments, before Helene crisply ordered the maids to fetch candles and light the way to the bedrooms.

CHAPTER 4
Willing Seduction

Helene Birencourt, ignoring her guest's discomfort and holding a small lantern, led the way along the open veranda. Behind her, supported by Mebele, came Elizabeth, hands busy comforting the stripes lacing her bottom. Jenni held a second lantern, the flickering lamplight turning the naked girl's body to soft bronze as they moved along.

Inside the bedroom Helene turned to look at her latest conquest, her eyes bright with anticipation. 'Leave us,' she smiled at the two native girls. 'I'm sure you have other duties to attend to.

'Come here, my dear,' Helene continued, her hands gently caressing the firm peaks of Elizabeth's breasts. 'I expect you cannot understand why I caned you so severely just now. You have to learn the balance between pain and pleasure. Can't you feel the warmth, the unbearable tingling building in your body and the need for release? This kind of release...'

A hand dipped to the delta of the young blonde's thighs, a single finger teasing inwards, teasing the soft lips and drawing a moan of longing from Elizabeth. Helene laughed lightly, her finger slipping into the hot wetness before withdrawing to continue caressing the firmly thrusting breasts. She knew the girl was on the brink as she rolled each peak to and fro.

'M-Madame... Helene, I w-want you...'

'Go on, my darling,' the woman urged, twisting the swollen nubs more urgently, 'tell me what you want.'

Elizabeth gasped, her breathing hurried as Helene continued working her to a pitch of intense arousal. 'I want to spend again... like before... please, Helene, please...'

In silent answer the woman kissed Elizabeth's lips very gently, feeling them parting in inquisitive response. She moved her hands, continuing the slowly sensuous stroking of the girl's breasts and nipples whilst urging Elizabeth gently backwards to the bed.

Elizabeth gasped as the edge of it caught her behind her knees. Unbalanced, she sat down abruptly, the contact making here squeal as her sore bottom reminded her of the recent caning.

Certain of her control, and the young blonde's willing surrender, Helene shed her own clothes to reveal a tanned and firmly toned body to the girl's flustered gaze.

Elizabeth's eyes widened in surprise as she saw that Helene Birencourt's mound, and the deep cleft of her sex, were quite smooth and naked so she could see every detail. Catlike, Helene watched Elizabeth's reaction; drawing her hands up her thighs very slowly so that her fingers gently parted her nether lips to show the moist, pink inner folds to the breathless gaze of the spellbound girl on the bed.

'Do you like what you see, Elizabeth?' Without awaiting a response she touched the soft blonde fur at Elizabeth's groin. 'Here it is the custom for women to remove their body hair. In hot countries it makes you so much more comfortable. Tomorrow, the maids will pluck you clean too. It will hurt a little, I'm afraid,' she smiled with private delight, 'but I think you'll find it... *stimulating* as well.'

Suddenly intent on their shared pleasures, Helene bent so that her breasts swung firmly forward, inviting the blonde's attentions. She sighed in satisfaction as Elizabeth cupped the full globes before her, and the sigh deepened as Elizabeth, unbidden, instinctively started licking each nipple to a glistening, aching stiffness.

After a few minutes the two women broke apart, breathing heavily with their own arousal. Helene moved Elizabeth, laying her back on the bed. Then sensing the girl's urgent need she knelt beside her, one hand stroking Elizabeth's breasts, the other tracing a path from the deep hollow of the blonde's naval to the V of her thighs. Elizabeth surrendered to her touch as the delicious feelings grew stronger. Helene was watching the increasingly urgent movements of the girl. Her lips curved in a smile of satisfaction as she saw the involuntary parting of her knees, the little surging hip movements as Elizabeth's arousal grew and grew.

Helene teased her fingers around the delta of Elizabeth's sex, running her nails lightly over the plump lips of her cunt, tickling the damp blonde hairs and those tender folds beneath.

'Is that nice, my dear?' Helene whispered softly, one finger tracing, featherlike, up and down the soaking groove of Elizabeth's sex.

'Oh yes, please make me come,' the blonde urged innocently. 'Don't stop now, please. Deeper, *please*.'

Elizabeth threw her legs apart, lifting and spreading her knees, giving her seductress full access to her body. Helene paused, then gently slid one finger into Elizabeth's vagina, sliding her finger deeper and deeper, watching the signs of Elizabeth's increasing pleasure as she rode the intruder like a slim penis.

After a few minutes of such expert masturbation Elizabeth was lost, totally engrossed in her own world of sensations, rocking her hips and gently crying and moaning with pleasure. Her fingertips trembled, whitening under the effort of holding her knees up and apart, digging into her skin as she prised her body open to welcome Helene's delicious touch.

Helene knew it was time to make Elizabeth come once again. She bent, kneeling between the straining, outspread knees, resting her own hands high on Elizabeth's parted thighs to flicker her tongue over the wet folds of the girl's cunt.

Elizabeth, quite unused to being brought off in this way, jolted as though a spear had lanced through her body. She lifted her head, eyes wide with excitement as she gasped at Helene, 'Oh, what are you doing to me? Oh please, don't stop now, go on, go on, please, harder, yes, *yeeeeesss*.'

The Frenchwoman, using her tongue like a flail, teased the tender flesh. Concentrating on her victim's clitoris she used her tongue to flick it rapidly before sucking the tiny bud so it swelled to even greater prominence.

Elizabeth cried in ecstasy as she reached climax. Her hands clawed at Helene's hair, forcing her lips harder and harder into the soaking heat of her sex, desperately trying to increase the delicious torment washing over her.

Feeling the spasms of Elizabeth's orgasm jerking through her, Helene increased her efforts. Using the skill of experience she was forcing Elizabeth on, over her first peak and on to a second without a break.

Knowing that she was lost in the pleasures of riding the maddening sensations, Helene slipped a moist finger deep into her lover's anus, plunging it rapidly in and out. Elizabeth, squirming more violently at the sensation of the wicked finger deep inside her bottom, shuddered uncontrollably for a third time, coating Helene's face with her juices as a longer, deeper orgasm claimed her.

Relenting at last, Helene slid her finger out of Elizabeth's anus and lifted her glistening face. She smiled, watching as Elizabeth slowly came back to reality. Helene kissed Elizabeth very softly, allowing her to taste the tang of her own juices as their lips and tongues touched.

'Well, did you enjoy that, my darling?' she whispered huskily.

'Oh yes,' Elizabeth panted. 'Oh, I didn't realise, your mouth, your tongue... I've seen the maids do it, but I've never...'

'All the better for you to learn, then.' Helene smiled, stretching up so that Elizabeth was able to look down the lush curves of her body as she knelt between her kegs. The dark-haired Frenchwoman laughed in delight, moving up the bed so that she was straddled across Elizabeth's body.

'Do you think you would be able to put your lessons into practice?' she enquired, rocking her hips so that her own arousal left a moist trail on Elizabeth's belly. 'Or are you just too exhausted?' Elizabeth, still tingling with her own release, looked up at the figure above her and smiled back in turn, deliberately putting out her tongue and suggestively flickering it to and fro.

The invitation was unmistakable; Helene kissed Elizabeth once more then eased herself gently upwards. Elizabeth wriggled to lie flat, arms sliding under Helene's widespread thighs until her lover was poised above her face, knees pressing into the mattress on either side of her head. Looking upwards from between the straddled thighs, Elizabeth watched as Helene leaned forward to grasp the carved rail of the bedstead, the movement tilting her body so that the lips of her sex parted and brushed against her young lover's eager mouth.

Elizabeth's tongue peeped out as Helene sank slowly back, bringing the succulent lips of her sex down onto the face of the girl below. She gasped and jerked as Elizabeth immediately probed the soft folds of her body, sighing in satisfaction as she felt her beginning a maddening swirling flicking movement at the entrance to her vagina. Braced by the bedrail, Helene began rocking gently, her body reacting to the delightful sensations as she rode Elizabeth's face.

It was clear that her pupil had learned her lesson well because, within minutes, Helene was beginning to shudder and buck frantically, calling out in excitement as the first spasms of her climax began.

Like Helene only a few minutes before, Elizabeth understood the message in the erratic gyrations, the wordless cries and the slippery wetness of the figure above her. She moved her tormenting attentions, concentrating on the fleshy hood and the nub it concealed. Intent on making Helene spend, Elizabeth used all her wiles, nibbling and flicking the little stem and forcing Helene over the peak, whether she wished it or not.

With the writhing figure pressing down against her face, Elizabeth copied Helene once more. Reaching into the wet cleft of her buttocks, she also slipped one finger deep into the moist heat of the woman's rectum. Elizabeth waited, feeling the sudden gripping tension as Helene reacted to the unexpected invader, and then began a slow pumping movement, working her finger deeper and deeper, matching each thrust with Helene's frantic rocking.

'Oh yes, my darling, yes, harder,' the woman urged passionately. 'Oh yes, you little treasure, yes I'm there, I'm there, please go on yes... yes, yes, *yes!*' Helene, crying with pleasure, gave in to the flood of bliss rolling over her. Despite the difficulty of breathing Elizabeth kept up her experimental assault, working with lips, tongue and driving fingers to hold Helene screaming at her peak for long minutes.

Eventually, unable to take any more, Helene slumped off Elizabeth's body onto the bed, curling up in a shuddering ball as the sensations overwhelmed her.

A silence fell across the room, and entwined in the tangle of sheets, Elizabeth wrapped her arms round Helene before falling into a deep and satisfied sleep.

CHAPTER 5
Personal Services

Elizabeth woke as the sun was streaming in through the blinds. Wearing a soft blue robe with native designs on the border, Helene Birencourt swept into the room without ceremony. 'Awake at last,' was the first thing she said. 'Now, we must look after your grooming, just as I promised last night,' she paused, looking at Elizabeth with a teasing expression. 'Don't tell me that in all the excitement you've forgotten?'

Elizabeth blushed deeply, realising what Helene was talking about, and the blush deepened as she remembered clever fingers stroking the golden hair of her sex, and her own surprise when she saw Helene's smooth body for the first time. 'Oh yes, Madame,' she whispered, 'but I didn't think... you mean now, this very morning?'

'Silly child,' Helene chided lightly, 'why wait? I've told Jenni to prepare the things. If we do nothing, why, all her labour will have been in vain. Come, Mebele will help get you ready.'

Elizabeth just lay there, caught up in a sudden mixture of emotions; confused at the speed of events but excited by the thought of the treatment to come. Deciding to make the best of the situation she threw back the covers and rose elegantly.

'You look as enticing as you did by candlelight,' Helene complimented, thoughtfully caressing Elizabeth's bare arm with the tip of one finger. 'Perhaps... but no, there are things to attend to first.' She moved to the door with her usual natural grace, and then with her manicured fingers poised on the handle, turned to look back at Elizabeth. 'Well, don't just stand there,' she enticed, 'come along.'

Elizabeth wondered if she was expected to parade naked through the house, when Mebele appeared and startled her out of her reverie by draping a cotton robe around her shoulders, enveloping her slim figure from throat to toe. Still feeling uncertain, Elizabeth followed Helene obediently out of the bedroom and down the hall to the bathing room.

The décor was tiled with bright, intricate patterns. Fretted arches allowed light to stream in, and the clear water of the small pool set in the floor looked cool and inviting. To one side a stone slab was raised slightly above the floor. Beside it a couple of stools and two wicker chairs stood in a semicircle. Jenni was there, standing by a table stirring a thick, honey-coloured mixture in a copper bowl above a spirit lamp, the smell of the toffee-like mixture filling the room with a rich scent of lemons and sweet herbs. Next to the bowl there was a dish of water and a glass pot of amber liquid.

Helene beckoned Elizabeth to the table. 'Look.' She pointed to the liquid. 'First, a little honey on your skin, just to help the mixture. It clings to your soft hairs, then we pull it away, one tug and all the hair comes with it.'

Helene looked at Elizabeth, trying to suppress her own thrill of anticipation as she spoke. 'I know, yes, it will hurt, but...' she smiled, stroking Elizabeth's cheek in an intimate caress. 'Only for a moment, and then your flesh will respond deliciously to the slightest touch, as you'll find out...'

'Oh yes, Helene,' Elizabeth breathed, mesmerised by the idea. 'I want to be like you. Show me what I have to do.'

'It's ready, Madame,' Jenni informed her mistress, 'we can begin when you wish.'

'Very good.' Helene smiled at her servant. 'Lie on the table, Elizabeth, on your front to start with, I think.'

Mebele slipped the robe from Elizabeth's shoulders and the girl lay down on the smooth stone, folding her arms to cushion her cheek, then flinching slightly as Helene stroked the thin red marks of last night's caning.

'Still sore, my darling?' the woman enquired silkily. 'But remember how hot you were afterwards...' Her nails tickled the tender skin again in unspoken promise, before Helene settled herself in the chair nearest the table.

Seeing Helene's knowing expression, Elizabeth wondered just how many other girls had been involved in these sexual games before her. She was quite certain that Jenni was very used to such happenings. Probably, beneath her simple top and skirt, she was naked like Mebele tended to be. She felt her nipples stiffening against the cool stone as an image of Jenni being caned, or fingered to a climax by Helene, sent a thrill of excitement into the pit of her stomach.

Jenni placed the pot of honey on the edge of the table, a soft brush standing in the golden liquid. But to Elizabeth's surprise it was Mebele who picked up the brush, carefully wiping the excess honey off on the rim of the pot before painting the sticky unguent all over Elizabeth's back and legs, as Elizabeth realised that Jenni couldn't apply the honey because she was busily kneading and working a small ball of the sticky, scented mixture in her hands.

Helene noticed the flush of growing arousal on Elizabeth's face. The brush swept and curled across the soft bronze skin, the honey glistening on Elizabeth's golden down, her body glowing in the sunlight as though lovingly crafted from polished glass.

'That feels good, I know it does,' Helene whispered. 'Now, just relax, my dear. You'll feel Jenni pressing, then a sting as she pulls away.' Lulled by the words, Elizabeth calmed as the ball was moulded to her, then gave a sharp intake of breath as the first strip was jerked free. And Jenni didn't give her a chance to react, immediately smoothing the sugar ball onto the next area for treatment.

The maid's expert movements and the fact that Elizabeth's downy hair was so fine meant that the work on her back and legs was completed in only a few minutes, even though Mebele gently eased the cheeks of Elizabeth's bottom apart so that the sticky mass could be applied properly to all parts of her anatomy. This time, as the mixture was torn away, Elizabeth did gasp aloud at the stinging burn between her legs.

'When you are ready, missy...'

Elizabeth gathered her thoughts as Mebele helped her to sit up, then she edged herself back into the middle of the slab before lying back. Helene was right; it felt as though her skin had been lightly whipped all over. She settled back, trying not to wriggle any more than she could help. Then some remaining sense of modesty made her bend one knee slightly, half crossing her thighs and almost concealing the delta of her sex. Self-consciously she also let her hands rest across the swell of each breast, trying to conceal the hardness of the tips from the knowing gaze of Helene and the two maids.

'Give me your hands, my darling girl,' Helene ordered, standing and reaching down to grasp Elizabeth's wrists. 'Jenni can't work properly with them there, now can she?' She pulled Elizabeth's arms away from her body, stretching them back until she was holding them above the blonde's head, the backs of her hands pressed to the slab.

Enjoying the way the tension was pulling Elizabeth's breasts into even greater prominence, the woman looked to her maids. 'Go on,' she said quietly to them, and Mebele started painting a film of honey into the delicate flesh of Elizabeth's exposed underarms. Helene's grip tightened, and in return she felt Elizabeth's fingers tighten on her own wrists as the soft bristles began to tickle the sensitive hollows under the girl's arms.

Elizabeth writhed on the stone table, biting her lip as the tickling continued. All thoughts of modesty were forgotten as her legs parted a little in her efforts to relieve the maddening torment. Mebele, knowing exactly the kind of anguish she was causing as she brushed each hollow, deliberately swirled the bristles, increasing the tickling so that Elizabeth was soon whimpering aloud as she squirmed.

Then the girl slumped as Mebele desisted and moved away. But Jenni immediately leaned over, a fresh ball of the mixture in her hands, and once more Helene felt Elizabeth's fingers digging into her wrists as the sticky mass was spread into the dip of her left arm. 'Prepare yourself,' she whispered, and then without further warning, Jenni snatched the gluey ball away in one clean, tearing movement.

'Aaah!' Elizabeth's hiss of pain, and the sharp stab of her fingernails into Helene's wrists, revealed how much she had felt that particular application.

'Gently, my dear, gently...' Helene coaxed. 'It's only once more on this side and then we must do your other arm. I know it hurts, but the sting soon disappears. There's a bath waiting for you when we finish. Your skin will feel like silk once the treatment is completed.'

'But it stings so, Helene,' Elizabeth whimpered. 'Aaah no, not again please, wait a little... aaaaah!'

Jenni completely ignored the pleading cries, and using all her skill she worked the lemon-scented sugar along each arm in turn, ripping away to the accompaniment of further gasps from the young blonde stretched out on the cool table.

Now it was Mebele's turn again, coating Elizabeth's breasts and flat tummy with the fragrant honey. Helene could sense Elizabeth's anticipation as the brush licked around each firm mound in turn, and the audible gasp of disappointment as Mebele left the jutting peaks completely alone.

Elizabeth suddenly cried aloud, her body arcing up off the slab in excitement. It was all Mebele's fault; she had gripped Elizabeth's nipples and pulled them upwards, stretching the blonde's breasts into taut cones so that Jenni could work the mixture across and around each one in turn.

Helene smiled, well aware that Elizabeth's reaction was to the unexpected touch, rather than any discomfort. She could see, by the way that Elizabeth was curving her spine, that she was surreptitiously enjoying the firm tugging of Mebele's fingers.

'Oh!' Elizabeth cried as the delicate skin on her left breast was treated, then she managed to control her reactions, only allowing a hissing gasp of pain to echo in the room as the gooey coating was pulled away from her right breast. Mebele gave the rigid tips a final, teasing flick with her fingers as she straightened up, and Elizabeth thought each would burst, so swollen and so sensitive they felt.

The two maids rapidly finished the easier areas of Elizabeth's stomach and legs. Then, Jenni began kneading and shaping the last piece, ready for the final, and most delicate application of all.

'Wide apart now, so Jenni can finish the task,' Helene ordered the tormented, supine girl. 'Mebele will hold your legs.' She watched closely as Mebele helped Elizabeth to open herself completely, knees bent and thighs wide apart, the fine golden hairs lustrous around the split swell of her sex. 'Now here's the brush again...' she went on, commentating on proceedings. 'That's nice, isn't it? Can you feel it tickling your cunny, darling?'

Elizabeth stared down the length of her body at her glistening sex, the golden hairs throwing back glints from the tropical sun streaming in though the tall arches behind the table. Panting a little with a mixture of excitement and apprehension, she enjoyed the firm pressure and the clinging warmth as Jenni worked the sugary mass across the edge of her hairline and into the junction of her left thigh.

Helene leaned forward, planting a kiss on Elizabeth's slightly parted lips, then taking their mistress's movement as the signal, Mebele pressed down on the parted thighs as Jenni stripped the mixture free in one long pull. Helene's kiss and Mebele's hands effectively smothered Elizabeth's sharp squeals and jerking reaction, the double assault of pain and pleasure catching the pinned girl in a storm of conflicting emotions.

Elizabeth, on fire with the burning itch in her groin and the sensual stimulation from Helene, hissed with excitement as she felt the lips of her sex being fondled by another pair of gentle fingers. Mebele was carefully stretching the tender folds to ensure that Jenni could reach every inch of her body. Her fingers tickled between the lips of Elizabeth's cunt, slithering in the soaking groove and taking Elizabeth almost to the point of spending as the teasing sensations increased. Jenni worked even more delicately, pressing and stripping the sugary coating from the very edge of Elizabeth's labia in a series of short movements. Then suddenly, just as Elizabeth's hips began their insistent writhing, it was over.

Finding herself released, Elizabeth lowered her legs from the cool slab and stood up, a little shakily, taking Jenni's offered arm to aid her balance, and Mebele held a hand glass so she could see the reflection of her newly naked self. Turning and twisting she lifted her arms before running her hands delicately over the strange, smooth swell of her sex mound.

Then Helene interrupted her musings. 'Enough admiration, Elizabeth; time to bathe and be rid of the last traces of that sticky mixture.'

Without heed of Helene's earlier warning, Elizabeth stepped down into the warm pool, lounging back in the enfolding water, before erupting up again with a shriek, her skin bright red. 'It stings!' she wailed, but to her amazement, instead of rushing to her aid, the three onlookers were laughing gaily.

'Oh, dear girl, I did warn you to be careful!' Helene giggled, once she had recovered herself a little. 'Remember, I said it leaves your flesh particularly sensitive for some hours. Try again, very slowly and gently this time. I think you'll find it bearable now.'

Gingerly Elizabeth lowered herself back into the water, and this time she was able to sit down without the squeals of discomfort, although Helene noted her biting her lip endearingly.

Once immersed Elizabeth slowly relaxed, letting the water soothe away the sting and irritation. After some minutes Jenni helped her up the two steps, steadying her so that she could step gracefully onto the cool marble floor.

'Jenni, Mebele, it's time for you to indulge your mistress,' Helene instructed. You'll need a towel over the chair and the cream. I believe she's ready for your particular personal attentions.' Jenni gave a little bob of assent, and then fetched a small jar of white, sweetly scented cream, while Mebele spread a towel over one of the chairs, patting it down in the middle and moulding it to the seat.

Helene again took Elizabeth's hand. 'Now, to complete the work, my darling, come here and sit down.' Elizabeth, edging back and down onto the towel-covered seat, looked up at Helene's handsome face, then winced a little when, without warning, she felt a chill shock as Mebele, standing behind her, spread the scented cream over her shoulders and down across the upper swell of her breasts.

The maid's clever fingers moved steadily lower, sliding down her mistress's flanks before cradling the firm globes. 'I don't think... I mean I, oh... Helene, should she...?' Elizabeth stuttered, her hands lifting to clamp over her maid's to forestall their cunning movements, embarrassed by the reaction of her own body and suddenly afraid of what Helene might think.

'Elizabeth, darling, don't tell me you're not excited,' the woman teased. 'Why, you nearly spent on the table when she was fingering you just now. Silly girl, let go of her hands; she's only doing as I instructed, so why not enjoy it?' Helene slowly raked her gaze from Elizabeth's flushed face, down to where the two stiff nipples were partly hidden between the two girls' interlocking fingers. 'Besides, after all that wriggling on the table, you want to relieve all those naughty feelings, don't you?' Helene licked her own lips deliberately, staring purposefully at the beautiful body sitting before her.

Elizabeth gave up the unequal struggle. She let go of Mebele's hands, letting her arms fall away and resting her palms on the arms of the chair. Taking a deep breath she let her last inhibitions flow away, submitting to the demands of her body and the gently coaxing voice of Helene Birencourt. Immediately the slick, moist fingers returned to their work.

Mebele's caresses became more urgent and direct, her hands slithering over the firm curves, rolling and pressing the erect nipples with every movement. Elizabeth's breathing quickened, the flush mounting in her throat and shoulders as her hips rocked gently.

Helene began to breathe harder too, excited by the sight of the beautiful coloured girl's intimate fondling of the young blonde in the chair. 'Jenni, go on now, go on...' she whispered, and immediately the young maid knelt before the chair and began running her oily hands up and down Elizabeth's thighs, making sure her fingers stroked across the soft bulge and into the sensitive creases of her body at the top of each caress. Elizabeth's mouth peeled open as she panted under the double assault.

Keeping her eyes on Mebele's fingers, Jenni slowed her own movements, concentrating on the delta of newly stripped flesh at the base of Elizabeth's belly.

The slow, deliberate arousal continued until they could all see Elizabeth subconsciously edging her thighs apart, beginning to lift and push her hips to meet the probing fingers.

'Now, darling,' Helene whispered, 'it's time to let them finish. Gently, lift your legs over the chair's arms so Jenni can attend to you properly. You don't really want her to stop, now do you?' Hearing the soft moans of acquiescence, and looking at Elizabeth's closed eyes and flushed face, Helene urged, 'Go on, girls, make her spend for me, you know how I like to see them come.'

The kneeling maid swiftly pushed apart Elizabeth's legs, lifting and bending her knees so she could rest them over the wooden arms. Mebele helped, holding each knee outspread so Jenni could kneel even closer to the erotic splay of the English girl's body. Helene edged closer too, observing as Jenni delicately traced her fingers around the split purse of Elizabeth's cunt and along the soft valley shadowing the darker whorl of her anus.

All gazed intently at the glisten of moisture while the tender flesh parted, responding as Jenni stroked the naked lips. They watched entranced as growing arousal revealed the little bulb of Elizabeth's clitoris, nestling between the folds of her sex. Stroking the area with her oily fingers, Jenni leaned even closer, letting her hot breath play directly on the little nub.

Elizabeth rocked her hips forward, desperately trying to open herself and increase the tormenting contact she could feel.

'Make her come, she's ready for you now.' Helene's whispered command was harsh with passion.

With her fingers Jenni split the engorged lips, holding the pink flesh apart to open the soaking folds so she could use her tongue to lap and tickle Elizabeth's core, and Elizabeth couldn't care that she was spread obscenely across a chair whilst others watched her shameful passions. 'Go on, please go on, please, please,' she begged deliriously. 'Oh yes, yes, *yeeeeesss...*'

Hearing the urgent gabble Jenni increased her attentions, teasing the opening of her victim's vagina before thrusting two fingers deep into it. Elizabeth climaxed immediately, pulling her knees hard back to her breasts and thrusting forward to impale herself more deeply on the driving fingers and the flaying tongue. 'Yes, go on, oh yes!' she wailed without shame. 'I'm there, oh Helene, I'm coming, I'm coming, *I'm coming!*'

Helene Birencourt gazed enrapt as she watched her young pupil shuddering in the chair in front of her. This was her particular delight, her secret prize, to be a voyeur as her servants brought a beautiful girl to a state of intense, uncontrollable ecstasy, just for her enjoyment.

Mebele, aware that Elizabeth was instinctively trying to close her legs as the orgasm swept through her, clamped her hands tighter on each knee, forcing them back against the chair as Jenni continued to wriggle her tongue in Elizabeth's cunt.

Elizabeth, sobbing in the throes of her release, gave up the struggle as another wave of bliss engulfed her. Jenni then subtly changed her tack, continuing to flick her tongue across Elizabeth's clitoris while her fingers sought the secret opening of her body, smiling wickedly as she slowly slid one finger deep into the girl's bottom, working it in and out in time with the desperate, heaving movements in the chair. Mumbling incoherently at this new impalement, Elizabeth allowed herself to be brought to another, shattering climax.

As Helene produced, apparently from nowhere, a gently curved wooden phallus and handed it down to the kneeling Jenni, Mebele pressed even more firmly into the crooks of Elizabeth's knees, pushing to keep the girl vulnerably open. Jenni continued fondling the moist petals of Elizabeth's sex as she accepted and then licked the polished shaft, her tongue slithering over the wickedly raised carvings of veins that writhed across its surface. Then taking a firm grip on the sculpted column she pressed the bulbous head into the entrance of the exhausted girl's vagina, causing her spine to arch and her naked breasts to thrust out in unison with the slow intrusion.

Helene teased the girl's oily nipples. 'Elizabeth, are you ready?' she whispered. 'Jenni's going to make you spend all over again, can you feel her pressing into your cunny, darling?' Her hands moved, fingertips rolling the aching, erect nubs. 'No, no, you can't stop her...' Elizabeth shook her head deliriously and mumbled under her breath, her cheeks flushed. 'Oh no, my dear; no it's not too much at all. You've only come for me twice so far. Now... feel her pushing it up inside you... ah yes,' Helene kept her mouth close to Elizabeth's ear, her whispered coaxing helping to build the excitement as the three attendees prepared the perspiring and trembling blonde for another forced orgasm under the ministrations of their expert hands.

'Oh Helene, p-please, I don't think I can...' Elizabeth begged feverishly. 'Ooh, it's too big... no, please... *aaaaah!*'

Elizabeth's head rolled back in ecstasy as Jenni cleverly manipulated the thick shaft, her cries of protest due to Jenni deliberately making sure the ridges carved across its surface rubbed and fretted against her most sensitive flesh, the domed head prising open the tight opening, lancing up into her body.

The intrusion brought another startled gasp of pleasure from the young woman, now fully impaled on the cunningly decorated rod. She twitched helplessly as Mebele's hands pressed her knees even further apart, holding her young victim ready for her third pleasuring at Jenni's hands.

The kneeling maid pulled the long shaft slowly out of her victim's body, watching until the bulb began stretching the entrance once more. Then she slid it back, quite slowly, feeding the full length deep into Elizabeth's body and drawing a long groan of pleasure from her as the raised pattern rippled deep within her.

'My darling, do you like that?' Helene cajoled huskily. 'Oh yes, that's so nice, isn't it? Feel Jenni sliding it into you again. Is that nice, darling? Ah, that's it... that's it.'

Jenni gradually increased the rhythm of her arm, pumping the thick rod in and out

24

like a piston as Elizabeth began to ride the shaft for herself, hips grinding in an effort to draw it even deeper with each stroke.

'Oh please, please, faster, faster!' Elizabeth's cries became a kind of chanting rhythm as she responded to the dildo's stimulation.

'Tickle her clit again, Mebele, she's nearly there,' Helene ordered, her manicured fingernails flickering across the girl's nipples. 'Come on, darling, spend for me now, darling.' Mebele slid one finger down between Elizabeth's labia, vibrating it from side to side as she found the trigger spot the top of her cleft.

'Aaah yes, yes,' Elizabeth babbled. 'Yes, I'm there, yes, yes, I'm going to *come...*' Wailing, the helpless girl threshed in the chair as the three took her over the peak again. Jenni continued pumping the dildo in and out while Mebele's fingers strummed a continuing avalanche of ecstasy from the girl's clitoris. For long moments the two held the feverish blonde on the crest of her orgasm, then they relaxed, letting her lie back, totally exhausted, in the chair.

Helene Birencourt straightened up and studied with satisfaction the semiconscious beauty slumped in the chair. 'Thank you, Jenni, Mebele, I think you can leave your mistress with me now.' She smiled, observing Mebele's flushed face and hurried breathing. 'I believe you've served Mr Elford before?' she asked, and the maid nodded. 'Good, he's in the guestroom. I'm sure you'll be able to entertain him for an hour or so. You'll not be needed for any duties again this morning.'

CHAPTER 6
Under Instruction

The maids stirred Elizabeth from her rest just before lunch. All she was allowed to put on was the white robe she'd worn that morning. Very conscious of her newly naked sex, she hurried along between the two maids, hands holding the robe together as best she could. The room they entered had bare white walls, and was sparsely furnished with two wicker chairs and small tables.

In the middle of the room, though, standing alone on the polished stone tiles, an ominous apparatus drew her attention.

Although different in design to the one she'd been forced to mount in Sir Roger's own punishment room, Elizabeth recognised it immediately. It was a whipping frame!

Just less than waist high, one end sloped sharply while the other curved down more gently to where she could see some kind of brass fitting glinting in the sunlight. The crest was padded with maroon leather that shone with the polish of long use.

Elizabeth puzzled over the stout pegs jutting from both sides and the padded brackets set so cunningly behind them on the black wood. As she understood their purpose a picture of her own body strapped over the padded pyramid flashed into her mind; she felt another flush of arousal at the mere thought of it.

'Soon, very soon...' Helene's voice in her ear made her jump. 'But first you must see the instrument of your chastisement since you are to learn obedience as Sir Roger has insisted.' Helene was now dressed entirely in black. A laced corset emphasised the swell of her breasts while her midriff was bare, revealing the enticing hollow of her navel. A long black skirt was wrapped around her hips and her hair had been swept back into a severe bun. Elizabeth felt hypnotised by the air of power and dominance radiating from the woman who had seduced her so completely within a few short hours.

Jenni handed her mistress a carefully tied bundle of rods, water dripping from them. 'Last night the cane, now you must feel a different touch,' Helene told the blonde girl. 'These are green twigs, cut this morning...' She stroked the tips across the girl's thigh, watching the sudden flush of goose pimples as Elizabeth shivered at the contact. 'At first the pain of the stroke will be everything and then, in a little while, that other warmth you crave will fill your body. Have courage, my darling. Come here, it is time for your lesson.'

Gentle hands led her to the frame. 'Stand astride this end, hold the top, then lift your knees over the pegs and lean forward a little,' Helena instructed.

Elizabeth started to obey, but the woman's grip tightened on her arm. 'The robe, my dear, the robe.'

Elizabeth shivered despite the heat of the day, as Jenni slipped the soft material from her shoulders. Again Helene's hands guided her forward and Elizabeth felt the polished wood pressing against her thighs as she straddled the black frame. With both hands braced on the leather top, she let Helene lift her knees over the rounded pegs, mounting her like a rider on a pony. Jenni, crouching by her side, lifted each ankle into a padded bracket, locking her legs in place.

'Just bend forward and hold on, darling,' Helene said quietly, pointing at the brass handles mounted on the very edge of the sloping front. There was an insistent pressure in the small of Elizabeth's back as she bent forward until she could reach and grasp the brass grips. She was bent double, the smooth crest of her buttocks uppermost. She blushed scarlet once again, realising how lewd she must appear with her thighs parted astride the frame, exposed so that the soft purse of her sex was clearly visible between her tautly stretched bottom cheeks.

Soft hands traced across her bottom, fingers dipping into the telltale dampness so she whinnied softly with desire. 'Now the choice is yours,' the woman told her. 'Hold without restraint for twenty, but if you let go of the handles Jenni will bind your wrists to the bar and we will start again without limit until you scream for mercy.' Helene's tone hinted at her own simmering excitement at what was to come. There was a pause, the woman allowing the girl to absorb her words. Then she raised the wet green twigs...

Thwack!

The implement blazed a fiery path across the proffered summits, each one bringing its own extra bite to the blaze of the powerful stroke. Helene watched the convulsions as Elizabeth stifled her cries at the first taste of the rods across her bottom, and then let the full sting of the blow develop before bringing the second stroke whipping down onto the same tender spot.

'Aaahh...' This time the gasps were more audible, more heartfelt as the twigs caught flesh already inflamed by the first cut. Despite the delicious wriggling, Helene could see she was determinedly maintaining her grip on the handles - so far.

Thwack! Thwack! Thwack...!

Helene plied the rods with a slow, regular rhythm, building the scalding heat in Elizabeth's bottom so that her writhing on the black frame increased, knuckles white with the strain of gripping the handles.

Helene smiled; now to take her to the limit, to make her understand fully how things must be. She skilfully changed the angle of the stroke, sweeping against the soft under-meat of her thighs, letting the thin tips flick agonisingly across the soft purse of the girl's sex as the stroke landed.

'Ooooooh!' The drawn out moan interrupted the heavy silence of the room, as Elizabeth wrenched her head towards Helene in entreaty. 'Jenni, soothe her a little; she still has the other half to bear.' The maid knelt by the girl's head, stroking her perspiration-dampened brow and whispering in her ear as the next stroke sliced across the same area of vulnerable flesh.

The beating continued with Elizabeth squealing as each new stroke brought another blazing stripe to her reddening bottom. Then it was Helene's voice in her ear. 'That's nineteen, my darling, and I'm going to cut the last one in now, so be ready. Oh yes, you can let go of the bars once it's done. And I rather think you'll want to, anyway.' There was time for one deep breath then the rods whipped into Elizabeth, flaying into the softness of her cunt like red-hot wires.

The sobbing girl surged upright, hands jerking back to rub her blazing flesh as she gasped and choked at the pain of the final stroke, then the rods clattered to the floor as Helene held Elizabeth's shuddering figure in a tight embrace. 'Jenni, undo her legs and then use the cream... quickly now!' the woman ordered.

Elizabeth shuddered as her legs were unhooked from the frame, then squealed as the coldness of the cream touched the blotchy red skin of her bottom. 'Shhhh, it will help, let her finish for you,' Helene comforted. 'Otherwise you will not be able to sit down at all today.'

Helene Birencourt looked at Elizabeth's tearstained face. 'You did very well,' she went on. 'I'm proud of you, my darling. Now, can you feel the warmth building inside you?'

Elizabeth, her arms still tightly around Helene's waist, her tear-streaked cheek nestled comfortably against the woman's slightly heaving breasts, was about to deny any feelings at all when she realised her sex was wet and a delicious warmth was permeating her body. She hugged Helene more even tightly, gasping with pleasure as she felt the maid's knowing fingers teasing the naked lips of her sex.

Within seconds she was on the brink of yet another orgasm, and then the after-effects of the beating and Jenni's knowing fingers brought her to a sudden, silent, shuddering release.

'There, there, I told you, didn't I?' Helene purred. 'Now, you have a visitor. Put your robe back on and Jenni will escort you.'

CHAPTER 7
Entertained by Mr Elford

The room seemed empty as Elizabeth, left alone by Jenni, looked around, unsettled by the silence. Plain walls with archways opened back onto the veranda and the courtyard. Dominating the room was a wide bed, white sheets and a scattered mound of lace-edged pillows. Elizabeth glanced quickly right and left, her eyes flickering rapidly over a tall chest and plain chair against one wall, a dresser and a simple washstand against the other.

Before she had a chance to turn again two hands, pincer-like in their harsh grip, dug into her shoulders. She squealed, rocked with the shock of the unexpected touch. Then the tall figure, stepping forward from concealment behind the door, spun his captive around.

'Well, well, as prompt as usual,' drawled Richard Elford. 'I trust you are enjoying your new home, Elizabeth? Oh come now, my dear, don't be so startled,' he went on without awaiting a response from the girl. 'You enjoy playing games, they tell me.' He moved closer, edging the young blonde back towards the wide expanse of the bed. One strong arm encircled her waist, the other moved down her front, fingertips caressing the full swell of one breast through the thin cotton, and before she could summon any words at all he lowered his face, kissing her long and hard on the lips.

Then just as abruptly he broke away, laughing, pushing Elizabeth backwards so that she staggered and fell onto the edge of the firm mattress, gasping at the pressure on her bottom. Then standing over her where she sat, her hands behind her on the crisp white sheet for support, her legs slightly parted, Richard Elford looked down at his onetime lover. 'Oh dear, is that uncomfortable? Helene and I are old friends, but I overlooked how she would be taking you in hand. Let me see.'

He turned Elizabeth over, bringing another squeal from her as his fingers lifted her gown and traced the scorching red marks of the recent beating, his hand slipping between her thighs as she wriggled. 'Well, well, and soaking wet too. Don't tell me she made you spend as well?'

Elizabeth buried her face in the sheet, scarlet with the embarrassment at the evidence of her own arousal. Richard Elford smiled at the sight of the flaring red buttocks and the flush of Elizabeth's discomfiture, continuing to idly stroke her. 'A pity I wasn't here a little earlier,' he said. 'I'd have liked to see you bent across the frame. Still, plenty of time for that.'

He turned her again and Elizabeth found herself looking up at the handsome rake, who had clearly been awaiting her presence, as his feet were bare, his only clothing a pair of britches and a white silk shirt, open to the waist and hanging loose over his slim hips.

Richard Elford pondered a previous girl, very much like Elizabeth, whom he and his friends had taken to the very depths of depravity. Her submissive appetite for punishment had been her downfall. So stupid to threaten their private circle with ruin! And not only that, but so foolish as to tell him of her plans of exposure in advance.

He closed his eyes, recalling that last delightful session; the hot, isolated warehouse further down the coast, the slow beating, Giselle's naked body threshing against the leather ties, a harsh gag reducing her outraged squeals to a frantic mewing as the bamboo rod flayed her buttocks without respite.

He remembered the way two native girls had worked the beaten figure to climax after climax until even they were sated. Then the arrival of Mehmet and his servants with the wicker hamper, and Giselle's look of horror as she realised how she'd been trapped.

Still locked in the past, he enjoyed the familiar tightness in his groin as he also recollected Mehmet's cruel laughter whilst cutting the girl free from the bed only to lash her arms and legs together once more before forcing her, doubled up, into the cramped confines of the basket.

And finally his own delicious revenge as he knelt beside her wicker prison, carefully explaining in cold detail the fate that awaited her; a sea journey, the auction block and then her painful future as some prince's pleasure slave.

Oh yes, he had enjoyed her last desperate writhing and the despairing look before the lid was slammed down and buckled tight. It had been a problem solved and a profit on the deal, to boot!

'I see you have tasted Helene's hospitality for yourself,' he said, a hand tracing the naked swell of her sex mound, stroking the newly plucked skin and making her shiver with shameful excitement. 'Hmmm,' he mused, 'I see she has wasted no time with you. Tell me, did she or the maids pleasure you?' Whilst awaiting an answer he stripped his shirt from his shoulders in one brisk movement, throwing the bundled silk carelessly into a corner of the room. As he did so Elizabeth sat up straighter, the heat of her own passions and his teasing touch suddenly overriding everything as she reached tentatively for the buttons of his britches, stroking the iron bulge of his erection through the straining cloth. Richard then worked the tight fabric down over his hips, allowing the thickening rod of his manhood to spring free, jutting proudly towards her flushed face.

Then impatient to be rid of the impeding garment, he thrust the britches down his thighs, forcing the tight band of material over each knee before dragging one foot free, and then the other.

Elizabeth gripped him, stroking her dainty fingers against the hard length of his penis. Pumping her fist softly up and down the warm column of flesh she used her nails to scrape lightly over the slick purple helmet, teasing the tiny opening so that his manhood jerked and stiffened even further. He gasped in delight as she opened her lips to engulf the smooth crown, and another, fiercer intake of breath followed as he felt the first flicker of her tongue.

Warming to her task, Elizabeth took more and more of his erection deep into her mouth, just as she had the previous night, her head moving up and down as she brought him towards his climax. Richard Elford, enjoying the wet warmth of her attentions, looked down the muscled length of his body, watching Elizabeth's bobbing blonde hair and busy hands; one gently fondling the soft weight of his testicles; the other clasping the thickness of his penis, now slick and shining with her saliva. Then without warning she sat back, her eager face turned up to his. 'Do you wish me to go on, sir?' she asked mischievously, her fingers moving, building the sensations in his groin. 'Or will you hear more about my visit here?'

Richard smiled, gave a gentle push, and Elizabeth fell back on the mattress, legs parting shamelessly, deliberately showing him the fullness of her pouting sex lips. He slid one hand between her thighs to probe the wetness of her, his strong fingers stroking her flesh, opening and teasing her ready for his further attentions. Leaning lower, watching her face as she responded to each touch, he worked her slowly to a frenzy. 'Well, go on then, tell me how you've been pleasured as your new mistress's guest here.' He slid his forefinger into her body, probing deep into her vagina, moving it gently so that she turned and heaved on the bed in her excitement. 'What, nothing to say? Come, come, my little minx, you were going to tell me how she made you scream with pleasure this very morning.'

'Oh Richard, please,' she panted, 'I cannot speak if you... oooh, if you wish to hear then mercy for a m-moment, please...' Elizabeth inhaled deeply, desperately trying to control her arousal as two fingers now thrust within her. 'Oh no, please, Richard, I'll spend if you go on. I'll tell you how it was, I promise, but your fingers... please...'

Chuckling at her murmured pleas he relented, letting his fingers slide from her sopping cunt and allowing her the brief respite she craved. 'There, I've done as you wanted. Now, tell me about your pleasuring. Or shall I finish what I began?'

'Oh yes, Richard,' she sighed, easing her legs further apart as his fingers returned to continue the gentle fondling of her cunt. 'But slowly, if you wish to hear my tale.' Her hand lifted instinctively, finding the hard rod of his penis.

'Mebele played with my titties first, as you might have guessed.' Elizabeth lost herself in the story, the images of the morning and Richard's insistent fondling keeping her at a peak of arousal. 'Helene could see I was close to spending, so she told Jenni to bring me off. Well, once she started on my cunny I was lost. I spent almost at once, but Helene told them not to stop. She does that; she tells them to go on so she can watch what happens next, so she could observe my face as I realised Jenni was going to make me spend yet again.'

Elizabeth ground her hips surreptitiously as his hand worked skilfully between her thighs. 'Richard,' she gasped, 'have a care or else I'll... oh yes, Richard, yesssss...' her soft voice faded as Richard Elford, aware of her rising excitement and involvement in her story, thrust his two fingers deeper into her clutching vagina.

'And what happened next?' he coaxed, deliberately twisting his fingers and smiling at the surging response of the beautiful young blonde under his spell.

'I-I s-spent again,' Elizabeth stuttered, fighting to control the rising tide of bliss being stirred by the probing fingers. 'First I tried to stop Jenni, but I didn't really want to. Then finally she used a dildo while Mebele held me down in the chair, and they made me spend for yet a third time.'

Elizabeth's words changed as the remorseless fingering finally drove her over the top. 'Oh Richard, please, don't stop now,' she panted urgently. 'Harder, harder, oh please, *please*...' Elizabeth wailed as she came, stretching her head back, arms rigid at her sides, Richard playing her adroitly as her intense orgasm overcame her. With immense satisfaction he felt the muscles of her vagina gripping and pulsing round his fingers as she squirmed under his touch. Kneeling astride her waist as she lolled back on the white sheet, he gazed down on the glazed eyes and beautifully drained expression of the young beauty, exhausted and vulnerable to his licentious desires.

A cruel look crossed his face. 'And now, my dear, it's my turn to have a little pleasure,' he vowed, and before Elizabeth could even gather the strength to react, he moved swiftly aside and hooked his arm under her legs, lifting and bending them so her parted knees were pressed tightly against her naked breasts. Then leaning forward, his weight pressing her immovably into the softness of the mattress, he stared into her startled eyes. 'Ready, my dear?'

Before she could reply he thrust his hips, letting the smooth domed crest of his penis slide against the wetness of her cunt.

Elizabeth tensed. 'Oh no, please Richard, no, please no,' she murmured, but her ramblings went unheeded. The lazy probing continued as her engorged wet lips caressed the purple helmet of his manhood. And just to torment her further he began to move his hips with shorter, more rapid strokes, concentrating on fretting the little pleasure bulb at the summit of her slit.

Pinned below him Elizabeth twisted in vain, tormented by the unbearable sensations from tissues already sensitive to distraction from her climax only a few moments before.

Richard panted, taunting her while continuing to let his penis slide to and fro over her cunt. 'It seems you can feel that particularly well,' he adjudged. 'And it's pointless struggling, my dear, for very soon it will be your turn to ride your pleasure all over again, whether you wish it or not.' He pressed harder, savouring her desperate writhing. 'You see? I told you there's no use in resisting me. Just a little more and then you can welcome me fully.' He pushed his hands outwards on her knees, forcing her thighs even further apart and making her sex even more accessible.

'It's too much, Richard, too much,' she babbled deliriously. 'Have mercy, please, not there, please...'

Suddenly the friction stopped as he withdrew, and gasping for breath she relaxed... but too soon, as the bulbous head of his cock pressed yet again into the opening of her vagina. 'Oh my God, gently please, Richard, *gently*.'

Braced over his victim he heard her words, but his own pleasure drove him on. Looking down with rising excitement he watched her mouth open as she felt the head of his penis stretching her, then came the sudden gasp, almost of astonishment, as the rounded bulb sank inside her body, giving her another sudden jolt of sensations as it did so.

Feeling the succulent warmth engulfing his shaft he began to move faster, letting the thick column sink deeper and deeper at every stroke. Below him Elizabeth continued to gasp and cry but he could hear the changing tone in her voice as the friction forced her to respond once more.

His groin docked against her and he had the full length of his manhood sheathed within the beautiful girl. Then rearing back until he was almost upright, Richard Elford began pumping his hips with long, steady thrusts, each time drawing back so that the glistening shaft slid free until only the curved helmet nestled between her labia, then driving forward and down again until the wiry hairs of his groin agitated the very core of her sex.

The remorseless rhythm began driving Elizabeth back irresistibly to yet another peak. Her hands gripped her own knees, her body arching up to bravely meet each powerful thrust.

'Yes, go on Richard, harder, harder,' she urged deliriously, her cries becoming almost a chanted refrain as Richard Elford braced his hands on either side of her head, all thoughts of teasing banter gone as he pounded into her, driving towards his own release as his stout phallus drove deep into her delicious body.

'Spend, you little bitch, spend again,' he demanded through clenched teeth. 'Come on, let me hear you... yes... now, now, *now!*' He grunted, every muscle quivering with tension as he felt his seed spurting deep into the hot, clinging glove of her body.

As he came Elizabeth cried out as well, bucking against him as she reached yet another climax. They threshed in a writhing tangle for long moments before the passions ebbed and silence fell, broken only by their heaving, gasping efforts to regain both breath and composure.

Richard was first to recover, smiling thinly at the young blonde beside him. 'Thank you, my dear, you really are most talented, you know,' he said. 'I'm sure you are going to be a real asset to this household.' He rolled away, sprawling on his back across the crumpled sheet. Elizabeth, eyes tightly closed and breasts still heaving with the effort, curled up beside him.

CHAPTER 8
Noises in the Night

That night Elizabeth relaxed alone, enjoying the delightful sensation of her fine silk nightdress sliding teasingly across her naked skin, still tender and so sensitive to the touch, even hours later. After all the painful and pleasurable experiences of the day, she couldn't decide if she was disappointed or glad that there had been no further advances from Helene. Richard had left soon after their encounter, but she knew she would be seeing him again.

Elizabeth blushed in the semi-darkness, remembering her wanton behaviour with the maids, the pain of the flogging over the frame, and the frantic lovemaking with Richard. After such a day she had expected Helene's games to continue, but there had been no more. To her surprise there were only the usual pleasures of a tropical evening and languid conversation over a quiet supper.

Drifting amid delightful memories, her hands roamed her body, triggered little shivers of arousal as they touched the sensitive mound between her thighs. She dozed, lost in a delightful twilight, one fingertip just stroking the soft lips of her sex as the moisture gathered.

It was a noise that brought her back to the present. Not loud or alarming, but different enough to jar her out of her erotic dreaming. She listened. The noise came again, a sudden sound, as though someone had gasped in shock - or delight. She opened her eyes fully, looking round the shadowed room. Nothing stirred at all.

Awake and more curious than scared, she sat up. In the moonlight she was able to see the expanse of polished floor and the dark corners of her bedchamber. A dim strip of yellow light showed beneath the connecting door to Helene's room, and as she looked at it the sound came again, longer and more intense this time. It was a woman's voice, not angry or fearful, but relaying pleasure. They were clearly sounds of passion; sounds Elizabeth knew only too well, and they were coming from the adjoining room.

Unable to resist the temptation any longer, Elizabeth folded the covers back, swung her feet to the floor and tiptoed silently across the darkened room. As she moved, the clinging silk of her borrowed nightdress slithered against her skin, and she felt her nipples hardening, outlined beneath the sheer fabric as her excitement grew by the second.

Edging close to the door and intent on finding out what might be happening in the room beyond, she ignored worries of possible discovery. She carefully placed a palm against the door, intending to stoop low enough to peep through the keyhole, but she almost gave herself away then and there as, fortunately without a sound, the door moved against her hand. She stifled a squeak of surprise, but it swung open a few inches before she was able to seize the handle. The low light from Helene's room seeped out as she held on to the handle for dear life.

She gulped, trying to recover her composure as she waited for the inevitable admonishment of discovery. But gradually, as the moments passed, her panic eased as her heart slowed from its frantic racing. The door still ajar she relaxed her grip a little, thankful to remain undetected by the occupants of the room.

'Ah, yes...' Much more audible now, it was clearly Helene's voice.

Desperate to find out what was happening Elizabeth pressed her face to the gap of the partly open door. At first all she could see was a confusion of abstract shadows, dancing shapes on the white wall behind the bed. Then lower, on the bed itself, the two interlocking bodies, writhing in the softly golden glow cast by two candles in silver holders, positioned on two bedside tables.

Slowly Elizabeth made sense of the scene before her. A coverlet lay discarded on the floor, and in the middle of the white expanse of sheet, Helene lay, the diffused light gilding the curves and toned muscles of her body, her arms stretching up, hands gripping the carved rail of the headboard in the gloom beyond the candle's reach. Her knees were raised and thrown apart, heels braced wide, opening the way for the figure crouching between them.

Watching the lurid writhing of Helene's body, Elizabeth could feel the heat between her own thighs as the dark head of the hidden lover continued to move rhythmically up and down. She could almost feel a wet tongue swirling against her own sex. Without thinking she sank down onto her haunches, tugging the soft fabric up her thighs, her knees feeling the coolness of the polished floor as she moved. One hand lifted the hem of her nightgown, the other burrowing between her thighs until she touched her own secret flesh again. Her fingers, edging deeper, teased the soft furrow of her cunt, letting her body respond to the scene being played out before her.

Breathing deeply from the arousal induced by her own fingers, slowly stroking the wetness of her vulva, Elizabeth continued to peer through the narrow opening. Clearly the man had nearly brought Helene to her peak, for now her knees were lifted back, her arms pushed down between them so she could entwine her fingers in her lover's hair, pressing his face against her, riding his features unmercifully.

Slumping a little further and leaning against the doorframe, Elizabeth was also on the verge of coming, her fingers dancing for her pleasure, thrusting into her vagina before sliding back to strum the rigid bud of her clitoris. All sense of caution now abandoned, she eased her knees apart on the polished wood, opening her body so her fingers could work with less hindrance, driving her to a frenzy of delight as she watched Helene arching, lost in the delirium of her orgasm.

The sensual cries that had stirred Elizabeth long minutes before were now continuous, Helene urging her lover on, her legs jerking as she twisted on the softness of the mattress. 'Yes there, there, oh yes, oh *yes*,' she wailed ecstatically. 'That's it, don't stop, yes, go on, go on...' the words disintegrating into a mindless babble as Helene Birencourt finally lost control as her climax claimed her.

Still hidden by the door, and spurred on by the erotic sounds and sights before her, Elizabeth too reached her climax. The fingers of her left hand, wrapped in her nightgown, were jammed hard into her mouth, trying to stifle her mewing cries as she worked herself over the brink with her other hand. One single finger, vibrating across the stub of her clitoris, took her over the edge. Eyes screwed tight shut in delight she shuddered helplessly against her own impaling fingers as the waves of glorious joy swept through her body. Half choked gasps and whimpers escaped the silken gag as she fought desperately to catch her breath, and stifle the cries of her private pleasure.

Slowly, very slowly, Elizabeth regained her senses, and awareness of her exposed position dawned as she looked down at her parted knees and bare thighs, the nightdress gathered up in folds around her hips. And as the reality of the situation dawned her hands flew to her mouth to stifle a gasp of dismay as she saw that her final movements had inadvertently pushed the door wider open, leaving her clearly visible should the lovers glance her way. She wondered how she could even begin to explain such unpardonable behaviour from a guest. Holding her breath and hoping against hope that the two figures on the bed might still be too occupied to notice her, she reached out gingerly with one hand, trying to catch the door and pull it to.

'Elizabeth, my darling, what on earth are you doing down there?' Helene's teasing voice dashed her hopes of an unobtrusive retreat. 'Don't tell me you like to play the *voyeur* as well.' Elizabeth looked miserably to the bed where the woman, languishing on her front with her chin propped on her palms, was regarding her with amusement in her eyes, one brow arched inquisitively, and a knowing smile just lifting the corners of her sensuous mouth. 'Oh, don't look so worried,' she chided playfully. 'Why do you think I left the door open? Jonathan, be a gentleman and help Elizabeth to her feet, she looks positively untidy crouching down there.'

Staring in befuddled confusion, the young blonde was barely aware of the tanned male rising, wearing nothing but a strip of white linen around his trim hips. The Honourable Jonathan Kingsford moved towards her in the candlelight, and she could see his lean, muscled figure more clearly.

Oh God, she thought, wanting to die of shame. Embarrassment choked in her throat as she looked up at the man, both of them almost naked and not yet even properly introduced.

'Elizabeth, what an unexpected pleasure,' the urbane man drawled. 'I've heard so much about you.' He extended a hand to help her up from the floor, and Elizabeth, mustering what dignity she could, let herself be pulled to her feet. She was embarrassingly aware of the way the silk was clinging to her body, outlining the rigid peaks and thrusting curves of her breasts. But she also caught the appreciative flare of interest and approval in his eyes as he studied her figure.

'Thank you, s-sir,' she stuttered, unexpectedly hoarse and stumbling at the touch of his fingers. He led her, unresisting but flushing pink and breathing quickly, to the side of the bed, looking down at Helene's smiling face.

'Oh, Elizabeth, forgive me please,' the woman said theatrically. 'May I present Lieutenant Jonathan Kingsford, of the governor's personal staff. Lieutenant Kingsford, this is Sir Roger Stanley's ward, Elizabeth Ashton.' There was a moment of stillness as they all realised the absurdity of the conventions in such a situation, but the moment passed as Helene burst into light laughter and both of them joined in.

'Darling Elizabeth, Richard and I have been lovers for two years now,' Helene went on, somewhat unnecessarily, Elizabeth thought. 'You haven't met him previously because he's been away with the garrison on patrol duties for the past two months, and only returned yesterday.' She giggled. 'I didn't know how you might react if I suggested we share his favours tonight so I...' she rolled over on the bed, turning to sit on the edge with her toes just brushing the floor, 'so I unlatched the door and left the rest to your own lusty curiosity.'

Reaching up she took Elizabeth's hands in her own, watching Jonathan running his hands lightly up her young guest's bare arms before stroking the golden strands of lustrous hair away from her damp brow. 'Now, my dear, as you've been properly introduced, Jonathan should have another chance to see how beautiful you really are. Lets get rid of that silly nightgown for a start, shall we?'

Elizabeth shivered in delight as she felt Jonathan's fingers easing the straps off her shoulders and peeling it free from her breasts. His lips nuzzled the softness beneath her ear while his hands cupped her breasts, freeing both from the last confines of the silk as he did so. 'Oh, that's so nice,' she whispered, almost too herself, as the strong fingers caressed her, cradling the soft weight as his thumbs grazed the stiff peaks with delicious assertiveness. Helene almost purred with satisfaction as she watched his expert fingers rolling and pulling at each of the girl's pink nipples, making them swell and stiffen as she surrendered to this new seduction.

'Slowly, Jonathan, remember she will need time before she's really ready again. Besides, you haven't finished removing her annoying nightdress yet.'

Jonathan laughed, giving each nipple a final pinch before sliding his hands to Elizabeth's sides, gathering the rumpled silk on the way, then slipping it down over the gentle curve of her hips until it fell in a puddle of shimmering fabric around her feet.

Elizabeth, golden in the candlelight and still holding Helene's hands for support, moved closer to the bed, stepping out of the crumpled silk and letting the cool air play across the delicate skin of her lower body. As she moved Jonathan, utterly bold and confident, stroked the bare swell at the base of her belly, dipping between her thighs very gently to cup the soft lips of her sex. She gasped as two fingers slipped inside her, slithering in the wetness of her recent passion, and Helene's hands were gripped with a fierce energy as she reacted to the tormenting intrusion into the moist slit of her cunt, still so sensitive from her recent climax.

'Jonathan, give the poor girl a chance,' Helene chided. 'We have all night. Leave her now and let me attend you for a change.'

Both the woman and Elizabeth eyed the bulge tenting the linen around his waist, but it was Helene, letting go of her young guest's hands, who reached up under the hem of the material, and with a dry mouth Elizabeth watched the cloth moving gently as Helene began fondling Jonathan's erection. Suddenly intent on joining in, she traced across the slope of his chest before running her fingers over the smooth ridges of his stomach.

Overcome by boldness, she hooked her fingers into the top of his wrap and before either of them could react, stripped the material away. Jonathan, now as naked as the two females, smiled proudly, enjoying his sudden exposure to their gaze. He arched back quite deliberately so that the upward curving shaft of his manhood swayed gently, thrusting out even more strongly from the tightly curled mat of black hair at his groin.

Helene used one hand to fondle the pulsing column, fingers barely encircling its girth, while the other was teasing the rounded bulb, sliding over the slick, purplish crest. 'You are next, my dear Elizabeth,' she purred, leaning forward and flicking her tongue over the bulbous helm, Jonathan groaning at each cunning lap.

Elizabeth watched Jonathan pressing against Helene's hands as she licked him, and Helene looked up, her face glistening with the dew of her efforts. 'Don't worry, we have plenty of time to let Jonathan recover, so he'll be able to take care of both of us tonight. Come here, my darling, feel what will soon be bringing you such pleasure.'

Elizabeth reached out, fascinated by the size and strength of his erection. Her fingertips slithered over the glistening bulb, shining wet from Helene's oral ministrations. Jonathan gasped, throbbing beneath her fingers. 'Ah yes, Elizabeth, but please have a care,' he warned gently. 'Do not take me too far too soon.'

She lightened her fingers in reply, watching the muscles in his thighs tensing and rippling as the twin assaults on his manhood served to arouse him further, his cock becoming harder and thicker in their busy hands.

Sensing that Jonathan was becoming almost too aroused Helene pulled her young apprentice away. 'No, my darling, stop now, let him rest a moment,' she instructed. 'Don't be disappointed; you shall be the first to ride that spear this evening. Come, Jonathan, onto the bed, lie down so that the dear girl may mount you.'

With two naked females intent on satisfying their passions with his body the officer obeyed, propping his head on a pillow so he could look down at the strong curve of his penis jutting up from the wiry thicket at his groin, his tanned frame contrasting with the white sheet. Eyeing Elizabeth's wistful expression he flexed his hips again, the shaft of his manhood arching back until the moistened crest brushed the toned bands of muscle of his stomach. Smiling at both of them, he folded his arms behind his head; ready for whatever Helene might wish to do next in this love game of hers.

CHAPTER 9
Turnabout

'Your turn now, my darling, come here, your pleasure saddle awaits,' enticed Helene, and Elizabeth, urgent with the need to feel that thick shaft thrusting deep within her, slipped gracefully onto the bed and straddled his hips. She reached down, caressing him again, cupping the soft weight of his balls before tracing the exposed underside of the shaft, drawing a quivering response as one fingertip tickled the underside of its swollen purple head. Her tongue moistened her lips, mimicking the tiny movement of the finger as she traced the line up to the little slit at the crest of his penis, already weeping the fluid of his arousal. She toyed with him, deliberately repaying his teasing, excited by the feel of his body responding beneath her touch, but her own needs were too urgent for long delay. Hands moving onto his chest to brace her weight, she lifted her hips very slowly, edging up to sit on the thick column, pressing it down against the firm muscles of his belly. She shivered at the feel of her labia sliding apart, folding around his cock, the warmth and pressure on her cunt making her gasp. That familiar wetness leaked as her breathing deepened at the extra stimulation of oiled flesh sliding upon oiled flesh.

The mattress dipped slightly as Helene moved and knelt beside them, intent on watching every movement as Elizabeth rocked on the erect flesh of her lover's penis; enjoying the struggle as the young blonde resisted his thrusting responses to the teasing friction.

Helene whispered into the curtain of fair hair, 'Gently, my dear, go gently. There, go on now, lift a little, and a little more...' She watched the trim buttocks tightening as Elizabeth followed her commands, letting her hips rise so the slick purple head of his penis could nuzzle up into the wet furrow of her body.

'Let me darling, let me,' came the hoarse whisper, accompanied by eager, searching hands. Elizabeth shivered deliciously at the touch of her mistress's fingers between her thighs, and Jonathan groaned as he felt those same fingers encircling his penis, raising and moving the swollen shaft, running the domed tip against the soaking slot of his new rider before guiding it into the hot wetness of Elizabeth's vagina.

'Take him, Elizabeth,' the stunning woman encouraged. 'Go on, my darling, take him now. Ride him for me - ride him hard!' Elizabeth bit her lip, a mixture of excitement and apprehension on her face, feeling the huge bulb of his cock stretching and opening her body, but with gasps of intense excitement she pressed down as Jonathan urged his hips upward, watching with delight as Elizabeth's mouth fell open in a soundless scream as the wide rim of his penis suddenly popped into the warm depths of her vagina.

'Ah yes, oh yes, go on now, go on *now...*' Elizabeth's cries became a pleading chant as she began to move more strongly, hips rising and falling as she urged the thick column deeper and deeper, and the Honourable Jonathan Kingsford picked up the rhythm, pressing upwards so the glistening pole disappeared completely with each thrust. Elizabeth shuddered as she rode her new steed, feeling a delightful extra torment as the wiry nest at his groin teased the lips of her cunt, still so tender from Jenni's attentions that morning.

'Ah yes, that's it,' Elizabeth gabbled deliriously, her eyes closed, her cheeks flushed. 'Oh, Helene, it's so big, so *deep*. It's never felt like this before. Don't stop, Jonathan, please don't stop.'

'Hush, darling, of course he won't stop,' the commanding woman promised. 'Go on now, sit back, ride him for me, my darling.' She pulled the girl's wrists. 'Now, bring your hands back here and let him feel those pretty titties of yours.' Helene's words were deliberately aimed at stoking the fires of arousal, her hands caressing her young lover as she lifted and fell on the impaling shaft of Jonathan's cock.

Elizabeth arched her body obediently, arms reaching back to grip his knees, her breasts lifting and thrusting so that the rigid points of her nipples jutted proudly in the soft, flickering light of the candles. Jonathan flicked his fingers across the quivering points, turning and twisting the tender flesh to induce more gasps from her as she thrust down even harder onto him.

Helene knew Elizabeth was on the edge of coming again, bottom cheeks clenching as she surged helplessly on the thick rod that drove deep into her cunt. Determined to make her spend quickly at her command, Helene probed into the wet cleft of her buttocks, one finger squirming against the puckered entrance of her anus. Then, already well aware of the intensity of Elizabeth's orgasms, her other hand crept over the straddled thighs, slipping into the warm slot of her vulva to search out her young victim's clitoris. Her finger wriggled delicately between the tender lips, Elizabeth's keening wail of pleasure and bucking convulsions signalling that she had found the spot she wanted.

Elizabeth's hands drifted forward, hooked fingers digging into Jonathan's arms as she curved over his body in undiluted ecstasy. Helene, loving every minute of her pupil's frenzy, moved her finger all the faster, the blade of her nail flickering unbearably against the tight knot of Elizabeth's clitoris. And she drove her other hand into the valley between Elizabeth's buttocks, a second probing finger thrusting like an arrow into the unguarded opening of her bottom. Working both hands with devilish skill Helene forced her young victim into a mad, wriggling frenzy.

The velvet suction, Elizabeth's internal muscles milking his shaft, broke Jonathan's iron control. His body arched up off the bed, lifting her as the jerking thrusts of his own climax overwhelmed him.

The mingled gasps of excitement echoed around the room as they both gave way to the avalanche of sensations carrying them over the edge. His fingers gripped and twisted her rigid nipples as her nails scored white lines over his chest, lines that darkened and swelled with blood as her fingers passed. Strands of damp blonde hair lashed his face and shoulders, Elizabeth's head flailing wildly in the throes of her release.

The girl's slim thighs clenched as she tried desperately to close her legs and shield her cunt from the maddening torment of those busy hands, but Helene's laughter joined the sounds of ecstasy as she continued to masturbate Elizabeth mercilessly.

'Oh yes, my darling,' she purred, 'can't you feel it, that fire getting hotter once again? Come on, my darling, come again for me.'

Jonathan, his own climax waning, cupped the lovely girl's breasts as, for the third time that evening, Elizabeth Ashton was forced into yet another shattering orgasm, and as it eventually subsided Helene, like a contented cat, lifted her glistening fingers and tasted the familiar tang of a female's passions.

'Just as I thought last night, my darling,' she said in sultry tones, 'you have strong fires within you.' She smiled, looking down at Jonathan's replete figure, still pinned to the bed by Elizabeth's shapely form.

Wearily, Elizabeth lowered herself to the cool sheet, immediately curling into a ball beside the handsome officer. 'Helene,' she mumbled dreamily, 'I am destroyed. I feel as though I've been riding for a week.' As she lay there, Helene softly stroked her damp brow, watching fondly as Elizabeth dozed.

Chapter 10
Riding for Pleasure

Mebele woke Elizabeth as the morning sun was just beginning to burn off the faint sea haze, lifting the temperature towards its usual scorching midday height. 'Madame says please to join her for breakfast.' The maid smiled as she held out a thin garment to her mistress. 'She says you not need anything but this to wear.'

Elizabeth recognised it immediately, the shift with the shoulder ties she'd last worn at Sir Roger's house the day she met Helene. The English girl stretched languorously, enjoying the slithering caress of the sheets on her body. She felt her nipples hardening as she wondered what games Helene was planning this time.

Mebele could see her mistress's excitement as she helped her into the flimsy shift, and then began to brush her mistress's soft blonde hair. 'Something special for you today, missy,' she said. 'Madame is going to give you a riding lesson. She asking me and Jenni to help you too.'

'A riding lesson?' Elizabeth echoed. 'But I can ride already. Does she mean we're taking a journey? What will I wear? Did she say anything else, Mebele?'

'No need for you to worry, missy, this is a special kind of riding. You see very soon. Madame Helene will tell you.' Mebele giggled at the blank look on her mistress's face as she finished tying the lustrous rope of blonde hair into a single gleaming tail. 'There, missy, all pretty for Madame. She waiting on the veranda for you.' Her fingers stroked Elizabeth's skin as she adjusted the shoulder ties. 'Better hurry now, missy, breakfast is waiting.'

Helena was taking her ease on the veranda as Elizabeth appeared. She smiled at the sight of her new conquest so obviously and eagerly obeying her instructions. Elizabeth sat down abruptly at the breakfast table, suddenly conscious of the way the hard peaks of her breasts were thrusting against the thin cotton, revealing her excitement to Helene's knowing gaze.

Once breakfast was over Helene clapped her hands to bring Jenni and Mebele hurrying to her side. 'Stand up, my darling,' she said to Elizabeth, 'it's time for your next lesson to begin. Put your hands behind your back.'

Experiencing a tingling anticipation, Elizabeth rose, clasping her hands together as she did so. Jenni slipped a soft leather tie round her wrists, knotting the tails to leave Elizabeth helpless once again.

Helene took her time studying the young blonde. 'And now another lesson for your senses, my dear girl. I suspect Mebele gave you a little clue earlier. I hope you slept well; you'll need all the stamina you've developed over the past few days. Oh yes, and a little repayment for last night.' She signalled to Mebele, who tugged the shoulder knots loose so that the thin cotton shift fell to the floor, leaving the young blonde naked.

Elizabeth could feel the urgent pounding of her heart as she listened to Helene's hypnotic voice. Was it to be another beating on the frame? The images raced around in her head and she squeezed her thighs together as she felt the delicious tingle of arousal in her loins. But the reverie was cut short as Mebele and Jenni took her arms, leading her across the courtyard to a gate set in the far wall. She had not explored this part of the villa and, for one wild moment, she shivered at the erotic image of being taken like a slave through the teeming streets to the market square, naked and with her hands bound behind her.

Jenni opened the gate to reveal not the street as she'd fantasised, but another smaller courtyard. A deep veranda lined one side, with a number of soft chairs and couches scattered upon it in the relative coolness of shade. The rest of the small area was paved with stone slabs. Even this early in the day Elizabeth felt the beads of sweat trickling down her body as the heat from the stones and the surrounding white walls made her pant for breath.

Then she twisted anxiously in the maids' clutches as she saw the truth of her 'riding lesson'. Set in the middle of the yard, the gleaming brown saddle mounted on a low wooden stand looked ordinary enough. But it was the sight of the two rounded prongs, the front one taller and thicker than the other, rising from the seat that made her fight against their grip. Helene walked over to the saddle, her fingers curling around the larger of the leather phalli.

'Oh yes, my darling, this is your next ride,' she said distractedly. 'Mebele, as this is her first time, I think we should ease the way for her a little. Please prepare the saddle for your mistress.'

Making sure that Elizabeth could see what she was doing, Mebele picked up a little flask and dribbled palm oil over the saddle, making sure each of the leather shafts was well soaked before using her fingers to coat the rest of it with a viscous film.

Helene then guided Elizabeth forward. 'Come on now, over you go.' She helped Elizabeth straddle the saddle, leg muscles straining to hold her body away from the twin shafts. 'Better sit down,' she went on, 'or would you like me to help?' Her fingers parted the lips of Elizabeth's sex to let the front shaft probe the opening of her vagina.

Elizabeth twitched, feeling the domed head opening her body, excited by the feeling as it slid upwards, filling and stretching her completely. Lowering herself gingerly, she had just begun to relax when she felt the stabbing intrusion of the slimmer, shorter shaft against the puckered bud of her anus. She stiffened, but Helene's hands pushed her down, the twin prongs sliding deeper and deeper until Elizabeth felt the warm and greasy curves of the leather seat tight up between her thighs.

Helene and Jenni pulled her ankles up behind her, slipping them into soft leather loops attached to the back of the saddle. Elizabeth moaned at the deeper impalement, then gasped as the cunningly placed ridge at the base of the front shaft provided an unexpected pressure against her clitoris. Wriggling to ease her leg muscles, she was only able to lift herself, with difficulty, a few inches up the leather shafts.

'Comfortable, my darling?' Helene asked unnecessarily. 'That isn't too bad, is it?'

'How long must I sit here, please?' Elizabeth pleaded, as the airless heat of the courtyard induced sweat to form in droplets on her body.

Helene chuckled. 'Be patient, you haven't even started your ride yet. Now you're seated so nicely, the girls are going to use bamboos on your bottom and titties; just enough to make you wriggle a little. For how long you ride is up to you, but,' she paused, a cunning smile playing on her lips, 'you will ride at least until you orgasm.'

Elizabeth wriggled frantically as Jenni and Mebele moved around her with thin canes in their hands. 'No, Helene, please no, I don't want to, p-please,' she pleaded.

'Of course at the moment you don't, but in a few minutes you'll be singing a different tune, I assure you.'

The woman turned and welcomed the new arrival to the courtyard. 'Ah, Richard, as punctual as ever, and just in time to enjoy Elizabeth's performance,' she said. 'Would you care to take a seat in the shade? There's wine, or fresh lime juice if you prefer.' Elizabeth looked up in horror then quickly lowered her head, trying to hide her face in shame as her supposed lover ambled closer.

He strolled slowly around the saddle, one hand running over Elizabeth's sweating flank and over the plump swell of her bottom, the cheeks now moulded around the intrusive rear phallus. 'You're looking radiant, my dear,' he mused. 'And Helene tells me you've been busy.' His hand fleetingly brushed the naked lips of her sex. 'Ah well, enjoy your ride and give us a good show. Excuse me if I find some shade, it's too hot for me out here.'

Angst and embarrassment reddened Elizabeth's countenance as the humiliation of her situation sank in. She watched vehemently as the couple retreated to the cool of the veranda, chatting and laughing gaily, sipping iced drinks and lounging in the inviting shade. Jenni and Mebele began spreading oil on her skin, interrupting her growing self-pity.

'Stop you burning and cutting up from the canes,' whispered Mebele. 'First it stings and then we make you happy very quickly. All the girls like riding for Mistress Helene in the end. Ready now, missy?'

Elizabeth, still glaring at Helene and Richard lolling at their ease on the veranda, was taken by surprise when Mebele swung her arm and sent the cane cutting across the curves of her bottom. She squealed as she rocked forward, rising off the saddle as the heat of the stroke bit into her buttocks, then it was Jenni's turn, cutting a stroke across the fullness of Elizabeth's breasts. She had waited for the girl's surging reaction to push her breasts out even more fully, before landing the first cut on the curve just below the poor blonde's nipples.

Elizabeth immediately jerked back again, trying to shield herself but, in the process driving the leather shafts back into her body. 'Ah, no...' she wailed at the second stroke from Mebele, and moments later another squeal of outrage echoed in the stifling courtyard as Jenni laid her second stripe just below the first.

Elizabeth quickly understood what they were doing. The rhythmic caning forced her to rock to and fro, up and down, so that the leather shafts slid remorselessly in and out of her anus and vagina. Already, beneath the immediate sting of the caning, she could feel the heat of arousal building up as she was forced to ride furiously on the saddle that impaled her.

'Noisy, isn't she?' Richard drawled, lolling back in his chair, watching the heaving figure on her leather mount. 'Hot work too, from the look of her.' He grinned at Helene. 'Already looks like she's been dunked in a pool of water, and the girls haven't even brought her off yet. Perhaps she's enjoying it too much to come.'

Helene shook her head, two fingertips absently tracing around her own nipple through the fine silk of her dress as she watched Elizabeth's alluring movements, enjoying the pleading cries that sounded over the regular *thwick* of the bamboo canes. 'She's almost there now. Richard, would you care for a small wager on how long it takes to bring her off a second time?'

'Not with your advantage of previously observing girls ride that apparatus of yours,' he chuckled. 'But you're right about the first time. Look at her go now, by God.' In the centre of the courtyard, beneath the increasingly ferocious sun, Elizabeth's thighs began to beat an urgent tattoo on the sides of the saddle, and the spasms of her climax threw her into a frenzy of movement, completely ignoring the stinging lash of the bamboos across her tender flesh as she lifted her face to the clear blue skies.

The maids smiled at their success, resting and catching breath as they watched the pleasure overtaking their victim. They waited quietly, ready and eager for the austere woman on the veranda to signal a recommencement of hostilities.

'Mebele, give your mistress a drink, then you may proceed,' Helene eventually ordered, and the coloured girl held a glass of limejuice to Elizabeth's parched lips, brushing the sweat-tangled hair away from her eyes as the young blonde gulped the cool liquid.

'That only one time, you come quicker now,' she told the disorientated girl. 'Mebele and Jenni going to pleasure you till you cry for us to stop, just like Mistress Helene tell us. You all ready now?' The maid didn't give the panting figure any chance of replying. Swapping sides, Mebele now let Jenni concentrate her attentions on the reddened curves of Elizabeth's buttocks, while she picked up the rhythm of sharper strokes to the heaving breasts as they swayed and quivered with the girl's jerking movements on the oily surface of the saddle.

'Oh Helene, p-p-please, no.' Elizabeth twisted hopelessly, her eyes screwed shut as the beating continued, but Helene and Richard could tell the blonde's protests were somewhat token ones, as it was quite clear she was quickly well on the way to her second climax. Within a few minutes her legs were again squeezing the sides of the saddle as her thigh muscles flexed at the effort of moving her up and down on the shafts that filled and tormented her. Elizabeth's head shook wildly as the sharp sting of the canes and the friction of the leather dildos within her drove her over the edge again.

Exhausted sobs of ecstasy echoed around the little courtyard a second time as Helene stepped out into the baking heat. 'Jenni, Mebele go and see to Mr Elford. I'll take over here.' She smiled at the two maids as they hurried over to Richard Elford.

'There, there, Elizabeth,' she continued, running her hands over the weary girl's wet skin, fingers teasing her swollen nipples and the angry flesh of her bottom, making the girl lift her head and gasp at the cool contact. 'Look, look there, watch Mebele and Jenni milking Richard for you.' Helene turned Elizabeth's face so she could see the maids, Mebele's fingers busy at Richard's groin while Jenni's head bobbed up and down, working her lips over the rigid length she had freed from his britches.

Elizabeth eased her position on the saddle, mewing softly at the movement of the leather prongs within her body, and at Helene idly toying with the lips of her sex. 'No, please, I can't, not so soon... ah, Helene, please have *mercy*...'

'Well now, this little button of joy tells a different story,' Helene teased, her forefinger delicately fretting Elizabeth's clitoris, and stroked the mane of wet blonde hair as the girl writhed against her touch, thighs once again tightening against the leather saddle in a rising tide of excitement.

In the shade Mebele's tongue was flickering across the domed purple head of Richard's penis as Jenni's fist worked the shaft with guile. Jenni moved to fondle his balls and the sensitive flesh between his thighs as Mebele took him deep into her mouth, sliding her head up and down, her cheeks hollowed with effort. Richard's cry of triumph rang out as Mebele's flickering tongue made him tense and ejaculate copiously.

'That's it, darling; go on now, for me,' Helene urged, her tone throaty with her own excitement. 'Ride for me, darling, ride harder, harder...' Helene's whispered coaxing and the relentless, tormenting finger, drove the saddled blonde wild, jerking frantically so that the leather shafts stabbed in and out of her body.

Finally the woman relented, slipping her fingers away, and the young blonde's head slumped forward as she fought to drag air into her tortured lungs.

She unhooked Elizabeth's ankles, freeing her legs so she could climb down, albeit extremely unsteadily, and stand on the hot ground. 'Oh, my legs,' she protested. 'I'm so tired, Helene, I'll sleep for a week.' She leaned on Helene's arm for support.

'Nonsense,' Helene chided affectionately. 'A little rest, a soak in a nice relaxing bath, and you'll be as right as rain.'

CHAPTER 11
Another Lesson from Sir Roger

It was ten days since Elizabeth first arrived at Helene Birencourt's villa, and already life under the control of her guardian, Sir Roger Stanley, seemed a distant memory. Helene's artful dispensing of both pain and pleasure was like a drug in her system, each day bringing unexpected discoveries as her mistress took her to new heights of experience.

Elizabeth, fully attired in a linen day dress, stockings and her white silk shoes, stood quietly in the main lounge of Helene Birencourt's villa.

Helene, still dressed in a black riding outfit with her hair tied back severely behind her head was sitting erect in one of the wooden armchairs. 'Elizabeth, Sir Roger has asked to see you tonight. As he is your guardian for at least two more years I cannot refuse his request, but...' she paused, and Elizabeth was taken aback to realise that Helene was unsure, unsettled by something. 'But I have grown fond of you, dear Elizabeth, and I would not wish to see you in danger. In truth, and perhaps I should not be telling you this, but I suspect that Sir Roger and Mr Elford might be involved in some kind of questionable business enterprise.' She faltered a moment, taking a deep breath, before deciding to continue.

'I saw a letter, yesterday whilst visiting Richard Elford, on the desk in his study while he went to arrange some tea for us. It was something I should not have seen, but your family name was mentioned, my dear. That is why I dared to read further. It was from a friend of Richard's in London, warning about an investigation into his business dealings and your guardian's affairs relating to your inheritance. At least, as far as I was able to ascertain.'

Elizabeth was stunned by this information, finding it extremely difficult to absorb. 'Were you caught, Helene? Is this why Sir Roger wishes to see me now? Did Richard discover you reading the letter?'

'No, my dear, no,' Helene reassured her. 'But that is not all. There have been other matters, not just the letter. They are friendly with a local merchant called Mehmet, a Turk, I believe. He trades in spices and gold, but it is rumoured that most of the goods he supplies are human. Not the usual trade, but a refined and particular market in beautiful young men and women, especially if they are fair-skinned, to be trained to supply the comforts and desires of rich and powerful men, in many countries.'

Carefully monitoring Elizabeth's reactions and dazed expression, Helene pressed on. 'Your guardian also does business with Prince Kemal, who wields much power in this region. He shows a cultured face but there are dark stories about him. He is rumoured to be deeply embroiled in the human trade, as Mehmet's patron, if the stories are to be believed.' She studied the English girl intently. 'Of course, such stories may be no more than malice from those who have been less than successful in their ventures here, but, dear Elizabeth, take great care. Remember, we are on the edge of the world here, and someone of your sex and colouring would command a high price from those with no ethics.'

Elizabeth shivered, as the meaning of the woman's words sank in a little more. 'Don't worry, Helene,' she said, with less conviction than she felt. 'Thanks to your warning I will be most vigilant, although I suspect that tonight's summons is more to do with Sir Roger swapping gentlemen's bawdy tales with Richard than anything else. But I wonder what the letter meant, all the same. I know my father left his affairs in order, and that there is considerable land and property in trust until I reach twenty-five.'

Helene thought for a moment. 'Go to Sir Roger with the warning I have given you. I will try to find an opportunity to again be alone in Richard's study, to see if I can find the letter and discover who sent it and what else it said. Then we can decide what to do next. Tell Mebele to pack your things, she can go with you.'

Elizabeth was surprised by how easily she settled back into the routine of Sir Roger's household. The first evening and the following day passed uneventfully. Elizabeth, carefully guarded by two servants with staves and cudgels, and accompanied by Mebele, spent the morning at the market, haggling for some lengths of cloth and a collection of silver bracelets.

Despite pinning her blonde hair up under a wide-brimmed hat, Elizabeth felt more conscious of what she now perceived as the calculating glances she was getting than usual, especially from some of the merchants in the Arab quarter. Helene's words about her hair colour and complexion had set her nerves on edge, and she was grateful for the looming presence of the two male servants, resplendent in their scarlet jackets and white sarongs.

Back at the villa there was a brief message to say that she was to remain in her room until Sir Roger summoned her later that evening, and Elizabeth couldn't help but wonder what his true intentions might be...

The tropical dusk was falling when the door of her room swung open. 'Your time, Miss Elizabeth, he is waiting,' beckoned Mebele, and Elizabeth rose from the chair upon which she sat, moving towards the door.

'A moment, missy,' Leila stopped her, 'Sir Roger also ordered...' Elizabeth paused, wondering what they were waiting for, and was too slow to react when, with a flurry of activity, Mebele suddenly produced a thick black hood from behind her back and tugged it down over the startled girl's head.

'Wha-what are you doing?' Elizabeth shrieked in muffled bemusement and anger, her world reduced to an impenetrable blackness. 'Let me go. Let me go at once! How *dare* you?' In the shock of being hooded and disorientated she didn't have a chance of resisting as Mebele also slipped a thin strap around her wrists.

Her cries of dismay echoed in the tiled corridor as the leash was jerked tight, digging into her skin and binding her hands behind her. Utterly helpless she felt both maids grip her upper arms, guiding her to the punishment chamber.

'Welcome, my dear, I'm so glad you've joined me for the evening.' The thick cloth muffled Sir Roger's voice to the struggling figure of his ward, once more held in front of him. 'Leila, I believe your mistress is well aware of her situation, you may remove the hood now.'

Elizabeth blinked as the bag was pulled off, the room exactly as she remembered. The only difference being the softer light of lamps and candles rather than the brightness of the bars of sunlight patterning the floor through slatted screens. Sir Roger, looking very pleased with himself, was sprawling in a woven rattan chair, the sloping back at such an angle that he was lounging back, one leg on a low footstool, the other bent so that his bare foot was squarely on the floor. A silk robe, startling in its vivid colours, was loosely belted around his waist. Instinctively, Elizabeth knew that beneath it he was naked... naked and ready for whatever perverse 'entertainment' he might have in mind for her on this occasion.

She gasped with relief upon seeing the polished bar had been removed. The floor was bare, apart from her guardian's lounging chair and footstool. But she suspected, whatever else happened, that chair was not there for her relaxation!

Sir Roger chuckled as he watched Elizabeth looking anxiously around. Waiting until she had scanned the whole room he said quietly, 'You may be wondering why I instructed you to return from Madame Birencourt's establishment at such short notice.'

He paused, enjoying the moment before going on. 'You see, my dear, it's very simple; in recent weeks our dear Helene has become more than a little indiscreet. And since I'm sure she did not keep matters to herself,' he paused again, his voice taking on a harder edge when he continued, 'I feel obliged to remind you of the necessity to keep out of the business of others. And it is a lesson that is going to give me great pleasure in conveying.' He looked at Elizabeth with cold eyes, and then smiled mirthlessly. 'Oh, but how impolite of me. Mebele, Leila, fetch a chair for my ward.' Obviously warned in advance of what was to happen, the two maids hurried to a corner, and Elizabeth's heart raced as she saw the 'chair' they were bringing from the shadows there. Shaped and jointed from black wood it had the look of age and barbaric native ceremony about it. The front legs, carved to represent twisting serpents, were set wide apart. The side rails tapered inwards to a single post, again intricately carved, that rose chest high in a curving arc from the floor to form a narrow backrest.

Elizabeth cringed with fear as she saw the chair had no seat, the only support it offered being two thickly padded horns jutting inwards, one from each front leg. Anyone trying to sit down would find his or her lower body and buttocks completely open and unsupported.

The two maids placed it in the position Sir Roger indicated. 'Come along, my dear, be seated so we may discuss matters in a civilised fashion,' he said casually. 'This may be your last chance to perform for me in all the ways I enjoy most. So I know you will try extra hard to please tonight.' Sir Roger lolled back, a picture of relaxation as he let the robe fall away from his sturdy legs.

'I do not know...' Elizabeth began, as she looked at the strange chair in dismay and confusion.

'Leila, Mebele, pray assist your young mistress, who seems to be suddenly unfamiliar with simple furniture.'

The two maids seized her arms, when Sir Roger spoke again. 'But before they help you, my dear, I fear your clothes will be in the way of your enjoyment of this new toy. You will undress, or the maids will do it for you.'

Elizabeth looked at Sir Roger in despair, twisting in the grip of the two maids, and Sir Roger smiled appreciatively at the feeble rebellion. Not that her entreaties would affect his cold heart at all, but it did make things more interesting to be faced with a challenge to his authority, no matter how fleeting it might be. 'It seems you misunderstand your situation, my dear,' he said. 'Challenge me, and you will disappear as though you had never even existed. Whatever you may think, it is I who commands here. Now, do you disrobe without question, or do you choose a more unpleasant course?'

Elizabeth submitted. Mebele undid the strap binding her wrists and then the girl

45

reluctantly began to unfasten her clothing. The two maids lifted the gown over her head, leaving her to unfasten the ties holding up her under-shift and bodice. Nervously, Elizabeth bent to unclip and remove her stockings, and only then did she allow the thin cotton shift to slip to the floor. Finally, uncomfortably aware of her guardian's growing impatience, she slipped down her lacy drawers and stepped out of them.

'Stand straight, my dear, let us see that pretty figure properly,' he ordered, and determined to appear unafraid Elizabeth stood proudly and openly before Sir Roger.

He gazed at the sweet curves of his ward's slim body. He could see that, despite her protests, her delightful nipples were significantly erect. Certainly she would be feeling the first moisture of anticipation and excitement in her loins, as she awaited whatever torments the chair might hold for her.

His eyes widened as he observed Elizabeth's newly shaven sex mound. The naked V at the junction of her thighs meant he could see every detail of the pouting lips and the deep slit of her sex. 'Well, well my dear young lady,' he said pensively, 'I see Helene has been at work, and your new appearance will increase our pleasures greatly.

'But time is wasting with this idle chat - secure her.'

Instantly obeying, Leila and Mebele lifted her, and spreading her legs at the same time, they lowered her so that her thighs settled in the curved horns on either side of the stout wooden frame. Although her feet rested on the floor Elizabeth instinctively braced herself by putting her forearms flat on the wooden arms and pushing hard against the curved backrest. As she did so she realised her first thoughts were right; her buttocks were left completely exposed by the chair's devilish design. Not only that, but the carefully shaped curve of the back forced her breasts out, displaying them even more blatantly to Sir Roger's stern gaze.

Working hastily but efficiently, Leila and Mebele fastened the strong leather straps attached to the frame. One tightened hard across each of Elizabeth's thighs just above the knee, holding her firmly onto the supporting horns. Each ankle was bound securely to the front legs of the chair, and then her wrists and elbows were buckled tight, forcing her arms down against the smooth wood.

Then knowing their prisoner was securely held, the two maids took more time to position and secure a wider band across her belly, cinching it tight to brace her body against the curving back. Finally, Leila secured a soft leather collar round her throat and through two slots in the wooden upright, making sure it was loose enough so as not to interfere with her hurried breathing.

Sir Roger smiled broadly as the maids stepped away to leave his ward bound and stiffly upright before him, her thighs held wide, her body ready for his attentions. Elizabeth twisted and wriggled in vain; despite her weary efforts the supple straps, creaking softly at her anguished straining, held her immovable in the grip of the diabolical frame.

Sir Roger looked into the pleading eyes of his ward. 'My special chair is new since you were last here, my dear,' he told her conversationally. 'So, you won't be familiar with its purpose. I acquired it from a trader some miles down the coast.' He paused and smiled grimly. 'You should be flattered, my dear, he claimed it is very old and was used in a distant tribe's more exotic rituals. I understand that only the most beautiful and passionate girls were ever permitted to show their endurance by being placed in the Seat of Pleasure.'

He savoured the moment, and the delicious look of apprehension on her beautiful face, before going on. 'Now it is your turn. I can't offer a roll of drums and crowds of eager worshippers but, as for endurance, I am sure that Leila and Mebele will be able to use all their skills to test you to the limit.

'But I fear you may well wish to escape those attentions very soon.' He looked at her closely before taking away her final hopes. 'You see, as a change from a simple beating, I have discovered it can be just as tormenting for someone to experience too much pleasure... something you are now about to find out for yourself.' He watched Elizabeth's writhing increase. 'I suggest you save your strength; you'll need all the stamina you can muster. For myself, I'll relax a little and let Leila attend to your needs.'

Hearing her master's words, Leila moved close, eagerly reaching to stroke and tease the unprotected breasts of the beautiful young blonde strapped helplessly to the chair. Elizabeth strained uselessly, the only effect achieved being to move her nipples against the maid's practiced fingers, and while Leila caressed her mistress all that could be heard in the room were the heaving breaths of the pinioned girl and the repeated creaking of leather as the straps flexed under the tension of her movements.

Sir Roger watched as Elizabeth's body responded, despite all her efforts to remain detached. 'I can see you are enjoying yourself already, so let me tell you what will now happen,' he said to her. 'While Mebele attends to my needs we will both watch as Leila makes you spend, and spend again. Enough times for the very pleasure you desire to turn to torment as your body clamours for release.' He leaned back in his chair so that Elizabeth could see the bulge of his manhood within the soft material of his robe. 'Then we shall see how the application of a little judicious pain can bring you back to a peak of pleasure yet again.'

'Please sir, for pity's sake show some kindness,' she pleaded. 'This humiliation is too much to bear. You cannot mean it.'

Sir Roger chuckled. 'Doubtless, my girl, but it is what I intend. Tonight you will entertain me by being pleasured as I command. Now Mebele, attend to me.'

Elizabeth slumped in her bonds as the summoned maid moved to Sir Roger's chair, and he slipped a hand under the hem of her cotton shift. Watching through half closed eyes, Elizabeth was able to tell from the sudden intake of breath and shuffling movement of Mebele's feet that Sir Roger was fingering the dampness of her cunt. The black maid moaned softly, moving her hips in a subtle circle under his slow manipulation. 'Take it off,' he ordered. 'Let me see you,' and Mebele obeyed hurriedly, pulling the cotton shift over her head before dropping it aside.

Just as Elizabeth had expected, beneath it she was completely naked. Trying desperately to ignore her own excitement, the vision of the maid standing submissively, feet apart, her fingers rolling the rigid stubs of her nipples as she was masturbated so openly, toyed with Elizabeth's senses.

Mebele's tight bottom clenched and flexed, her hips beginning to make instinctive thrusts, her knees bending and parting to open herself more fully. She was beginning to moan softly, her feelings growing more intense as Sir Roger worked his fingers deeper. Her fingers opened and closed, rolling and squeezing, teasing the points as she worked to increase her own excitement, seeking to drive herself over the brink of pleasure - but such immediate pleasure was quickly denied her.

Sir Roger was much too wily a rake to allow one of his servants to achieve her satisfaction so easily. Suddenly withdrawing his wet fingers he snorted at her sensual movements and whimpers of frustration. The maid's hips still churned in a slow circle as she leaned over to lick her own juices from his raised fingers. Knowing very well what he expected, she recovered her breath a little then knelt, parting the silk robe as she did so.

Elizabeth watched in awe, panting with her own rising excitement as Mebele freed Sir Roger's erection, the thickly veined shaft spearing up from the nest of dark hair in his groin. Mebele needed no further instructions, parting her lips over the polished crest before slowly engulfing his full length in her mouth. Sir Roger lazily thrust his hips upward, giving a deep sigh of satisfaction as he felt the sliding wetness close around his cock.

Once Leila saw Mebele's head moving gently up and down over Sir Roger's groin, she gave a final twist to the nipples she'd been tormenting and knelt at the side of her helpless captive.

'No, please no,' Elizabeth moaned. 'Please leave me alone.'

'I have my orders, missy,' Leila said softly. 'Besides, I know how much you enjoy a woman's touch.' She reached behind the chair with one hand, running over the toned curve of her young mistress's buttocks until she could play with the deep valley between them. Moist fingers traced the tender groove, eyes watching carefully for those telltale signals as her fingers brushed across the crinkled rosette of Elizabeth's anus. She smiled to herself as the blonde reacted to the intimate caress, watching as the girl's mouth opened in an 'O' of silent protest as one of her fingers pushed gently through the little ring of muscle and began to move and turn within the depths of Elizabeth's bottom.

Minutes passed as Leila twisted and pressed her finger in and out. 'Oooh, oh yes, what are you doing to me?' came the broken, whispering voice. Helpless to prevent it all, Elizabeth began to move her hips against the tormenting invader in her rear.

'What your guardian ordered, missy, I am to make you spend and there is nothing you can do to stop me.' Seeing from the gently thrusting hips that Elizabeth was already well on the way to riding her first orgasm, Leila slipped her other hand between the chair arm and the blonde's pinioned leg. Very gently she curved her fingers, reaching up to fondle the plump lips of Elizabeth's naked sex, open and unprotected between her widespread thighs.

Keeping the gentle rocking movement of her left hand going, Leila began to trace her fingers up and down the wet groove of the girl's cunt, making sure that her nails scraped lightly across the sensitive tissues at the mouth of her vagina. As Elizabeth got steadily wetter Leila slipped two fingers up into her, easing them in and out in time with the movements of her other hand. Gradually the cunning maid began to move both hands more quickly, allowing her impaling fingers to stimulate the deepest centres within Elizabeth's body.

The pleading words grew louder. 'I can't stand it, please, please don't, the bound girl mumbled. 'No more, please stop, please.'

Sir Roger looked across as he heard the babbling voice of his luscious ward, and the sight stirred his senses; her arched body, her tanned and naked flesh gleaming with moisture in the candlelight, held upright in the diabolical chair. She was muttering and gasping, continually writhing in the bonds, her firm breasts quivering with her efforts to prevent the betrayal of her own body.

Close to one side the figure of Leila appeared to be holding her arms around one of Elizabeth's thighs. Her apparent stillness was an illusion, for Sir Roger could just detect the slow flexing of her arms and the subtle pumping of one hand where it cupped his ward's sex. The effect of the maid's insistent masturbation was clear from Elizabeth's panting breaths, closed eyes and flushed complexion.

As he watched, Sir Roger saw Elizabeth stiffen and brace herself against the straps, her cries becoming more urgent. 'Oh yes, go on, don't stop,' she mumbled, held her breath, and then shuddered, signalling that Leila had brought her to a surging orgasm.

She continued fingering the slick wet lips for a moment more, before kneeling back on her haunches. Smiling, in cruel satisfaction, she looked up at the breathless young lady now slumped against the straps. 'There, missy, that's what you really wanted,' she whispered, stroking Elizabeth's thigh. 'Soon we'll try something a little different to make you scream with joy all over again.'

Sir Roger pushed Mebele upright then lay back fully, sweeping the dressing gown clear of his thighs and signalling to her that she should straddle him. The maid needed no second bidding, stepping astride him so that she was poised over the stout phallus. Her hands encircled the shaft, moving the slick head against her body as she squatted, the bulbous tip probing the entrance of her vulva. Slowly she sank further, adjusting her position and grimacing a little as the thickness stretched her, pressing deeper into her body, opening and filling.

Once firmly embedded she waited, not daring to move before Leila began again. Both Mebele and Sir Roger could observe the frame, watching the show as they enjoyed their own excitement. She felt Sir Roger stir inside her as Leila removed her dress, clearly enjoying being watched as she began to work on Elizabeth's body once again.

'Be careful you do not forget your task, Leila,' he warned, and reminded of her main duty, she got to her feet, a little unsteadily, to fetch two items from the cupboard by the door before kneeling once more by Elizabeth's side.

She whispered to the dreamy figure in the chair. 'Here, missy,' she said quietly, 'see what I have to please you with this time.' Leila held up the two objects, and the English girl's face reflected both her exhaustion and the sudden awful anticipation of what Leila might be going to do to her next. The small ivory cylinder, with its cunning ridges and smoothly tapered tip was all too familiar, since Sir Roger had often encouraged Mebele and Leila to use the dildo to make her spend during recent months.

The other item wasn't clear until Leila turned her hand and she saw the maid was holding a feather. Elizabeth shuddered because, although she'd never experienced it, she remembered Richard Elford describing to Sir Roger how they'd spent a night tormenting a victim with a feather like the one Leila was holding.

'No, please,' she pleaded with the naked figure kneeling closely by her side.

'You got no choice, missy,' Leila told her, lust thick in her voice. 'Quickly now, choose; which one to make you jiggle first? This little man that made you scream the last time, or maybe first you want some stroking from my feather? Come on, missy, time for choosing.'

'I can't, I won't, I don't want to spend again,' Elizabeth mumbled wearily. 'Leila, please let me rest.'

'Ah, you want a surprise, so I choose for you, missy.' Leila pretended to study both objects for long seconds. 'I think the little man first, missy,' she announced. 'But let me make him all wet for you first.' Leila sank lower, sliding the little dildo between the soft lips of her own cunt and gently moving it back and forth, coating the smoothly crafted shape with her juices. After a few moments she removed the gleaming cylinder, holding it up to Elizabeth's gaze before moving it between her thighs.

'See, missy, so smooth and easy, just like a silk tongue tickling your cunny. Can you feel that, missy? Does the little man still stir your body as he has before?'

She stroked the very tip of the ivory phallus against the soaking groove of Elizabeth's sex, running it from the cleft of her buttocks, over her anus to the junction of her labia. Gradually she increased the pressure so that Elizabeth began to gasp once more as the stimulation built steadily. With her free hand Leila parted the plump lips very, very gently so that the slick point of the dildo could slide up into the moist heat of her young mistress's body.

Mebele was also gasping with her own pent-up desires as she watched her colleague's slow masturbation of the blonde English girl. She rocked gently up and down, scarcely moving on the thick shaft filling her vagina. Beneath her, Sir Roger also watched, entranced, kept at a peak by the velvet sheath of Mebele's body.

Very soon Elizabeth's spasms revealed she was on the edge of coming once again, and the involuntary cry was torn from her as she sobbed and strained against the leather straps.

Straddled across the other chair, Mebele began to rise and fall more vigorously, responding to the erotic diatribe and uncontrolled movements Leila was cleverly coaxing from Elizabeth. Sir Roger twisted the delicate flesh of Mebele's breasts as he too began to reach his climax. Finally they spent together, Mebele falling forward, exhausted, onto Sir Roger's chest as her internal muscles milked the last of his seed from him.

While the two watching slaked their lust, Leila continued the teasing torture, dragging the young woman remorselessly to another orgasm and leaving her gasping and drenched in sweat, hanging in the straps with drops of moisture falling to the floor beneath her splayed body.

This time Leila was allowing no respite for the helpless girl. Using the ivory shaft to massage her own clitoris, she picked up the feather and began to stroke the softness against the parted, succulent divide of Elizabeth's sex.

'Oh no, please stop, I can't bear it,' the bound girl murmured, shaking her head deliriously. 'Stop... stop I tell you.' But Leila smiled wickedly as her mistress suffered the overload of sensations her nerves were being forced to bear.

Elizabeth jadedly lifted her head, orgasmed yet again, and then without warning she fainted, slumping down so that she hung limply in the straps.

'Damn me, that's excellent,' Sir Roger enthused, then clicked his fingers at Mebele. 'Fetch me a glass of wine, and one of my cigars.'

Mebele scrambled from her master's lap to bring him a glass of claret from the sideboard. Sir Roger sipped thoughtfully, then leered over the rim of his glass. 'Leila,' he paused, studying the lolling figure, 'a glass for your mistress, I think. Stir her blood a little before we continue with our little game.'

Leila struggled upright to fetch the wine, the feather and the glistening ivory cylinder lying discarded for the moment. She then stroked Elizabeth's hair until she finally began to stir.

'Wh-where am I?' the blonde mumbled, writhing against the straps in frustration. 'You monster,' she said, reality returning. 'You devil, let me go. Let me go at once, sir!' she shrieked, but Sir Roger lounged back in his chair, sipping his wine and smoking the cigar Mebele had served him with, completely at ease.

'Tut, tut, my dear, another childish outburst, I fear,' he mused. 'You really must learn greater self-control,' he teased, mocking her sudden rage. 'Leila, my ward is undoubtedly recovered, so after that silly tantrum, please remind her of her predicament. A little more attention to those elegant titties would serve, I think.' A smile of malicious delight crossed Leila's face at her master's instructions. She whispered something to Mebele, handing her the glass of wine untouched by Elizabeth and moving to the rear of the chair.

The maid's head dipped close to Elizabeth's. 'Better now, missy?' she whispered, hands stroking the young blonde's shoulders. 'Time to play with these again...' her hands moved, but this time her fingers were hooked into cruel talons, curved to pinch and twist the tender nipples.

Anger evaporated as Elizabeth pleaded with her guardian, Leila, anyone at all, just as long as the maid left her breasts alone. But Sir Roger ignored her, watching avidly as Leila used her nails to score bright red lines over each smooth curve, insidiously scraping across her jutting nipples. He smiled contentedly upon witnessing his ward's instant change of tone, letting Leila's agonising treatment continue until he saw the tears rolling down Elizabeth's cheeks. At last he waved the maid away with a languid hand.

'Ah, a little more contrite now, are we?' he said. 'Well, let me see; Leila has made you spend already, but I think you can show us your pleasure at least once more before we finish this delightful session.' Sir Roger ignored the outraged gasps from Elizabeth. 'Leila can continue working on those delightful tits of yours, then Mebele really should have a chance to show her skill with your little ivory friend. I will just lie back and enjoy your performance. There, that's fair, isn't it?'

'No, its monstrous,' Elizabeth argued. 'I'm not a paid whore, Sir Roger. Have mercy, what pleasure can you gain from this? Release me, *please!*'

Mebele, following her friend's request, handed Leila a many-tailed whip. Leila flicked the lash out, letting the tails snake down across the upper slopes of Elizabeth's breasts. 'This comes next, missy,' she whispered, and watched the cords dragging across the slopes of Elizabeth's flesh. 'Ah, but can you feel the little knots?' The maid paused, letting the knotted tails trace over the red welts left by her fingernails. 'They sting like the devil, catch every part of your fine titties. Oh, missy, you'll be singing like a mad lady very soon. You wait, you'll think your titties are on fire.' The tails irritated as Leila moved the whip to and fro. 'You ready for Leila, missy? You want to start?'

Elizabeth felt her flesh prickling as the knotted strands moved over her breasts, but despite every effort there was nothing she could do. And worse, her traitorous nipples were hardening once again. And before her the added torment of seeing the smirking presence of Sir Roger, lounging naked in his chair, his thick penis curling back from the thicket of hair at his groin, already partly erect again against his belly.

She missed the imperceptible nod Sir Roger gave Leila, and wailed in shock as the cunningly knotted thongs flayed across skin already sore from the previous session.

Thwick!

Leila sent the next stroke cutting home, making sure she laid the tails across the tips of Elizabeth's breasts so that some of the little knots seared like points of molten fire over the peaks of each nipple. Elizabeth jerked and actually rocked the heavy wooden

51

frame, the legs clattering against the polished boards as she fought the pain blazing through her body.

Leila continued to bring the thin strands whipping across, scoring a network of fine welts on the hot flesh before her. Elizabeth, sobbing, threshed against her bonds as with the cruel expertise of long practice, Leila now used slower strokes, swinging upwards so the knotted cords flailed into the soft flesh beneath each taut underside. Instantly the girl's cries became shriller as scalding lines sliced into her most tender flesh.

After twelve strokes Leila paused, one hand resting on the back of the chair, the whip's vicious little strands trailing limply to the floor. Twelve strokes had reduced Elizabeth to a wreck, her mouth slack with pain and the effort needed to ease her tortured breathing. But the pause was only a cruel respite; in her pain she knew with awful certainty that the two maids hadn't finished with her yet.

Mebele now added aching pleasure to the web of pain. Running a hand over the swell of Elizabeth's buttocks, she smiled at her fellow tormentor, expert fingers tracing the deep divide, teasing the tender furrow, reaching lower until she could stroke the soft opening of Elizabeth's body just as Leila had done.

Elizabeth, still locked into the pain in her breasts didn't react at first. It was only the stronger sensation of two fingers slowly probing up into her vagina that forced her to concentrate on Mebele's assault from below. 'No, oh please, haven't you done enough to me?' she pleaded, but her words had no effect on the steady movements of Mebele's hand, a fondling that was already making her traitorous body respond once again.

Mebele giggled over the soft squelching of her fingers. 'No need to pretend, missy.' Her fingers stirred and flexed in the succulent warmth. 'All soft and wet, missy, ready to ride your little man again. Where would you like it first?' She probed into the girl's vagina. 'Or here, perhaps?' The devilish fingers slithered back, stretching the circle of her anus. 'Tell Mebele, missy, tell her how you want your little friend to please you this time.'

'Leave me alone...'

'Mebele chose for you, missy,' the maid said, ignoring her mistress's protests, picking up the little ivory phallus just as Leila had done, then reached between Elizabeth's thigh and the wooden arm of the chair with one hand, carefully moving her fingers to hold the moist lips apart. Working like a seamstress with the most delicate material, she used only a feather touch to slide the dildo to and fro against the moist slot of the young blonde's sex, and she, breathing in shallow gasps, heaved in her leather restraints as the tip met her flesh.

A charged silence fell in the candlelit room as Mebele worked intently, a silence only broken by intermittent gasps and stifled sounds from Elizabeth, sounds forced from her as ecstasy built, the pain in her breasts becoming a dull throb, fuelling the growing arousal in her loins.

'Leila, a few strokes more,' Sir Roger instructed, 'but softly this time, just to tease her onwards. She is nearly ready to spend again.' Sprawling in his chair, his own rampant arousal now obvious, his cock once again arching up like a carved rod.

Leila stroked Elizabeth's shoulder. 'Now, missy, feel my little cat licking you again.' Achingly slowly she swung her arm, letting the tails just flicker lightly across the reddened skin before her. Breath hissed from Elizabeth's throat as she felt the hot lines tracing over her breasts again. But this time was different; this time the fiery sting of each strand was almost welcome, stoking the fires inside her.

Sir Roger noted the change as pain merged into pleasure once again, his own lust stirred by the rhythmically wet sounds of Elizabeth being moved inexorably towards another climax. 'Leave her, Leila,' he ordered. 'Come here and attend to me while Mebele makes her climax.' His voice was thick with desire.

Leila obediently dropped the whip and hurriedly straddled her master's erection, easing the purple head between her sex lips then sinking down to engulf his length in one ecstatic movement. Despite her need and excitement she cried aloud, biting her lip as she felt the fleeting, stretching pain of his manhood within her. Hands braced on her master's shoulders, she rose and fell on the thick shaft, always careful not to block Sir Roger's view of his ward as Mebele forced her to climax yet again.

The careful thrusting twists of the ivory dildo increased, pushing deeper, and speeding the movement she urged her young mistress over the brink. 'Come now, missy, can you feel it? Are you ready? Quickly now, look at Leila as she fucks Sir Roger.'

Mebele gave Elizabeth no chance to resist; the delicious friction in her sex and the sight of Leila riding Sir Roger like a wild thing conspired to drive her over the peak. She screamed in wonderful release as the pleasure waves engulfed her. Far stronger and more intense than before, she shuddered and bucked against the straps, desperately trying to make Mebele continue. The convulsions of her orgasm were enough to finish Sir Roger and Leila; their urgent coupling also brought to a climax.

Eventually Mebele moved, rising to her feet and looking to Sir Roger for instructions. 'Shall I untie missy now, sir?' she asked.

Sir Roger sat up, pushing Leila to the floor. 'Yes, yes,' he said slowly. 'Get her to her room. You will have no trouble with her now. Lock the door, once she is secure.'

CHAPTER 12
Voyage into Slavery

Elizabeth Ashton stood against the handrail of the trading brig *Nightingale*, watching the bowsprit rising and falling against the first rays of the morning sun. The wind was steady and delightfully cool. Two days out from the harbour, she was experienced enough to know that within hours the pleasant breeze would die and the sun would become unbearable, heating the decks until even the pitch softened in the seams and a patch of shade became the most valuable thing onboard.

The morning after her last experience with Sir Roger had been an uncomfortable awakening. Elizabeth found herself wracked by cramps, aching from the events of the night before. But a bath and gentle stretching exercises, Mebele's hands this time soothing and gentle as she rubbed cream into the sorest places, did much to restore her spirits.

Elizabeth, now fearful of her guardian, had been unprepared for his announcement at breakfast. They were sitting in the shade of the deep veranda enjoying fruit and fresh coffee while the birds scolded loudly and small lizards scuttled about along the line of shadow cast by the overhanging roof.

'Business affairs call me away for a few weeks, Elizabeth,' he told her. 'I've chartered a brig to make a number of visits along the coast. Since you are staying with me I have arranged for you to come too. It's a chance to see the country, my dear girl. I don't know exactly where we'll be putting in, but there's a man I have to visit at Lome.'

He stopped, realising Elizabeth was still unfamiliar with the settlements along the Gold Coast. He waved a hand in a vague direction. 'It's about a hundred and fifty miles along the coast, east of here across the delta,' he explained. 'Impossible by land, all swamps and marsh, fever country, but an easy journey by sea as long as you keep your wits about you. What do you say?'

Elizabeth balanced easily as the ship corkscrewed across the long ocean swell, rolling into what she'd heard the captain call the *Bight of Benin*. She knew from her long voyage from England just how little privacy there was onboard ship, and since her guardian was also a passenger she reasoned that at the least she'd be safe from his attentions on the voyage.

There was a hail from the mainmast and scurrying confusion as the sails were trimmed and the ship headed in towards the thin green line of the coast. In a few hours Elizabeth was able to make out the yellow sand and a white line of the surf along the bottom of the tree line. Gradually, small white shapes of buildings, the darker patchwork of huts and the wispy spirals of cooking fires rising into the morning air became clearer as the vessel entered the river's mouth.

By the time they anchored and Sir Roger had been rowed ashore, it was midday and the heat was stifling. The wind had died and Elizabeth stayed on deck under an awning, watching the continual procession of small, brightly painted craft and canoes crisscrossing the water between the anchored ships. Warned in advance by Captain Soames, she steadfastly ignored the constant entreaties of men and boys in canoes and log rafts, trying to sell her anything from fruit to brightly coloured cloth.

It was three hours before Sir Roger returned, sweating and red from the heat, accompanied by a tall man dressed in the white cotton *thob* and ornately decorated waistcoat of a wealthy Arab. They strode across the deck to where Elizabeth was standing in the shade. 'Prince Kemal, my ward, Miss Elizabeth Ashton,' Sir Roger introduced them. 'Elizabeth, his Highness has offered us the hospitality of his palace for a few days while I conclude my business here.'

The prince bowed low, taking Elizabeth's right hand in both of his own, brushing it with his lips as he did so. 'Sir Roger did not do you justice, beautiful lady. My home is yours for as long as you desire. Will it please you to come now? My servants will see to your luggage. I have a boat already waiting.'

Neither he, nor Sir Roger, noticed the frozen expression on Elizabeth's face *'He wears a cultured face but there are darker stories about him...'* She could hear the echo of Helene's words in her brain as she went through the required responses of etiquette. Sir Roger was being too nice, too accommodating after his warning about meddling in his affairs. As she was helped down into a boat, Elizabeth was revising her view that a sea voyage had been a good idea.

They were rowed across the anchorage to some steps. At the top of them an open carriage awaited, with servants holding its steps as others helped them up. Then making their stately way through the teeming maze, Kemal kept up a flow of local information and stated how pleased he was to welcome Sir Roger to his home once more. That last remark deepened Elizabeth's anxiety.

The carriage halted by an anonymous wooden door in a whitewashed wall. It swung open and Kemal ushered them into a large enclosed courtyard, blazing with colour, the sound of fountains and running water drifting on the scented air. Elizabeth, looking around in enchantment at the unexpected contrast to the dusty, chaos of the town streets, could see archways and long tiled corridors opening off the courtyard. Broad steps led up to the floor above and everywhere there were flowers and shrubs, even tall trees, growing in pots and beds. The noise of the water was coming from a large octagonal pool, tiled in a deep, brilliant blue interlaced with white and gold patterns, into which a small fountain spilled a steady trickle of clear water.

'Oh, it's lovely!' Elizabeth couldn't help but exclaim. 'Your palace is delightful, Prince Kemal.'

The prince tutted and wagged a slender finger at her. 'Kemal, only Kemal, beautiful lady,' he said. 'It gives me joy that you like my humble home. As you will see, I enjoy owning beautiful things.' He clapped his hands, and from the other side of the courtyard two girls approached, moving silently on bare feet. 'Selima, Sula, these are my guests. My home is theirs, bid them welcome.'

Elizabeth stared at the clothes the two girls were wearing, or rather, the clothes they were not wearing, as they bowed. Both were in close-fitting bodice tops, cut low so that the upper swell of their breasts was obvious, but it was not the tops that made Elizabeth pause. At first sight she thought they were wearing some kind of skirt, tied at the waist and ankles. Then she saw that the garments were loose trousers, like long drawers, but that they were made of the sheerest cotton so that their legs were clearly visible through the almost transparent cloth.

The only aid to modesty was the tiny jewelled triangle each wore, held by thin cords round their waists, serving to cover their sex but somehow making them seem even more naked in the process.

Kemal noticed Elizabeth's stare. 'Please, I trust my servants do not offend you?' He oozed charm. 'In this climate, and in the privacy of one's home, clothing such as theirs is very usual. Besides,' he looked straight into Elizabeth's eyes, 'when there is beauty, should one not be able to appreciate it without restriction?'

He bowed again to her. 'Unfortunately, I have matters of urgency to discuss with Sir Roger. I am sure you must be fatigued after your voyage. Why not let the girls show you to your rooms. They will help you bathe and, why, if you wish, you may try some of their clothing for yourself.'

For Elizabeth the prospect of being able to wash and relax for the first time in days was too tempting to refuse. 'Thank you, I'd be very grateful of a chance to refresh myself,' she said, and the girls immediately seized a hand apiece, leading her away to another part of the palace.

'She is perfect, exactly as you described, my friend,' Kemal said to Sir Roger, licking his lips, looking across the courtyard to where the three girls had vanished. 'I will be fighting away offers within days once the word gets round. Are you sure she suspects nothing?'

'The bitch doesn't trust me at all,' grunted Sir Roger. 'Only came with her to make sure we reached here without some other blasted interruption. She has to go, Kemal; knows too much, and too willing to tell what she knows, I suspect. Still, a few days to get her up river, then the job's done.'

'As you say, a few days only.' He paused. 'I had thought we would share some entertainment tonight. I have a girl who must be punished; you will find it to your liking, I think. Shall we let the beautiful Elizabeth join us? After all, she might as well see what she is to expect in the future. You did say she had taken part in such entertainments before, did you not?'

Sir Roger smiled at Kemal's suggestion. 'Capital idea,' he agreed, 'simply capital. Yes, that should set her thinking. And yes, she's used to both the whip and the rod, as you'll see soon enough. Tonight should be different; let her know what's coming, and who's in charge.'

CHAPTER 13
Helene's Ordeal

Richard Elford, face alight with cruel anticipation, walked into the room. 'Well, well, look what we have here,' he mused. 'A damned thief, if I'm not mistaken. So, Madame, are we to receive an explanation at all for this disorder?'

Behind him, also grinning unpleasantly was a slim, dark-haired stranger. Both men were still dressed formally, the stranger in Arab robes and chequered headdress, Richard sporting a silk shirt and a waistcoat rich with gold thread and fashionable colours.

Helene, crouching on the floor, was totally lost for words. Gawping at the two men now barring her route to freedom she tried to imagine what had gone wrong. Why was Richard here? How did he seem to expect to discover her here? 'Richard, you are supposed to be... I mean... I thought that?'

'Well, well, our French bitch is lost for words,' he scoffed. 'This gentleman is the man you've been making such clumsy enquiries about in recent weeks. Mehmet, the figure grovelling before you amid my private papers is Madame Helene Birencourt. You will have a chance to get to know her more intimately in a little while.' Richard laughed quietly, enjoying the look of horror on Helene's ashen face when she heard Mehmet's name. 'As to my presence here, I think that explanation can wait until we have taken you downstairs. There is so much I want you to tell me.'

'You evil monster, you planned this little charade from the beginning,' Helene accused. 'Well, you can bluster all you like but I'm not going anywhere with you, or your slimy friend. It's the governor who'll hear of this! Out of my way... or shall I rouse the household?' She was so intent on lashing out at Richard in her fear and rage that she didn't consider Mehmet. His arm whipped round, the leather cosh slammed against her head, and Helene crumpled to the floor, quite unconscious.

'Do not worry, Richard, a few minutes only I assure you, a headache but nothing worse,' he assured his accomplice. 'The cellar, yes?' Richard nodded, watching as Mehmet picked up the inert body. He checked the corridor was empty before leading the way to the very back of the house, where stone steps led down to the underground network of vaulted chambers that had once been the cells and holding rooms of the slave pens.

The underground passageway was lighted with lanterns set into the brick walls at regular intervals. After ten yards or so the two of them ducked as they went through a low archway. The chamber was bright with candles, and opposite the point they'd entered another archway gave a glimpse of more stone steps, leading up.

A series of arches pierced one wall, each opening into a small cell, bare but for a frame bed, straw mattress and a wooden bucket. An iron grille barred each opening. The opposite wall was braced with stout vertical beams, all fitted with ancient hooks and ringbolts. Those same ominous fixings could be seen at intervals along ceiling beams. A tall cupboard stood next to the stairway arch, and apart from two plain wooden chairs, a padded bench and a menacing wooden frame set with straps and leather padding, the chamber was empty.

'Any one will do, Mehmet,' Richard said carelessly, walking across to a niche in the wall and pouring some wine from the bottles and glasses placed there. Sipping the rich red liquid appreciatively, he watched Mehmet use a foot to swing open one of the iron grilles before dropping Helene, now beginning to mumble and stir, onto the thin mattress.

The Turk lashed her wrists with a thin leather thong then slammed the grille closed. He secured the heavy bolt, yawned and stretched, easing the muscles cramped by carrying Helene's weight for so long.

'Exactly as you said, Richard, my congratulations.' Mehmet frowned. 'However, this is not some forgotten relative or unknown maidservant. Helene Birencourt is well known to many people. She cannot simply disappear without enquiries being made.'

'I know, Mehmet, I know. But matters have reached a crisis. You know we were all but finished here anyway. That's why we had to act today. Once Jenni came to tell me that the bitch had seen the letter, and talked to Elizabeth as well, we had no choice. I've made sure all is ready for a quick and comfortable trip. Back to Tunis or Algiers and we can pick up the other end of the business quietly and easily. I've kept as much as possible in gold and jewels and this property is only rented till the month's end. We can be on the brig and away as soon as Sir Roger returns from his dealings.

'Kemal can deal with the Ashton girl through his usual network, and Helene can come with us. She'll fetch a handsome price, with the maid as a tasty bonus. And until then she can provide us with some sport.'

Mehmet grinned at the thought of the 'sport' to come. 'Excellent, Richard, she's safe here. There are things we need to do today if we are to move our mutual interests further north so soon.' Nodding in agreement, Richard Elford followed Mehmet out of the chamber and up the stone steps.

Helene came round to a splitting headache and the prickle of coarse material against her cheek. Trying to gather her wits, she sat up; panic and anger mingling as she gradually remembered the scene in the study. But where was she now? The little cell was dim, the only light filtering in from the candles in the chamber beyond making the iron grille look black and immovable. Standing up, she found that only two short paces were enough for her to press her body against the bars.

She looked across the gloomy brick chamber beyond. Even with the lights around the walls the place had an evil, brooding atmosphere. She knew this was Richard and Mehmet's lair, part of their evil business in the flesh trade that she'd discovered so much about in the last few weeks.

Screaming in anger and frustration, she rattled the bars in a mad fury of anguish and rage. But no one came. Her voice, muffled by the thick damp walls, faltered and faded to a whisper. Helene Birencourt sank onto the thin mattress in tears, dreading what the future might bring.

Hours passed before Helene again heard the sound of footsteps. Looking through the grille she saw the shadowy figure of Richard entering the chamber, followed by Mehmet, and a third figure wearing a long, hooded cloak. From his staggering gait, the latter had apparently been drinking.

'Ah, dear Helene, awake again and all ready for me, I see,' this man said. 'Mehmet, please arrange Madame Birencourt so we can talk more comfortably.'

'Keep away from me, keep away,' she said, wide-eyed with fear, shaking her head and backing away as Mehmet opened the grille, ignored her threats, picked her up and carried her out of the cramped cell, and dropped her, still shouting and kicking onto the grimy floor. Taking a strong cord from his pocket, he laced it through her wrist tie before fetching a chair to pass the other end through one of the black ringbolts in the overhead beam. Stepping away from the struggling figure on the floor he then pulled steadily, dragging Helene's arms upwards as he did so. She scrambled to her feet; trying to lift her arms faster than Mehmet could pull them.

'It's no use, my dear, just accept that you cannot escape,' Richard murmured as her arms were dragged above her head. 'That'll do I think, Mehmet. The ankle straps will spread her enough to bring her up on her toes.' Mehmet tied the cord to one of the fixings at the side of the macabre chamber. The two men, and the small hooded figure, watched intently as Helene panted, cursed and wriggled, trying desperately to ease the pressure on her wrists and find some way of freeing herself from the bonds.

'Now, now, dear lady, I've just told you,' Richard mocked her futile efforts. 'Mehmet's far too adept at this sort of thing, so stop fighting it. Now, to make sure you cannot use those pretty feet to injure anyone.'

Mehmet knelt, swiftly buckling a leather cuff with a short chain attached round her left ankle. Jerking her leg out wide, he clipped the chain to an iron staple set in the stone flags. With one leg secured he repeated the process, less urgently, with her right ankle, forcing Helene into a wide straddle as he fastened the second chain.

Both men then sat down next to the hooded figure, relaxing and studying the fine lines of the woman before them. Held on tiptoe by the tension on the ankle ties, Helene Birencourt waited, toned legs spread wide and the single cord stretching her arms to their limit above her head.

Gradually the sobbing breaths eased and Helene was able to feel the full effects of her position. 'You monsters, you animals, how dare you threaten and treat me in this way,' she cursed. 'Let me go at once... at once, I say!'

Richard stood and glibly caressed her cheek, then ran his hands over the familiar slopes and hollows of her body. Helene closed her eyes, cursing and crying as she tried to move, even just a little, to escape his crude fondling. 'Dear Helene, you will not admit your position, even now. Well, it is time you met my other helper this evening.' He beckoned the hooded figure forward. 'Take the cloak off so you can be seen, my dear,' he said, without looking at the shrouded figure by his side, his eyes fixed on Helene's.

The dark cloak fell to the floor and Helene nearly fainted as she saw her own maid, Jenni, standing before of her. 'You little traitor, you bitch!' she hissed vehemently.

'How dare you betray me to this scum? You're, you're *dismissed*. I will have you jailed for this.'

'My, my, such a disappointing reaction,' Richard gloated. 'Jenni has been keeping me in touch with your activities for months. Now you understand how I was able to forestall your deceitful little robbery. It's so much more fun when you can see your opponent's cards, don't you agree, dear Helene?'

He stood back, studying the bound figure before him. 'I think we should use Jenni's services again tonight,' he said, eventually looking at the pretty maid. 'Perhaps you would be good enough to ready your mistress for the next part of the evening's entertainment. I fear she will not be able to manage things for herself in her present position.'

Jenni smiled wickedly as she bobbed a curtsey to the two men and moved closer to her mistress. 'Mr Elford was able to appreciate my true worth, Madame,' she said. 'Besides, you were the one who insisted I entertain him properly.' She undid the ties of Helene's gown as she talked. 'Soon, Madame, I show you how well you taught me to please other women.' She giggled, quickly freeing the black overdress from her mistress, leaving her in only white undergarments.

'Don't touch her bindings,' Richard Elford warned as Jenni paused. 'There is a small knife by the cupboard. Use it to cut her things away. Let's see how the bitch looks in the raw.'

Jenni obeyed, working swiftly until the ruined underclothes fell away. Both Mehmet and Richard stared hungrily at the perfection of Helene's figure, every muscle tensed in an attempt to relieve the inexorable pull of the bonds, breasts lifted and thrusting, the painful straddle of her legs emphasising the smooth swell of her sex mound, curving inward to the deep split of her sex.

'Ah, Richard, my friend, again you are right; for this one a fortune awaits us,' Mehmet crowed, reaching out to let his fingers trace Helene's hollowed stomach. 'Very fine, very fine indeed.' His other hand moved, teasing the peak of each breast in turn as she tried vainly to twist away from his touch. 'See how she rouses even now. Someone will pay much in gold to have such a body at their command.'

'I agree,' Richard concurred, 'but first the penalty for her meddling ways. Let me tell you how it will be, my dear Helene. Contrary to popular belief, I *am* a vindictive man, as you well know by now. Therefore I intend to make sure you feel the pain that you deserve, some small repayment for the trouble you have caused me.' He stopped, holding her jaw in a harsh grip before turning her head and looking deep into her dark eyes. 'Later you will be suitably gagged and bound and shipped to my new home in...' He checked himself. 'Let us just say, one of the ports of the Mediterranean that takes a more liberal view of goods we trade than they do here.

'You will be sold,' he went on candidly, savouring her fearful trembling, 'and the price will be gratifyingly high - for me. For you there will be another kind of life, at the whim of your new owner.'

He waited, enjoying the look of fear and loathing in Helene's face. Behind her Mehmet continued to grope the smooth curves of her bottom, his hands delving between the cheeks every so often to make her wriggle and twist against them.

'You devil!' she spat passionately. 'I won't let you get away with this, you filth! I won't. Do what you like, but you are *finished* in this colony, you and your evil friends. Selling people like animals! I *hate* you!'

'Oh, how tiresome, Helene, and so irritating.' He feigned boredom, stifling a supposed yawn behind an elegant hand. 'Be silent, or I will have Mehmet gag you.

'Now, if you have quite finished with your wearisome little outburst, Mehmet will teach you the need for obedience, a first lesson for your future, shall we say? And for our amusement, Jenni can show us those *intimate* skills you have taught her so diligently.'

Then, wineglass in hand, the young rake settled comfortably in a chair, carefully positioned so he could watch everything happening to his beautiful prisoner.

Jenni, under orders to take her time, began by licking each of Helene's nipples. A feathery touch, caressing and wetting each peak, she followed by closing her lips around each raised nub, sucking and tugging so it swelled and hardened. Then, adding another maddening stimulation, her fingers grazed the deep hollows of her upraised arms, tickling lightly but unmercifully so that Helene gasped and choked, the leather ties creaking in protest as she writhed in her bonds.

With Jenni occupying Helene's attention, Mehmet strolled to the tall cupboard, then pondered over the collection of whips, canes and scourges it contained. At last he pulled out a fine long rattan, thin and so flexible he was able to bend it in a complete circle. He grinned, letting the pale yellow rod sing through the air, the crisp *zip* making Helene jerk, even as she writhed in a desperate attempt to avoid her student's crafty fingers and tongue. As he shut the door Mehmet paused, looked at Helene's shuddering figure once again, leered, and picked up a small cut glass scent bottle filled with oily liquid.

Moving behind Helene, he watched as the maid's fingers trailed lower, grazing across the exposed lips of her mistress's sex, using skills that belied her age to tease her mistress into a state of maddened arousal. 'Jenni,' he said, 'leave her for a moment.'

Mehmet tilted the little bottle, letting a trickle of oil fall across Helene's shoulders so that runnels of thick liquid oozed down the deep curves and swelling rounds of Helene's back and bottom. 'Work that in for me now.' The candlelight gleamed off the sheen of oil and perspiration, shadows and highlights, as Jenni's dark hands smoothed the scented oil into the softly tanned flesh, and Helene's muscles flexed against her arousal and her strict confinement.

Circling his victim, Mehmet dribbled oil onto the swell of her chest, and Jenni followed, her hands moving until Helene's breasts glowed too, the light emphasising the high curves, the jutting peaks glistening and casting dancing shadows around the dingy chamber. The last of the oil dribbled down her belly, and Jenni cleverly coated her mistress's flanks and thighs, leaving mixed dewdrops of oil and perspiration in the secret folds of her body.

Mehmet handed the empty bottle to Jenni. 'Now the punishment Richard promised you,' he whispered, letting the rattan caress the air in front of her. 'So thin it looks like a toy, yes? Do not be deceived; this will be like fire across your body, lady.' Helene twisted her head away, burying her face in the curve of her arm. 'No use trying to hide, my lady, you will sing out soon enough. They all do, trust Mehmet, he knows...'

'Just watch, my dear,' Richard whispered to Jenni as Mehmet measured his distance from the polished figure held in a taut inverted 'Y' before him. 'The oil increases the intensity of the strikes, but it also guards against any damage to her skin. Mind you, she'll think he's ripping it off in strips in a moment.'

Helene, still fighting to ignore the sensations roused by the touches she'd received, bit her lip as Mehmet taunted her, sniggering as each swish of the rattan made her wince. Her anger boiled at watching Jenni and Richard taking their ease in front of her, relishing her plight.

She detected their sudden stillness, their avid looks, and that minute warning gave her a fraction of a second to prepare as Mehmet swung his arm.

Thwick!

The rattan curled like a living thing across her buttocks. She felt the pressure of the impact and, for a split second, there was nothing, but the next instant a blazing line seemed to sear across her body. She arched forward, buttocks clenching, every muscle rigid with tension as the stroke bit. Moments later Helene sagged back, mouth falling slack as a deep grunt of agony forced itself from her, the pain boiling up from the first raised weal. 'Aaah no, no...'

Thwock!

A fuller sound this time, the rattan biting across the crest of her bottom before the pause, the arching thrust and the gasp of agony.

Thwock! Thwock! Thwock!

The stripes marched relentlessly down into the soft crease at the top of her thighs, returning across the blazing curves of her bottom once again. Helene whimpered and cried at the agony, indeed feeling as though the rattan blade was flaying the very skin from her body.

To the watchers it seemed as though she were mounting some phantom lover; her legs spread in invitation, her body thrusting and tensing, her mouth agape as she mewed like someone on the verge of sexual release.

By the tenth stroke her control had broken, the stifled grunts replaced by a keening wail of suffering as each new cut bit home. At fifteen strokes Mehmet let the rattan fall more softly, building the ecstasy of pain by crossing lines already scored around Helene's rear. He signalled for Jenni to join him, crooking one finger in an obscene gesture, inviting the maid to take Helene over the peak of pleasure. Adding humiliation to misery as she was forced to spend, riding her maid's finger and spurred to a climax by the fiery bite of the whip.

'Let me feel you, mistress,' Jenni's hand moved between Helene's open thighs, fingers slipping between the engorged lips into the soft warmth of her body. 'Oh mistress, so wet, so hot and ready for me, I didn't know the cane would bring you on so.'

Her fingers wriggled deeper into the soaking cleft of Helene's body, probing up into the entrance of her vagina with an expert touch, bringing a different kind of groan from the tethered woman. 'Oh yes, that's so nice, isn't it mistress?' the maid coaxed. 'A little deeper?' Her hand moved, pushing further, fingers stroking against the delicate membranes inside the tethered body.

Helene thrust forward again, this time trying to ride Jenni's hand, striving to increase the sensations stirring within her. Jenni sank to her knees, finally touching the place that made Helene Birencourt shiver and cry out with delight.

Mehmet heard Jenni's words and the cries of excitement, and resumed the steady caning, now intent on stoking a different kind of blaze. Helene's buttocks, already barred with dull red welts, clenched and wriggled as he laid a fresh network of lines across the tender skin. This time the noises were a rising crescendo of need, the gabbled demands for more and more sensation. Helene, caught in the web the two had woven for her, was now desperate to reach a climax, desperate for the feelings to continue so she could ride them to the limit of her endurance.

'Harder, Jenni, harder, there, there, yes, press deeper, deeper,' she babbled. 'Aaah, hit me, yes another, go on, another. Don't stop, please don't stop, I'm there, I'm there, yes... *yes!*'

Helene Birencourt clamped her eyes tightly shut and lifted her hot face to the low vaulted ceiling. Hips jerking, she rode the pain of the beating and the wonderful sensations of Jenni's fingers twisting and pressing inside her cunt. 'Yes, I'm there, I'm there...' The refrain died at last into a heaving, gasping silence as she collapsed, hanging limp against the ties that held her erect. Her two tormentors stopped and stepped away, letting her dangle like a broken puppet from the ceiling hook.

'Oh yes, most impressive, my dear Helene.' The words from Richard Elford, accompanied by a sardonic clapping, lifted Helene's glazed eyes to meet his cruel and mocking stare.

'Damn you, Richard Elford, damn you to hell,' she murmured, still breathless from the intense pleasure and pain. 'Do what you will, but you will never break me... you or your filthy helpers.'

'Helene, my dear lady, it is obvious you are overwrought. Mehmet, untie and return her to the cell. She can have the rest of the night to contemplate her next performance.' He pointed a languid hand to a corner of the chamber. 'You mount the saddle of my whipping horse in the morning. A flogging and the feel of Mehmet's cane across those pretty titties will soon alter that fruitless defiance.'

Mehmet loosened the rope and Helene slumped to her knees on the floor. With her ankles and hands still tied it looked almost as though she had thrown herself down to plead for mercy at his feet.

Richard Elford used one polished boot to roll his victim over and onto her back. 'Take the time to rest, my dear Helene. When we have finished here your real journey begins.' Ignoring her whimpers at the stretching and movement of muscles long cramped by her bondage, Mehmet dragged her back to the cell, pushing her inside and bolting the grille.

Richard then flicked his fingers at his cohort in a covert signal, and turned to Jenni, who was collecting the remnants of Helene's clothes. 'Thank you, my dear, I never doubted your talents,' he told her. 'Take those to Mehmet; he will dispose of them for us.'

Jenni, sublimely unaware of her peril, walked across to where the Turk was standing by a second cell, and she never even had a chance to scream. Seizing her by the throat with one hand he opened the grille with the other and flung her inside. Slamming the iron bars closed with a crash, he then picked up the remnants of Helene's clothes.

The two men looked at the terrified maid grovelling on the dirty floor. 'Ah well, too bad, Jenni, especially after all the enjoyment we've shared,' Richard said scornfully. 'I'm afraid I must send you on the same journey as your mistress. After all, with what you know and the despicable manner in which you've betrayed her, how can I rely upon your loyalty?' The two men listened in amused silence to the torrent of insults and pleading assurances from her as she shook the unyielding bars in fury. 'Ah, promises are all very well, but Mehmet and I have survived because we don't take chances. Come, my friend, we have much to do. Sleep well, ladies, you will need good rest before your journey.'

One by one the candles guttered down, flickering and flaring in the moments before the light sank and vanished as a fading blue glow. The chamber grew steadily darker, shadows seeming to slither across the uneven stones as the weak lights disappeared in turn. Helene had given up her vigil by the bars. Sitting on the thin, lice-infested mattress she tried, without success, to ward off the damp night chill. From the next cell Jenni's anguished sobbing interrupted the silence as she absorbed what her greed and duplicity had brought her to.

'Jenni, don't cry, please don't cry,' Helene comforted in the darkness. 'It doesn't matter. What you did doesn't matter any more. Listen... please listen, Jenni, we've got to work together.' The sobbing eased and faltered as Helene went on. 'There's sure to be a chance at some time for us to get away, to escape. We must be ready, both of us. I know Elford; I know what he's like, but he doesn't know I've left a message for Lieutenant Kingsford. Hold on to that. He will try and help. The governor will have to listen to him now.'

'Oh mistress, I've been so silly,' Jenni sobbed apologetically. 'He told me how he loved me and that he would help me get back to my village. How can you ever forgive me, mistress? To do that to you, to betray you to him. Oh, mistress...' A fearful silence fell as the last candle began to flicker and splutter into extinction. Helene then heard a timid scrabbling on the stones of the cell wall.

Edging her way to the corner of her own cell, she pressed her cheek against the cold iron bars, and putting her hand around the dividing wall between the cells she felt Jenni's fingers steal into her own. Without words she gave a squeeze.

As the long night began, she hoped her brave words to Jenni were more than bluffing in the dark. Helene prayed silently that Jonathan had understood her message and that he would be able to convince the governor, Lord Roberts, that action was needed. From the darkness she felt the returning squeeze. At least, tonight, neither of them would be completely alone.

CHAPTER 14
The Gilded Cage

The girls led Elizabeth into a room rich with hangings and brightly coloured tiles. A low divan against one wall was stacked with cushions and draped with sheets of soft material; gauzes, silks and rich cotton covers. Rugs of all kinds dotted the floor, almost obscuring the polished mosaics and deadening each footfall. Low stools, small tables and couches were scattered across the remainder of the space. Archways pierced each wall.

Without warning the girls ran off through one of the openings, leaving Elizabeth staring around in confusion. The bright colours and a strange sweet smell that filled the air, almost overlaying the scent of the flowers outside, emphasised the strangeness of this different world.

The touch of fingers undoing the fastenings at the back of her dress startled her out of her daydream. The girl Kemal called Selima had returned unnoticed by Elizabeth, and was now intent on undoing her bodice. Immediately on the defensive the English girl turned and pulled away so quickly that her leg, catching the edge of the divan, made her overbalance so she went stumbling back before sitting down abruptly.

'What do you think you're doing?' she demanded, anger and fright both sharp in her voice.

Selima cowered back, head bent, hands clutched against her chest as though she'd been struck. 'So sorry, lady, no trouble, please, no trouble, yes?' she gabbled penitently. 'Master say you like bath. You cannot bathe with clothes on. Selima only try help you be ready for bath.' The girl looked so worried and timid that Elizabeth immediately wondered what punishment she'd expected to receive, and felt pity for the pretty girl.

She held out a hand, smiling in friendship. 'I'm sorry, Selima,' she said. 'I didn't mean to snap at you. Yes, I'd love a bath, if you'll help me get ready.'

Selima cautiously smiled back, relaxing as though a threat had been lifted. She grabbed Elizabeth's hands, helping her up from the divan, and with the English girl's cooperation, the dress and underclothes quickly turned into a jumbled pile on the floor.

Revelling in the sense of freedom, Elizabeth stretched in delight. She felt Selima's hands stroking her, but it didn't seem to matter at all. 'You are very beautiful, lady,' the servant said, with refreshingly innocent sincerity. 'Such fair hair, I have not seen this before. Are all women in your country pale like this, with the golden hair?' She let her fingers comb the lustrous blonde strands, eyes wide with amazement.

'Not all women, Selima, some are dark like you, some are...' she broke off, unsure how to explain red and brown hair properly. 'There are many different colours,' she finished lamely. 'Did you say there was a bath for me?'

Selima smiled again, clasped her hand, and Elizabeth gawped at the room beyond one of the arches as she was led through to it. The room was based around a large bath, sunken and oval, filled with scented water, with two steps leading down into it at one end. Bright colours decorated the walls and a wide rim surrounded the bath itself. Sula, another servant girl she'd seen briefly before, was standing beside it patiently, holding a large yellow sponge and a bar of soap.

With Selima to steady her, Elizabeth stepped down and sat in the water, surprised to find it was only warm, rather than hot as she'd been expecting. The next moment she was being stroked and washed by two pairs of hands as Sula and Selima began to wash her with vigorous enthusiasm.

Selima concentrated on her hair, washing and rinsing the golden strands again and again. 'Oh yes, that's wonderful,' Elizabeth sighed, her eyes closed against the sting of the soap. She was revelling in the sensuous feel of fingers massaging her scalp then smoothing the thick mane into a shining rope down her back.

Sula, after watching Selima for a minute, used the sponge to clean and caress the rest of the English girl's skin. Moving her limbs as necessary, she let the soft sponge stimulate Elizabeth's body, feeling her relaxing and welcoming the sensations more and more as she worked.

Sula quietly changed her movements, letting the sponge go to use her hands. 'Better now, lady?' Her dainty fingers massaged the slippery skin with slow movements that stroked along Elizabeth's flanks and down each leg. Selima gave the golden hair a final rinse, and then her hands, too, began to stroke Elizabeth's body.

Lulled almost to sleep by the gentle touches, Elizabeth began to feel the familiar excitement growing. She realised, almost without caring, that the girls had moved on from simply washing her clean and were now deliberately arousing her, working her into a pitch of sexual desire. Welcoming the warm rush of sensations, her body twisted slowly in a swirl of water as she stretched, catlike, in her rising need.

Sula, quick to correctly interpret the involuntary stretching, as well as the sudden flush of colour on the pale skin, changed the rhythm of her movements. Her hands now concentrated on Elizabeth's thighs and the sweet fork of her body.

Selima, gently soothing Elizabeth's shoulders, could see Sula's submerged arm was now curving up between the English girl's legs. Watching Elizabeth's gentle movements she smiled as she saw her knees gradually parting, encouraging Sula to fondle her in an increasingly urgent caress, each time her hand slid upwards.

'Sula is good for you,' Selima whispered, supporting Elizabeth's shoulders with one arm, the other hand moving to stroke the slippery slopes of her breasts, still slick with the remains of the soap and scented oils the girls had been using only moments before. 'I know her touch is gentle. Let her bring you to delight, lady.'

'She is ready,' Sula whispered, adding a brief comment in Arabic as she used her other hand to ease Elizabeth's knees up, spreading them even more as she did so. Selima nodded her agreement, very slowly rolling one hard nipple between thumb and forefinger.

'Now, pretty lady, enjoy Sula's touch as she strokes those secret places,' Selima coaxed with a sultry whisper. 'You feel her, yes?' The swirls and ripples of water concealed the deft movements of Sula's hand, but she was now stroking deep between the lips of the English girl's body, concentrating on the lips of her sex, her clitoris, and the delicate opening of her anus.

'Oh, Selima, yes please, yes, she's so good,' Elizabeth murmured dreamily as Sula touched and stroked and teased the core of her body. 'Kiss me, please, Selima, kiss me. She's going to make me spend, I... oooh, yes there, just there...'

Selima silenced the cries, as Elizabeth wanted, leaning down to kiss her on the lips. 'Shhhh, lady, so nearly, now feel Sula tease your little button.' She half turned, whispering instructions to Sula, knowing exactly how to bring Elizabeth to the climax she wanted so desperately. The teasing hands moved more deliberately, the two girls locked into a game they'd played many times before. Selima increasing the rolling stimulation of Elizabeth's breasts, attending to each bud in turn as she continued to coax and whisper, making sure her sweet breath teased the soft shell of the blonde's ear.

Water splashed unheeded onto the tiled floor as Elizabeth's body braced up in an arch, responding to the sensations being dragged from her. Intent only on her own pleasure, she cried aloud, arching up again and again as Sula eased her forefinger into her bottom, then gasped at the glorious feeling as the young Arab's thumb slid forward, curving into the warmth of her vagina. For long moments only the one hand touched her body, rocking so gently, letting her ride the twin impalement as the sensations grew and grew. 'Oh, go on please, don't leave me here, go on...' She wriggled, desperately trying to force Sula to move her hand more quickly, trying to bring on her own release.

'Now, Sula, now,' Selima whispered, taking Elizabeth's shoulders in a stronger grip, waiting for the frenzy to come. Sula used her other hand too, easing the plump sex lips apart so that her fingers could wriggle between the soft folds of Elizabeth's cunt. The girl's body bucked violently, responding to a sharper delight as the little fingers moved within her secret flesh.

'Aaaaah, yes!' Elizabeth jerked, throwing herself forward as though Sula had touched a switch. 'Oh yes, *yes!*'

'Go on my lady, let your delight come fully.' The whispers caressed her. 'Bring her to her pleasure, Sula, tease her button till she cries.' Sula didn't need any urging from Selima. Water churned and splashed to the floor as she vibrated her fingers against the little nub. Elizabeth sobbed her joy and exhilaration at riding her release, her ecstasy echoing in the tiled room as the two girls milked her of every spasm of pleasure. Then slowly, as the frenzy began to ebb, Sula sat back, herself wet from Elizabeth's threshing, while Selima gently caressed the English girl's neck, tracing her lips over the downy skin below her ear.

Eventually the two girls helped her out of the bath, wrapping her in soft towels and leading her back to the room so she could rest on the divan.

'Selima,' Elizabeth stretched lazily as hands moved over her, dabbing and drying, 'why did you look so scared when I snapped at you earlier?'

'If I do not please you I be punished,' the girl said simply. 'The master would be sure that I did not offend you again. The master say what we must do, if we do not please him then we must be punished.' She paused and traced one finger along the fading lines crisscrossing Elizabeth's breasts. 'You are punished if you do wrong things. I know because here are the marks.'

Elizabeth blushed, but before she could counter the observation the dusky girl went on.

'Both Sula and I were bought for our master, Prince Kemal, at the slave market nearly three years ago.'

'You are slaves?' Elizabeth said, suspecting she shouldn't be surprised to hear this, alarming realisations beginning to dawn and fall into place. She had to press the girls. 'Sir Roger said Prince Kemal was a business friend,' she stated, watching them closely for any reactions. 'What exactly is Prince Kemal's business, Selima? Sula?'

'Lady, please, the master will come.' Once more there was genuine fear in her whole demeanour. 'Do not anger him or we will all be in trouble. Why complain, this be your life too, very soon?'

Elizabeth stood up from the divan, wrapping one of the towels around herself and securing it between her breasts.

'Lady, please for our sake, please,' pleaded Selima, panic etched on her lovely face.

'What to you mean, Selima, it will be my life too very soon?' Elizabeth persisted.

'It - it is what I heard,' Selima reluctantly confessed. 'Sula heard it too.' Sula nodded in vigorous agreement. 'Our master, Prince Kemal, has arranged for you to be taken up the river tomorrow. I hear him say it to the man who was with you, the big one with the face like fire. The master say that with such beautiful hair and such blue eyes you fetch a great price. Then I know that you be another of Kemal's women. And when he tell us to prepare you and dress you, we think that...' Her voice tailed off as Elizabeth, ashen-faced, slumped to her knees.

'Sold...?' she echoed. 'In God's name how can they do this? Oh, I've been so stupid. All his talk of business and... oh, Selima, Sula, I'm in terrible trouble.'

Elizabeth told them of her plight and how she knew that her guardian was plotting to be rid of her in some way or another. 'I must get away, tonight, before it's too late. If I can just get a message back to Helene, she can tell the governor and they dare not continue with the plan then.'

'Lady, there are guards everywhere,' Sula pointed out. 'If you escape it will go hard

66

for us, I know.'

'I'm sorry, both of you, but I cannot let him do this,' Elizabeth said determinedly, but feeling the rising tension and panic in the girls, she knew she had to calm things down. Whatever she might do she couldn't involve either of them, so deliberately changing the subject, she made a huge effort and smiled. 'But before I do anything, I think you'd better show me the kind of clothes I'm supposed to wear. We don't want to make Prince Kemal suspicious of anything, now do we?'

The girls seemed to relax a little, and Sula finished combing and drying Elizabeth's hair before coiling and pinning it up in a whorl, leaving her slim neck and shoulders bare. With increasing enthusiasm, the two girls then set about the task of finding some suitable clothes for the English girl - that would fit her voluptuous shape. They unearthed a low-cut brocaded top that fitted, although Elizabeth knew she was going to have to be extremely careful if she was not to fall out of it by accident. Gauze trousers were no problem, since they were loose and could be adjusted at both waist and ankle.

Before the trousers, Selima found a pair of the tiny triangular panties both girls were wearing, as a final shield to their modesty. As they helped and fitted her into the unfamiliar briefs, Elizabeth once more felt the flush of arousal as two pairs of hands teased the sensitive skin of her thighs and sex. Selima let her hand close over the swell of Elizabeth's mound as the final adjustments were made, and Elizabeth wriggled with pleasure as the fingers closed, squeezing her labia and sending a pulse of sensation lancing through her body. 'In time we will delight each other again, yes, lady?'

A gong abruptly interrupted further comment, and Selima and Sula prostrated themselves on the floor as Kemal entered.

'English lady, you are more beautiful than I remember,' he said silkily. 'My girls have looked after you?'

Trying hard to look confident in the revealing costume, Elizabeth looked at the two girls bowed low on the floor. 'They have been wonderful, Prince Kemal,' she said. 'So kind, and they have taken such care of me I feel quite refreshed. Is Sir Roger not with you? I thought he would be here.'

'Unfortunately he has been delayed,' Kemal said smoothly, but he did not reveal that the delay was to be permanent. The afternoon's business had degenerated into a fierce argument over money and two of Kemal's bodyguards had been a little too zealous in restraining a furious Sir Roger, with the result that he suffered a stroke and died within minutes. He now awaited his final journey in a weighted sack among bales of cloth that were to be shipped up river that night. Unlike the cloth, however, Sir Roger's journey would be completed after only a few miles, at a suitably deep point where crocodiles gathered in some number.

'He did say, though, that I was to look after you as his most precious possession,' the prince continued. 'I have a little entertainment planned for tonight, that I would be honoured if you would attend. Until then, Selima can show you to your room to rest.'

'Entertainment, thank you, you are too kind,' she said, her skills of deception improving as she gave no hint of the awful knowledge she had gained from Selima and Sula. 'But what should I wear to do you honour as your guest?'

Prince Kemal's eyes scanned the English girl's shapely figure, now displayed so revealingly in the meagre costume. 'What you are wearing now will be more than suitable,' he told her. 'Beauty needs no other adornment. Until later, beautiful lady, until later...' Bowing again, Kemal turned and left the room, and Elizabeth could almost feel the release of tension as the two other girls cautiously relaxed.

'Come now, did you think I would deliberately betray you to him?' She tried to lighten the atmosphere by changing the subject. 'Selima, where is the room Kemal mentioned? Perhaps I should take the opportunity to rest awhile.'

Selima once more took her hand, leading her back across the open central courtyard to another part of the building. Following obediently, Elizabeth said nothing further about escape. She knew it was much too dangerous to involve either of the girls. If she was going to get away, it had to be on her own.

The room, opening off a corridor beside the main courtyard, didn't look or feel much like a prison cell, as she'd feared. Tall window slits allowed air and light in from the outside, and the high ceiling helped to keep the room cool while the corridor and veranda provided shade and protection from the sun, now sinking behind the distant hills.

'I hope you will be comfortable,' Selima said. 'I will return to take you to the entertainment as our master has commanded.'

Two lamps behind glass provided a gentle light, enough for Elizabeth to take a good look around the new quarters. The window slits, apparently so invitingly open, were guarded by fine metal bars, curved into ornamental patterns and painted to match the white plaster of the walls. While there was no door as such, she had seen another metal screen on her way in, hinged so it could be secured across the passage. Doubtless it would now be barring her way out, and doubtless Kemal would argue it was for her protection and was actually barring others from entering.

Sitting amongst the inevitable mound of cushions and elaborately embroidered drapes, Elizabeth wondered if Kemal was so complacent that he thought she was still blissfully unaware of his scheming? Perhaps his views of women would blind him to any thought that she might be able to discover the truth, and have the courage to do something about it.

She fingered the dark blue drape pensively, a crazy idea forming in her head; it would serve to disguise her pale skin and fair hair until she was clear of the building. Elizabeth hurriedly wrapped herself securely, tucking the loose material out of the way so she could move freely if necessary. With no more time to think or ponder the wisdom of her actions, she tiptoed cautiously to the archway, peering out into the gloom.

Taking a deep breath she slipped along the corridor, heaving another sigh of relief as she saw she'd been wrong; the security grille was still flat against the wall. But relief almost led to disaster, for overconfident, she crept a little too quickly into the lemon-scented air of the main courtyard and it was only the tinkling noise of the fountain that saved her, that and the flickering lamplight on the walls. The cascading water muffled her padding steps, and it was the shadow of the patrolling guard, flickering across the white of the wall as he passed one of the lamps that gave her just enough warning to duck into the shelter of a raised flowerbed.

Elizabeth fought to get her breathing under control as she tried to remember exactly where the wooden door to the alleyway was situated. Slowly recovering from the shock of near discovery she managed to get her bearings from the position of the fountain, and eventually she located a deeper rectangle of shadow on the far side of the courtyard. Eyes intent on the slow pacing of the guard, she edged round the garden, keeping in the shadows and cursing every time loose stones or pebbles dug agonisingly into the tender souls of her feet.

Upon reaching the door there was another moment of panic as she tried to discover if it was locked, or simply bolted from the inside, and the relief of running her fingers across its surface and feeling the shape of a heavy iron bolt was immense. The fixings were slick with grease and she was able to ease the flat metal tongue from its socket without any noise.

Now the way was open for her! She pulled the door inwards, pausing before looking out into the alleyway she'd been in a few hours before. Summoning her courage she stepped out into the warm darkness, the whirring song of the night insects muffling her careful footfalls on the dusty road. Ten paces took her to the end of the wall and the black mouth of the cross-alley leading away up the hill...

'The sack, Ahmed, quickly!'

Kemal's harsh whisper was all she heard before a smelly darkness blanketed her head and upper body. One gasp was all she managed, then cruel arms clamped round her arms, immobilising her instantly. A vicious jerk and she was thrown to the ground, small stones digging into her legs and side as she crashed down, unable to break the jarring force of the fall. The voice was muffled but the gloating tone was clear enough. 'Clever lady, but Kemal is used to such foolishness. Ahmed, pick her up and take her back inside. Downstairs in one of the small cells will do for now. Secure her well, while I have a word with Selima. It seems she too must learn greater obedience. Her punishment will serve to educate our little English friend as to what awaits her.'

CHAPTER 15
Rescued by the Governor

In the darkness Helene and her maid finally managed to fall into restless sleep. Helene's plight made worse by the unexpected chill, unable to cover her nakedness, she was only protected from the damp cold stonework by the thin straw mattress.

The click and chink of metal on stone roused her. Light was coming from somewhere, somewhere up the steps, since the archway was clearly outlined in the dim yellow glow. Did she call, or would that merely signal an earlier start to her promised ordeal across the whipping horse? Desperation won out. 'Here, down here, please help, we are prisoners,' she called, her voice hoarse. 'Someone, please help us!'

The light brightened suddenly, shadows dancing on the walls, accompanied by the sound of hurrying booted feet. Before she could call again the chamber was full of figures; officers in black and scarlet accompanied by armed soldiers. Hidden amongst the throng Mebele clutched a bundled cape and dress.

'Here, Mebele, here by the wall, Jenni is in the next one,' Helene called frantically. 'Oh, thank God, thank you, thank you.'

And then a gruff voice was ordering the men to turn away as Mebele pushed the clothes through the bars.

'They're yours, mistress, we found them upstairs as we searched.' She peered through the grille. 'Are you well, mistress? He hasn't hurt you, has he?'

Helene nearly burst into tears at the concern in the black girl's expression and voice.

Ignoring the crumpled undergarments she struggled into her dress, trying to see what was happening beyond the bars, and gasped with relief as she recognised two of the men. 'Lord Roberts, Lieutenant Kingsford,' she said. 'Thank you.' The two men turned, hurrying across now that Helene had been able to cover herself. 'You don't know how relieved I am to see you all. Richard Elford, he is the devil behind this. Have you caught him?'

Jonathan didn't answer; concentrating on slipping back the heavy bolts so that the barred grille could be swung open. Ignoring any idea of propriety, Helene flung herself into his arms, hugging him gratefully before finally collecting herself and turning to Lord Roberts.

'We are pleased to find you so well, Madame,' the colony's governor commented dryly. 'You have to thank Lieutenant Kingsford and this forceful young woman. They were somewhat persistent in persuading me that your life was in very real danger. Ah, and this is the scheming minx who led you into the trap, I believe.' He peered coldly at Jenni's shivering figure as she was released from the other cell to collapse onto the floor, terrified out of her wits.

Helene looked down on her traitorous maid for a few moments 'She has been foolish and deceived by evil men. Whatever you may think, sir, Jenni will come home with me. Despite what has happened she still has a place there.'

Lieutenant Kingsford smiled and nodded approvingly, helping the wretched maid to her feet and signalling for Mebele to take her from the cellar.

Lord Roberts took easy charge. 'Captain, we have completed our main task,' he said. 'Now take your men and search the rest of these accursed vaults. You should find they connect with Mr Elford's residence. Join up with the search party. I'm particularly interested in any personal documents, letters and so forth. A complete report to me by the end of the day, understand?'

One of the uniformed officers snapped to attention. 'Yes sir, full search of vaults and house. Report to you at the end of the day, sir!'

'Very well, carry on. Now, lieutenant, since you have a personal interest in this matter, perhaps you would be good enough to assist Madame Birencourt so we can get out of this dismal place. I have a carriage waiting, we can be more comfortable once we have you safely home, my dear.' He led the way to the steps, Helene following with Jonathan, his arm around her waist to give support.

Once delivered safely to the villa, Helene retreated with Mebele to bathe before beginning to feel human once more, in fresh linen and a new dress. Mebele, taking Jenni's role, combed and pinned her hair, and in an hour or so she felt ready to meet Lord Roberts and Jonathan once more. 'Keep a close eye on Jenni for me, Mebele,' she instructed her maid. 'I don't want her doing anything stupid at this stage. I'll deal with her later.'

The courtesies over, Lord Roberts got down to the details Helene was so eager to hear. 'That maid of Sir Roger's deserves some reward,' he stated. 'She raised the alarm, having got worried about Miss Ashton, but as yet we have no news of the young lady's whereabouts. We know she sailed with Sir Roger two days ago, but exactly where to we cannot say as yet.'

Helene bit her lip, praying silently that Elizabeth was all right. The one remaining hope was that her colouring and hair would make her too valuable to harm. While she was alive, even if a captive, there was still hope.

The governor cleared his throat. 'She went to look for her mistress and saw Elford and that other rogue, Mehmet, going into the study and then carrying you out. She had the sense to look in there when they were gone and found the letter on the desk. Damn my eyes, the girl only has the wherewithal to think it might be important, so she takes it and goes to the barracks. Makes such a fuss at the gate the guard commander calls the lieutenant here. She tells the story and all hell breaks loose. Decided to take a hand myself since there were ladies involved. Don't want another scandal. Story will be all over town by noon, anyway,' he muttered gloomily.

Helene managed a grim smile. 'What's happened to Richard?' she asked. 'Have you got him?'

Lord Roberts looked even gloomier, but Jonathan answered. 'There's a warrant out for both of them, but they've vanished. If what you tell me of their plans is right, Mr Elford is at sea by now, together with Mehmet, or whatever he calls himself. I doubt if either of them will be troubling us again.'

Lord Roberts heaved himself to his feet. 'Leave all that to me, my dear, government business now,' he said brusquely. 'Well, I must be off. Pleased you're safe. We'll need to talk again once all these matters have been concluded. Damned lawyers will make a pretty penny trying to sort this lot out.'

'Thank you for all you've done,' she said sincerely. 'You don't know how grateful I am for your help.' The governor huffed and made his way to the door, his guard crashing to attention as he appeared on the veranda. He turned and eyed the two of them.

'Ah yes, Kingsford,' he said, 'don't think you're needed for a few days. Take some leave. Tell the colonel I said so. See that Madame Birencourt is properly looked after, eh!'

CHAPTER 16
The Seat of Correction

In the palace lamps and candles gleamed and flickered, even the discreetly hidden punishment chamber glowed with light. Prince Kemal ran his hand over the top of a slim wooden pyramid, fingers tracing the subtle undulations along the rounded, finger-wide ridge, enjoying the feel of the polished finish of the narrow saddle with its gently up-curving ends. It was a saddle that had encouraged many young women to adopt an eager obedience to his commands. Nothing to look at, he mused, just a three foot tall pillar of black wood, twelve inches wide from front to back with the sides sloping out to form a base of about two feet wide.

His hand stroked down that elegant taper, feeling the way the wood sloped out from the narrow wedge of the summit; so simple, so cunning... so utterly effective. Kemal's penis rose and thickened as he thought of the two females who would be riding his diabolical Seat of Correction in such a short while.

Each would be mounted in turn; legs spread down the tapering black sides, the soft

'V' of their bodies split by the narrow summit with its deceiving curves. In turn they would cry and scream for mercy, but then they always did, always promised him everything, if only...

Kemal shivered, his erection tenting his robes, thinking of that wonderful contrast between the frenzied pleading and the desperate, tightly clenched stillness. Each rider fighting to prevent the growing agony as their own body pressed down, their weight forcing them to torment their own most sensitive flesh without respite.

And always the added refinement of the cane, applied slowly to breasts or buttocks, usually both of course, each stroke bringing the fresh delirium of enforced movement, the sobbing victim rocking on the black, wooden saddle. For each one that awful understanding why the edge is so subtly carved, as the curves press and burrow into the deepest, most sensitive folds of her sex.

Tonight the correction would be wonderful, lingering and severe. Kemal sighed, welcoming the pleasure he would savour before a well-earned rest. The prince allowed himself one last caress of the smooth black pyramid as he looked around his punishment chamber.

The Seat of Correction rose from its low platform in the middle of the floor. Kemal mentally checked the rest of the fittings with a sweeping glance; a rope, leather cuffs dangling from the end, hung from a pulley in the ceiling above, the other end curving away to an iron bracket anchored to the white stone wall.

Apart from low divans curving along half the wall space, each covered with a selection of pillows and cushions; the octagonal room was almost stark in its simplicity. A copper cylinder next to the arched entranceway held a selection of canes and rods. Some bound with silver wire, some made of bamboo that had been delicately split and then re-bound, others of whalebone or dried and tempered leather. There was even the long, tapered tale of a stingray, carefully preserved and mounted in a leather handle. All showed the signs of wear and long usage. There was no other furniture, nothing except for a slim brass pedestal with a flat top, resting upon which was a large hourglass.

There was something amiss, he knew, but all seemed to be in order so what had...? He smiled, looking again at the sinister tapering shape on the plinth. Mounting blocks, that was it! Where were the mounting blocks that usually stood on either side of the pillar?

After all, what could be more delightful than insisting each girl position herself on that polished edge? The erotic thrill of watching her make the careful and intimate arrangement of her body, the expectation when quietly warning her to prepare, finally, the removal of the blocks and that wild tensing of the legs and muscles, that long heartbeat of silence as each girl settles onto the unrelenting edge for the first time, tugging uselessly at her bonds until she is forced into stillness by the bite of her narrow black saddle.

Kemal reached across one of the divans and moved a cushion so he could pick up the two little stands. He placed them carefully in position, ready to provide a temporary foothold for Selima when she was invited to step up and take the first turn in the evening's little show.

Satisfied, he lifted his arms and clapped twice. In seconds his chief guard and general organiser appeared. 'Ahmed, I believe we are ready to begin,' he said. 'Tell Sula to come to me here, then bring the English girl.' The squat manservant turned to go. 'And

Ahmed, make sure the guards try no tricks with the golden-haired one. Just tie her hands and leave her clothes on, it will be more amusing that way.' He pondered for a moment. 'Behind her back, I think will be best. When you bring her, secure her to one of the rings. Make sure she is in a position to see all that happens to Selima.' He gestured towards the walls where steel rings were set in the stone at regular intervals.

'And Selima, master?' Ahmed asked, a cruel and eager smirk on his dark, battered features. 'How do you wish her to be prepared? Stripped?'

'Ahmed, Ahmed, always the same, you are too quick,' Kemal mused, chuckling quietly. 'If we did it your way she'd be stripped, whipped and riding that thick cock of yours within a few minutes. Patience, you must learn the skill of enjoying such moments. Leave her dressed as she is. Once the other two are here you may bring her in. Yes, yes you are going to seat her first, but leave her untied. After all, how is she to undress for our entertainment if she is already bound?'

Ahmed left, smiling broadly, while Kemal finished preparing the scene for Selima and Elizabeth. He draped a dark red cloth over the pyramid, hiding the details but leaving the thrusting shape outlined by the velvet folds. None of them had even seen the inside of his punishment chamber, although Selima and Sula had doubtless heard stories about the Seat of Correction from the other servants. He smiled again, thinking of how her second-hand knowledge would be increasing Selima's fear as she huddled in the little cell she'd occupied ever since Elizabeth's abortive escape attempt.

At that very moment Selima didn't even know what had happened to her, or why. Thrown into a squalid cell without any word at all, she had been left in darkness until the door swung open hours later. Kemal, framed in the lantern light, had quietly told her she was to be punished for failing to do her duty. The door had slammed shut, leaving her in the darkness once more, imagining only too vividly what that punishment might be.

Sula, still dressed in the brocaded top and gauze trousers, crept into the punishment room a few minutes later. Her master lay at ease on the divan, propped up on a mound of pillows. 'Come here, Sula, don't be frightened,' he beckoned. 'You are not in any trouble tonight. Rather, I have chosen you to help me administer the correction that Selima and the English girl must suffer. You will do exactly as I tell you, is that quite clear? After all, you wouldn't wish to take Selima's place, would you?'

He laughed at the avid denials as Sula tried to remain bowed respectfully whilst casting anxious glances at the shrouded shape in the middle of the room. 'Enough, fetch me something to drink, I wish to be refreshed while we wait for your friends.' He chuckled again, watching Sula retreating rapidly through the archway to carry out his commands. Arranging his loose robes more comfortably, Kemal stretched out on the soft divan.

Creeping back on soundless feet, Sula offered the tray to him, the glass of fresh limejuice jittering slightly as she tried to still the shaking in her hands. 'Thank you, now get rid of the tray and come here, beside me,' he ordered, and Sula knelt by her master's side, reaching to take the glass as he finished drinking.

'So beautiful, so many beautiful girls,' he murmured, as one hand curved to rest under the small weight of her breast so that his thumb could flick the tiny bulge made by her nipple. 'You will not need this any longer.' It was a low, barely heard comment, but Sula knew she had been given an order, nonetheless.

She undid the clasp, the garment falling away from the small firm peaks of her breasts as she moved. Careful not to brush Kemal's hands and risk offence, she slipped the top off before resuming her position. The fingers cupped her once more, her master's thumb slowly rubbing the crinkled nub so that it swelled and hardened.

Elizabeth, wild-eyed with fear and anger, fought the implacable grip of Ahmed and another guard as she was forced into the room. 'Damn you, Kemal, how dare you treat me like this?' she hissed indignantly. 'I'll tell the governor, the garrison commander - everyone. I'll break you! You and Sir Roger bloody Stanley - he's gone too far this time!' She tried to lunge at Kemal, a futile attempt to wipe away his infuriating, gloating expression, but the guards held her easily, strong fingers digging into her upper arms, arms pinned behind her by the thin leather tie around her wrists.

Kemal studied the young English woman lazily, noting the spirited behaviour and language with approval. So much better to tame a fighter, he thought, than subdue one who collapsed at the first hint of pressure. 'Miss Ashton,' he said softly, so softly that she automatically stopped her blustering complaint to hear his words. 'Let me tell you things you must now understand. First, I regret to tell you that your guardian, "Sir Roger bloody Stanley", as you have so touchingly referred to him, is dead.'

He enjoyed the way she froze upon hearing the news. 'And whatever you may think, I did not kill him. We had our business differences, but unfortunately he had some kind of seizure whilst discussing them. There was nothing I could do.' He didn't add that he hadn't made any effort to aid him, either. 'This presents me with a minor problem, so I have decided to solve it, and save all those tiresome officials so much wasted effort, by ensuring that he disappears completely - tonight.'

'But, w-what about m-me?' she stammered, now definitely fearing the worst. 'I'm only supposed to be away for a day or so. People will be asking questions.' Her voice rose with anger and fear, as she understood his next words and their dreaded meaning.

'Ah yes, but which people?' he ruminated. 'The governor? Governor of what? He does not govern in this place. Here it is I who rule. And as for the late Sir Roger, he made both of us promises. Promises of gold, promises of opportunities to increase my business,' his voice hardened implacably. 'Also he made promises to continue to supply me with beautiful white girls for my trade. Therefore you, my foolish and gullible young lady, are one of his promises to me.'

He laughed, a sinister reaction that made Elizabeth shiver. 'And you are a promise that I intend to hold him to, even in his absence...'

'You can't, people will know, I have friends, important people who will wish to find out what has happened to me,' she babbled desperately. 'Can you risk that?' In her heart she knew it was all a feeble bluff. She knew no one. Even if Helene could follow the trail, it would vanish here. This was Kemal's world and in it she didn't stand a chance.

And Kemal confirmed the truth of this when he dismissed her words with a single flick of a hand. 'That is all noise and nothing more, my lady. You have no one, no one knows or cares, you are Kemal's now. And this evening you will learn Kemal's ways, or...' his voice grew colder, '...or you will bitterly regret your disobedience. Ahmed, secure her.'

Elizabeth was thrown down and her arms jerked behind her, away from her body. 'Wait,' Kemal insisted suddenly. 'Sula, take one of the longer cushions and place it next to her.' Sula hurriedly placed the cylindrical velvet cushion so that it spanned the width of the divan from front to back. 'Help your English friend,' he continued, 'she is to kneel astride it, if you please.'

Leering broadly at what his master intended, Ahmed held the ends of Elizabeth's wrist ties threaded through one of the steel rings, and Sula helped the blonde straddle the cushion. A harsh tug on the leather ties snatched Elizabeth's arms back so that she grimaced and had to bow forward.

'Oh yes, very good, Ahmed,' Kemal praised the squat brute. 'Make quite sure she is secure. I do not wish her to miss any of Selima's performance.' With a final tug the cruel servant clambered off the divan to stand by the archway, and Kemal noted the eager stance. 'Yes, yes, it is time,' he said, as though talking to an excited child. 'Go, fetch Selima here, but tell her nothing. Just bring her and then we will tell them both about our little demonstration.'

Elizabeth fidgeted, edging backwards until she could feel the rough stone against her toes, the strain on her arms now a fraction less. Sula had hurried back to lie by Kemal's side; Elizabeth noticed his possessive cupping of her breasts but realised the stroking was almost absentminded. Kemal's attention was fixed on the centre of the room with its sinister, dangling cuffs and the mysterious object concealed under a cloth of heavy red velvet. The English girl shivered despite the heat in the chamber. What devilish torment did he have in mind for Selima and her?

They all heard Ahmed's slapping footsteps well before he pushed Selima into the lighted well of the punishment chamber. He pushed her to their master, his hands gripping her upper arms so she couldn't lunge forward.

'Such a disappointment, Selima,' Kemal said. 'Have I not given you a life of comfort, ease and enjoyment?' It was a purely rhetorical comment; Kemal wasn't concerned with any reply from her. 'Yet, tonight I find one of my guests creeping out of the gates and threatening all sorts of terrible things about me and my household. Now, Selima, your master is wondering how his guest could have found out so much to concern her in the little time since her arrival?'

Selima shivered as his musings toyed with her fear. 'She learned it from someone here, someone who thought her disloyalty would not be noticed,' he answered his own question on her behalf. 'So, my delightful little telltale, it is time for you to make amends and learn a lesson in obedience. Both you, and this delightful English girl, will receive ten strokes of the cane from Ahmed, as punishment for your betrayal.'

Selima and Elizabeth gasped with relief, ten strokes, painful but nothing like the beating both had been expecting.

Kemal smiled as he observed the reaction, and walked to the shrouded shape on the platform. 'Before you rejoice too much, this is how I choose to deliver such reminders,' he elaborated. 'Some have named it the Seat of Correction.' He drew the red velvet away, revealing the slim black pyramid to the girls' shocked gaze. 'And now you will both have a chance to try it for yourselves; Selima will be first. Ahmed...'

Selima was hustled up onto the platform to face one end of the wooden pillar, and gazed at the tapering sides and the shallow curve of the top with terror. 'Once you are seated, your punishment can begin.' Kemal waved a hand towards the copper table 'See the sand glass. Since this is your first offence I will be merciful. You will ride the Seat of Correction for one turn of the glass, and then Ahmed will beat you as I have promised.'

He looked at the shivering girl, toying with her, watching avidly as she imagined what was about to happen. 'Oh, I almost forgot, there is no need for clothing,' he added, as though as an afterthought. 'So...' he waited for the inevitable hesitation. 'Of course, should you choose to be uncooperative we can turn the glass a few more times to help you pay attention.' His voice hardened. 'Do you understand me?'

'Yes, master, but please don't make me do this, please...'

'Two turns, perhaps?'

Selima, frantically shaking her head, struggled out of her top before bending to free the gauze trousers from her ankles. Finally she eased the triangular briefs off to stand naked in the soft candlelight, hands tightly clenched at her sides. She gasped when Ahmed stepped forward, pulling her arms behind her and wrapping the padded cuffs around her wrists.

'Selima, listen to me, position yourself well, make sure the peak lies between your nether lips,' Kemal advised. 'Believe me, you would not wish to have it otherwise. Come then, mount my Seat of Correction.' He used one hand to caress the globes of her buttock whilst steadying her with the other as she stepped up.

Elizabeth was watching with awful fascination, knowing this same fate awaited her. But looking at her friend astride the wooden pillar, she felt a sudden, wicked surge of arousal. She saw Selima bending her knees, lowering herself so carefully, the lips of her sex parting, almost embracing the smooth wooden blade.

'Are you quite ready, Selima?' Kemal asked.

Feeling the movement as he tipped the platforms away, Selima desperately adjusted her position, trying to hold on to the last remnants of support they offered. With her knees clamped tightly against the pyramid's sides, every muscle was rigid with the effort of trying to hold her weight.

'Aaah, it hurts, I cannot,' the serving girl pleaded. 'Please, I cannot...'

At that moment, seeing she was actually sitting on the gently curving saddle of the pillar, Kemal pushed the two platforms away completely. The girl moaned, arching her back, small breasts thrust out, her legs scrabbled vainly for some grip, anything to hold on to, press against or rest a fraction of a toe against, but the smooth surface offered no relief.

'Ahmed, a little support for her arms,' Kemal ordered, and the grinning guard hauled in on the line, lifting Selima's arms up and back. There was another quivering scream from her as she was forced to bend forward from the hip. Kemal could feel the fierce thrust of his erection at her cries, knowing how she was being forced to sit on the most tender parts of her body, her own weight squeezing her pleasure button against the cruel curves of the apparatus.

'Enough, Ahmed, enough,' he said. 'Now, my lovely young slave, perhaps you understand why girls do not choose to take a second ride.' He leaned closer, savouring the sheen of sweat across his slave girl's breasts and on her thighs and belly. As always he marvelled at the definition of muscles and tendons as Selima fought to hold herself as still as possible, legs braced as though to crush the very wood itself.

'You have a lovely body, my dear.' His fingers wiped the beads of moisture from her forehead and then tenderly stroked the globes of her breasts, and Selima's rasping breath was broken by stifled whimpers as she stirred on the wooden blade, grinding the cunning ridge against her sex. 'Oh, I am sorry, does that make you move?' he teased.

His hands continued to stroke her naked body, fondling her nipples before probing delicately in the junction of her thighs, touching the line where the lips of her cunt separated over the saddle peak. 'But I must not delay, I am a man of my word. Now, what did we agree? Two turns of the glass, or one?' He smiled at Selima's desperate efforts in front of him. 'Very well, one it shall be. Watch the glass now, Selima. Remember, your beating begins when the last grain of sand runs through.'

Kemal walked over to the copper pedestal, lifting the sand glass and reversing it with one swift motion. Neither girl knew that this particular glass had quite a large hole and would only run for about ten minutes. He needed Elizabeth to be in a fit state to travel tomorrow and Selima, despite his threats, was only here as an example for Elizabeth. He let a brief smirk cross his face. Of course, there were other sand glasses in the storeroom. They all looked the same but one took over two hours to run through completely... an opportunity for Sula, perhaps? He smiled to himself as the grains began to sift through.

Elizabeth's eyes were darting between the stream of sand and Selima's strutted figure. Despite the pain, Selima, eyes screwed shut and breathing in shallow pants, appeared to be managing the first few minutes of her ordeal quite well. Elizabeth was breathing almost as hard, aroused by the sight of her friend's gleaming skin, the little movements and the tensed, erotic splay of her body. The velvet covering of the cushion prickled the soft flesh of her thighs, and almost subconsciously she began to grip the cushion, pressing and moving so that she rocked gently, feeling the growing wetness in her sex as she rubbed herself on the velvet cylinder.

'You find what we do to Selima exciting?' Kemal's voice whispered in her ear, and before she could protest she felt his hand slipping across her belly to probe under the top edge of her skimpy briefs, fingers curving to dip between her thighs. 'Ah yes, so wet already, lady. What will you do when it is your turn to mount my little toy?' The fingers squirmed and delved, forcing gasps of pleasure from Elizabeth as she responded to his intimate touch.

'Oh please, don't, please, no more,' she begged. 'I shall spend if you continue, my master.' Kemal grinned broadly, drawing the slick fingers from between her legs. With her acknowledgement he knew he had won. Truly, this girl would fetch a rich reward in the days to come!

'Not so eager, lady, you will have your pleasure, but at my command,' he told her. 'Now watch your friend, the sand is nearly run and she must endure Ahmed's caresses. See how skilled he is, and remember; your own turn is yet to come.'

Ahmed had made great play of selecting a slim bamboo from the copper jar. One end was bound with green silk while at the other the cane was split into four, thin strands running back about a foot from the tip. Taking a few hissing practice strokes he ambled back to stand a little way from where Selima was now beginning to moan and struggle as she fought to hold her position.

'Ahmed, you may begin,' Kemal instructed. 'Selima, you will count for us, ten strokes, remember. Should you forget we begin again, with another turn of the glass as well.'

Selima could only nod between rapid, gasping breaths, whimpering in pain as Ahmed playfully tapped the smooth swell of her bottom, measuring his distance.

Swish, thwack!

The first stroke cut almost horizontally, slicing a line across both cheeks of Selima's bottom.

'Aaahhh!' The slave girl screamed, not only from the sudden blaze of pain as the split bamboos cut into her like fire, but also from the biting agony of her own movements rocking her sex against the narrow saddle ridge. There was a pause, everyone's eyes fixed on the figure shivering astride the black pillar. 'One...' came the ragged count.

Thwack!

The second stroke added another set of crimson welts barely a finger's width above the first. Again the scream, the pause and the trembling count. Elizabeth, close to spending in her excitement, pressed even harder into the velvet of the cushion as she watched the fine red lines of pain being etched across Selima's olive skin.

Seven strokes and Kemal raised a hand. 'Ahmed, are you going to neglect the other side? Take the last three there, it will be enough, I think.'

Elizabeth puzzled over Kemal's words. She knew from the grins being exchanged that the prince and his chief guard were playing some game, but what had he meant by 'the other side'? As Ahmed tapped the cane against the hanging curves of Selima's breasts she realised what was about to be done to her.

'Oh no, no you can't, please...' Elizabeth's cries were drowned by Selima's anguished wail as the first stroke cut across her breasts, the split strands tracing fiery lines over the peaks of her nipples so that she heaved and twisted on the torturous saddle blade.

The next stroke cut upwards into the soft crease where her breasts met her ribs, and Selima's strangled count of eight faltered and died. Elizabeth was transfixed with horror as Selima tried to gather herself, gasping and panting, reaching for enough breath to count again.

'N-n-n-nine...' only sounded a whisper as she slumped forward, heedless of the pain lancing up into her sex as she rocked on the wooden ridge. Ahmed smiled, waiting for her to lift her head. Selima fought to bring her body upright, heedless that the movement would thrust her breasts out once more. Ahmed waited, watching the cruelly striped curves ease forward, and then swung his arm. The hissing bamboo strands whipped across the vulnerable peaks, flaying skin already burning from the earlier strokes.

'Mercy, master,' Selima begged pitifully. 'Please, m-mercy, t-t-ten, master.' The muscles of her back and buttocks rippled and tensed as she fought for control. Gradually the movements lessened, the breathing quietened and Selima achieved some kind of balance on her painful perch.

'Very good, my dear, very good indeed,' Kemal congratulated. 'Ahmed, help Selima to dismount, I'm sure she will be suitably grateful in a few moments.' The muscular servant freed the rope, unbuckling the wrist cuffs so she could grab the two ends of the ridge, taking her weight off it. Hooking one thick arm round her waist, Ahmed lifted her before throwing her, hands clutched between her thighs, onto the divan.

CHAPTER 17
Agony and Escape

Still fighting her own turmoil of emotions, Elizabeth saw, despite the obvious agony she'd suffered, the curved blade of the Seat of Correction was glistening wetly with the juices of Selima's body.

Kemal untied her leash from the ring. 'Now, Miss Ashton, time to take your turn. Be grateful to Selima for easing your way, as you can see there was enjoyment hidden in her discomfort, after all.'

Ahmed dragged her to the pillar, and automatically Elizabeth lifted her foot to step onto the little platform. Her head was pulled round as Kemal grabbed her chin. 'Oh no, dear lady, you weren't paying attention, were you? I wish you to be naked.' Elizabeth stopped, frozen by the Arab's black eyes. She undid the top and let it fall, and realising that further delay was pointless she quickly removed the trousers and briefs, standing naked in the golden light. Automatically she crooked her knee and lifted one arm across her body to shield her groin and the fullness of her breasts from Kemal's gaze.

'The hands, if you please,' he said.

Elizabeth Ashton surrendered her last defence by putting her arms behind her back. She felt Ahmed's harsh fingers buckling the cuffs, then the sudden tension as her wrists were locked together. Urged forward by Kemal's hand, she stepped up, inching forward until she could feel her thighs being parted by the tapered sides. Teeth clenched she bent her knees slowly, feeling the warm wet wooden edge parting her labia as she lowered gingerly onto the narrow blade. She winced, wriggling slightly so that she was central on the line of the polished rail, and then she felt the platforms tip away. Her full weight pressed down, grinding her sex against the edge of the pyramid as her toes scrabbled on the smooth black surface.

'Aaah, no, put them back, please,' she moaned desperately. Worse than anything she had imagined, she locked her muscles, trying to hold her body rigid. Instinctively arching back she clenched her buttocks to seek some respite from the throbbing pain in her groin. Then relentlessly her arms were lifted, bowing her forward so the polished edge ground her clitoris against her pubic bone. 'Aaah, p-please, no...'

Prince Kemal flicked his fingers, ordering Ahmed to continue pulling. As the rope continued to force her forward, the English girl's breasts swayed delightfully. 'Enough, Ahmed, turn the glass and then you may take your relief with Selima,' Kemal told his trusty accomplice.

Elizabeth tried desperately to remain still. She knew only too well why she'd been tied much tighter than Selima. Every movement she made, every little effort to hold still, set her exposed globes quivering. A droplet of sweat rolled down one smooth curve before dropping off the rigid peak of her right nipple, to drip onto the base of the pyramid. Her muscles locked in agony she rode the black blade, and all that mattered was the hourglass and the trickling white sand that was busily measuring out her suffering in long, slow minutes.

Ahmed wasted no time in claiming his reward. He grabbed Selima from behind, forcing her facedown into the softly upholstered divan. Then without giving her a chance to struggle he buried the bloated bulb of his penis in the humid cleft of her buttocks and bucked forward, sinking his shaft into the tight passage of her vagina.

Relaxing on the cushions, Kemal watched the two erotic visions before him; the blonde English girl, quivering in every muscle, on the black wedge of the Seat of Correction; to his right Ahmed hungrily fucking Selima as she whimpered and clawed the cloth of the divan. He noted she was now arching her back, responding to Ahmed's onslaught.

'Stroke me, Sula, give me the pleasure of your fingers.' He lay back on one elbow as her dainty hands caressed the loose weight of his balls before encircling his shaft. He groaned quietly as she began to slide one up and down his fullness, using a delicate touch so that his manhood twitched and reared as she brought him to even greater arousal.

Ahmed needed little stimulus to reach his climax. So roused by the part he'd played in the events, and knowing the beating he was still to give, he lasted only a few minutes before shouting in triumph, jerking in a series of short thrusts as he came. Indifferent to her needs he immediately rolled away and got to his feet, adjusting his clothing.

'Enough, for the moment,' Kemal ordered, waving Sula away from her ministrations. 'I will test the skills of your tongue when the beating begins.' He whispered new instructions to Ahmed as the last grains trickled through the glass.

'Miss Ashton,' he called softly. 'It is time for your punishment. Perhaps I should warn you that the cane Ahmed uses is not as straightforward as it looks. I know you enjoyed the kiss of bamboo when sharing sport with Sir Roger, since he told me of your adventures himself. But do not be misled; this will be worse than you have ever faced. Oh yes,' he laughed softly, 'any movement will bring its own penalty, as you will discover. Ahmed, when you are ready.'

Elizabeth twisted her head wildly, trying to see her tormentor. 'Remember,' Kemal's voice teased again, 'remember the count. Forget and the stroke will be added.' He paused. 'Something I do not think you will want to happen, especially in a few minutes from now.'

Thwack!

Like liquid fire the split bamboo laced her bottom with agony. Elizabeth sucked in air, clenching desperately to ease the pain, then crying aloud at that other sudden agony as she jolted forward, grinding her sex against the fiendishly placed ridges of the Seat of Correction. 'One!' she gasped.

Thwock!

A deeper sound this time, Ahmed cutting upwards to bring the strands slashing across the soft groove underneath her buttocks, teasing and pinching the flesh where the edge of the pillar showed below the incurving swell of her bottom.

'Aaaaah, t-two,' she wailed, unable to ease the fire with frantic movements as she wanted to do so badly. Kemal, eyes feasting on the English girl's anguish, eased his robes apart, letting the length of his erection curve up, free for Sula's attentions.

'Attend me now,' he commanded, stretching lazily against the cushions as the third stroke brought another stifled howl from the blonde girl. Sula leaned forward, holding his thick shaft with one hand while her lips slid over the smooth crown, tongue flickering around the sensitive rim. The inscrutable prince ground his hips very slightly as the exquisite sensation teased his groin. 'Deeper, girl, take it deeper,' he ordered, and Sula slid her lips down the gnarled column, gagging slightly as he butted into the back of her throat. Her tongue flickered and teased him as she raised her head before engulfing the wet shaft once more in a tantalising rhythm.

Elizabeth was wailing and pleading, her bottom laced with a network of lines, raised welts cut by the strands making up the split bamboo rod. The wet *thwack* of the next stroke drew another agonised outburst of suffering from her lips. 'F-five!' she stammered. 'Please stop, it hurts so much!'

But despite her cries the young blonde felt something else; she slithered on the wetness of the wooden edge as the beating laced the agony with heat and rising excitement. Lost in her own world she didn't notice the pause as Ahmed moved around the platform, but the gentle tapping, just enough to set the full globes of her breasts swaying, jerked her back to awful reality.

Kemal, thrusting languidly into the wet warmth of Sula's mouth, felt a rising excitement as Ahmed prepared to follow his orders by delivering the last five strokes across Elizabeth's defenceless breasts, rather than the three Selima had endured.

'Ready, girl?' Ahmed asked in broken English, and before she could respond the cane hissed across to lace the upper slopes of her breasts with fire.

Thwick!

The next stroke, rising from below, nearly lifted her clear of the saddle as it cut up into the fleshy under-curves of each globe. 'No count, girl, that's two more,' gloated Ahmed, over the babbled pleading of the distraught English girl.

'Oh, please no, please, that's six and seven, please I've counted for you... *please*, you can't.'

'Too late, I'm afraid, much too late,' Kemal said softly from the divan. 'You were warned. From five I believe, Ahmed.' He smiled in anticipation. Not only were two more to be added, but also Ahmed was skilful enough to place the extra strokes exactly over the top of the two just given, doubling the effect.

Thwock!

'Six!' The count was wailed as the strands again seared the tops of her breasts. Stillness fell, Elizabeth fighting for breath while Ahmed took time to prepare the next upward stroke. This time the cane made a softer, wetter sound.

Thwap!

'S-seven, please... *seven!*' Kemal observed Elizabeth's mouth-watering globes swinging as she tried to ride the pain of that last deliberate cut. He wondered if she realised where Ahmed intended the last three strokes to go. He was thrusting into Sula's succulent mouth more aggressively now, hands clutching her hair as the driving images of Elizabeth's beating forced him over the edge and to his climax. 'Now, Ahmed, beat her nipples!'

Elizabeth managed a shuddering breath, bucking on the thudding pain of the wooden blade as she rode the agony of that last stroke. And her respite was only fleeting, Ahmed simply waiting for a pause in her spasms. Like Selima, Elizabeth instinctively arched back, trying to ease the biting agony of the seat against her cunt. The rigid stubs of her nipples jutted more prominently than ever, just as Ahmed wanted.

Thwack!

The split ends flayed the tender pink peak of each breast, flicking across the wide aureoles in scalding lines of pain.

'Aaahh... eight!' The squeal echoed as the English girl writhed helplessly, and the next stroke repeated the cut.

'Nine! No more, please no more!' To Elizabeth it was as though her flesh was being slowly peeled away by the dreadful bamboo strips. Her sight obscured by sweat and the tangled ruin of her hair across her face, she was only dimly aware of Ahmed raising his arm again.

'Enough!' Kemal's voice was firm but still replete with lust as he prevented Ahmed's final stroke from falling 'She understands well enough now. Take her down, my friend.'

Just as he had with Sula, the squat brute used one arm to lift her clear of the impaling pyramid before dropping her, curled and sobbing, in a heap on the divan.

'Now, perhaps you realise your position here,' said Kemal. 'You will thank me for my mercy in due course. Selima, attend her.'

Kemal took Ahmed to one side. 'Fetch two guards. The English girl goes back into the cells for tonight. The other two, amuse me while I consider what must be done, and Ahmed, be sure to see that Natawama and his men deposit the *special* cargo most carefully... enough weight to be certain there are no inconvenient reappearances. You understand me.'

Ahmed bowed and left the airless chamber, reappearing in less than a minute with two more guards.

'Miss Ashton, there are arrangements I have to make for your further journey. The guards will return you to your quarters.' Kemal ordered his men to drag the bewildered girl to her feet. 'Remember, it was Prince Kemal who showed you mercy in your ordeal.'

He watched as the young Englishwoman struggled to contain an outburst of anger. Even better, the lesson had been learned but that fighting spirit was still intact, Kemal mused, mentally revising Elizabeth's market value upward.

A few minutes later Elizabeth found herself lying on the remains of her own English clothes in another dark cell, the echoing slam of the door still ringing in her ears. At last she gave way to the anger, humiliation and pain of the past terrible hours. Why did she not stay with Helene? Her situation was utterly hopeless. She caressed her whipped breasts and buried her face in her arms, and slowly the sobbing eased as the tension in her body was released. After a while, curling up on the stone floor and using the remains of her dress as a makeshift pillow, Elizabeth Ashton slept.

It was the moonlight that awoke her. Not shining through a window, because the cell was below ground level, but in a pale strip of silvery light thrown around the edge of the door. Elizabeth stirred, then instantly she was fully awake. It simply wasn't possible... the door was open! Hardly daring to believe her good fortune she gingerly reached out to touch it.

It moved. Desperate now for speed before anyone checked on her, Elizabeth struggled into her drawers and shift. No time for the heavy dress, stockings, breast bands or bodice, and there was no sign of her shoes. With her heart thumping she eased the door wider. It seemed they'd slammed it and shot the bolt at the same time, causing it to strike the rim of its socket instead of slotting into it. Thank the Lord, she thought, that they'd been too intent on exchanging crude remarks about her to check that all was secure.

She was out of the cell and up the stone steps to the courtyard like a wraith. All too well aware of her previous failed attempt to escape, she kept a wary eye open for the patrolling guards, watching for the shadows to reveal their movements. This time she had no problem finding the gateway and within a minute she was once again creeping down the dusty alleyway towards the riverbank.

In spite of the urgency of her situation, Elizabeth made slow progress. Without shoes she kept stubbing her toes on small stones, her feet too tender to cope with the gravel at the sides of the narrow lane. Once she made the mistake of leaving the road to walk on what she took to be a grassy verge, but the first step left her hopping in agony as vicious thorns ripped across her soft skin.

Skirting the town she reached the edge of the estuary. A beach curved away where the river flowed out into the ocean, and she could hear the roar of the breakers on the sandbars of the entrance. Palms rustled and swayed against the brilliant stars of the night sky. With her eyes adjusting to the faint light she was able to see something of the litter and tangle of ropes, pots, wood and debris as well as the dark shapes of canoes and small fishing boats pulled up on the sand.

She was picking her way along the shore when she heard shouts behind her. Looking back she saw the bobbing glow of lanterns as Kemal and his men hunted her once more. She ran, feet sinking into the sand until she was able to make better speed along the waters edge itself.

She raced on, breath rasping in her chest with the effort. Behind her she heard a whoop of triumph and the lanterns began to bounce and flicker along the shore. They had found and were tracking her footprints. Throwing all caution to the winds she waded out into the silky warmth of the estuary, thankful at least that it wasn't the numbing cold of an English river.

Despite the dragging weight of her clinging shift, she managed to reach a canoe tied alongside a larger boat. Two struggling attempts to climb aboard, then success as she collapsed headfirst into the bottom of it, wrapped like a bundle of washing in the ruins of her clothes.

Still frantic to put as much distance as possible between her and her pursuers, she untied the rope holding the canoe to its bigger brother and pushed it out into the lapping water, and she was just scrabbling for some kind of paddle when she felt the canoe jerk and twist unexpectedly. She'd completely overlooked any possible currents! She was being swept away!

Looking back she could see lights clustered on the shore. She hoped the debate was about which way to go next, not a conference as to which boat to use to recapture her. A search of the canoe revealed only a crude rope, a calabash obviously used as a scoop of some kind, and a leaf-bladed paddle with a broken shaft.

Balancing carefully she sat up. Rotating slowly in the current she realised the shore lights were moving away and growing smaller by the minute. Whatever happened to her now, Elizabeth realised she was at least safe from immediate recapture, because she was being swept relentlessly out to sea...

CHAPTER 18
Helene's Sweet Revenge

Helene Birencourt stretched in the privacy of her bedroom, glad that all the fuss and questions were over for the day. She had shed the demure clothes, worn to ensure that Lord Roberts did not have further opportunity to think ill of her, and was now dressed only in a sheer silk gown, open down the front but held by a single cream ribbon. She had just finished brushing her glossy dark hair when a soft knock sounded on the door. 'Ah, Jenni, come in, we have much to discuss,' she welcomed the maid. 'I hope you are dressed as I instructed. Mebele gave you the message, I trust?'

'Yes, mistress,' the maid confirmed. She stood demurely before Helene, barefoot, dressed only in a short cotton shift. It was clear from the peaks and shadows visible through the flimsy material that beneath it she was naked.

'Now, Jenni, last night you obviously enjoyed what you did to me, so tonight I thought it only right that I return the favour,' Helene said. 'That's only fair, isn't it?' She watched as her adorable but traitorous maid nodded, eyes downcast and hands clasped modestly in front of her. 'Very well, begin by fetching the stool.' She pointed at the piece of furniture she required, positioned by one wall.

Jenni struggled to move the heavy stool. Set on four sturdy legs and originally meant as a piano seat for two people, it was about eighteen inches wide and three feet long, its top upholstered in rich brown leather. 'Good, just a little closer, I think. That will do nicely. Now, bring me the object placed on the corner table.'

This time Jenni was much more reluctant to face her mistress. When she did return she was carrying a cane, finger-thick with prominent darker ridges at regular intervals. It glowed with a vivid yellow gloss, polished with the sweat and friction of long and regular use. 'Ah yes, my little persuader,' the woman reflected. 'A friend you have met more than once before, isn't that right, Jenni?'

'Yes, mistress. But please, mistress, Jenni's sorry for last night. I didn't hurt you, it was Mehmet with the cane.'

'Shhh, don't get in such a state. It's very simple, Jenni. Either I punish you, as you heard me tell the governor I would, or I hand you over to the authorities. That will certainly mean you go to prison, and it could well mean a prison flogging as well. The choice is yours, you only have to say.'

There was a long pause before Jenni held out her hands, hanging her head as she gave the persuader to her mistress. 'I choose you, mistress, no prison,' she said quietly.

'Very well, now we'll do things a little differently this time. Come here and sit astride the bench. No, not in the middle; here, at this end...'

Jenni had to pull up her shift to straddle the width of the bench, inching back, her skin squeaking on the leather top as she wriggled until the curve of her bottom was just peeping over the edge of the seat. 'Good, now lean forward, right forward so you can hold the front legs.'

Helene suddenly stopped her. 'Oh dear, we are both becoming forgetful. I don't believe you'll need your shift any more tonight. Here, let me help you.' Helene lifted the rumpled folds of material away from Jenni's hips. She made sure her hands followed the curves of the maid's slim waist before lifting and tenderly caressing each shapely breast. Jenni shivered, raising her arms obediently for Helene to pull the diaphanous cotton clear of her body before throwing it on the bed behind her.

'Now you may bend forward, as far as you can,' the woman permitted, fingers pressing the young native's back, urging her down. Obeying the pressure of those insistent fingers, Jenni lowered until her breasts were flattened against the cool leather, hands reaching down and gripping the short wooden legs. The movement stretched the smooth curve of her upper body as well as lifting and parting the firm globes of her bottom. Helene ran her fingers over them, then smiled and picked up the yellow cane, using the tip to trace the indented line of her maid's spine.

Fascinated by the twitches caused by the cane's touch, Helene asked quietly, 'Jenni, how many strokes do you think you deserve?' The tip stroked the summit of one buttock before burrowing into the deep groove between the soft cheeks. 'After all, you seemed so eager to make me spend.'

The vicious implement worked deeper, sliding back and forth so the ridges caressed the opening of Jenni's anus, offered so blatantly by the splay of her position. 'I, I don't know, my lady,' Jenni said meekly. 'It was Mr Elford; he told me that since I enjoyed such games I should bring you off.'

'My choice then, it seems,' Helene mused. 'Ten would be fair,' she looked up as a thin line of light swept across the floor, her door opening and closing without a sound. 'Ten's fair, isn't it, Jonathan?' The cane, gleaming with the girl's moisture, tapped against her bottom as she spoke.

Jenni twisted round, looking for the visitor she had secretly been expecting, and peered up at Lieutenant Kingsford's tall figure as he dipped a hand between her buttocks, fingers curling to graze the pink inner leaves where they pressed against the leather top.

'Just as you thought, my dear, wet and very willing, isn't that right, my little spy?' he teased, trailing the moist tips of his fingers over the maid's tongue and lips, letting her taste the tang of her own excitement. 'Yes, ten would be fair. After all, we don't want her to be too tired, now do we?'

'Jenni,' Helene's voice was quiet but authoritative, 'you chose this punishment. I'm not going to tie you but you must hold your position. If you don't, Lieutenant Kingsford will hold you down and it will be twenty more strokes to remind you of the need for obedience, is that clear?'

Jenni nodded, her curly black hair moving healthily as she pressed her cheek into the leather of the stool. 'I'll try, mistress, honest I will.'

'Get ready, then.' Helene measured her distance. She wanted to make sure the stroke was full across both cheeks, knowing from her own experience that if delivered short, the tip of the cane could cause real damage.

Whick!

The soft curves bounced at the solid impact. Jenni's head reared back and she gave a hissing gasp, hands clenching around the wooden legs as the pain of the stripe developed.

Helene didn't follow up immediately. Putting the cane on the bed she stripped off her own robe and then knelt by the twitching body on the bench. She pressed the warm globes of her breasts against Jenni's back as she traced the first reddening weal with a delicate caress. 'Nine more... then we will see how I can repay the pleasure you made me feel.'

Jenni wriggled as Helene's touch inflamed the burning pain, excited by the promise of her mistress's words. Helene picked up the cane, pausing only to reach between the folds of Jonathan's gown to caress the jut of his penis. Freed from the impeding folds of her shift, Helene was now able to build up a steady rhythm, each stroke falling to carve a thin read line next to the one before, marching down to the most tender skin at the top of her maid's thighs. Each stroke was timed with the pace of an expert as Helene waited until there was that momentary, automatic relaxation of Jenni's bottom cheeks before sending the next blow slicing across the soft black globes.

By the eighth stroke Jenni was writhing desperately, legs tensed and hands clenching in a fraught effort to hold her position. Helene waited patiently for the turmoil to subside before sending the ninth cut diagonally across the existing marks.

'Aahhh, please mistress, please no, it burns, it burns, *please!*' the maid begged.

'Now Jenni, nearly over, there's just a special one left,' Helene coaxed, her tones dulcet, 'just to remind you of last night.' She turned, stepping to straddle the bench so she could look down on the smooth curves and open splay of Jenni's buttocks. 'Whipping in, I believe Sir Roger calls it. Hold on, my little one, this will hurt like the devil!'

Before Jenni understood what Helene intended she had brought the cane swinging down to slice deep into the valley between her maid's splayed buttocks, the cruel rod blazing a line of agony across the soft flesh of her crease and whipping against the sensitive lips of her cunt like liquid fire.

A wild squeal echoed around the room as Jenni hauled herself off the bench, hands between her thighs clutching the tormented core of her body. 'Oh, mistress, you've split me in two,' she wailed. 'I can't, I couldn't hold it, please no more, no more, please!'

'Silly girl, that was ten, wasn't it?' Helene chided. 'Perhaps you'll remember your place more readily now. Come on, sit down.' Jenni, helped by Jonathan, sprung up again with another whimper as the leather top brought fresh agony to the stripes across her rear. But Helene, intent on shared pleasures, pressed her maid down until she was full length, buttocks on the edge of the stool, thighs parted and her legs bent at the knees so her feet were braced firmly on the floor.

Helene knelt beside her maid, one hand stroking the tight curls of her black hair whilst the other trailed along one thigh, teasing the soft crease of her groin at each stroke. 'Jonathan will help us now,' she said quietly, and hearing his cue, Jonathan slipped off his robe and leaned forward, hands resting on Jenni's knees so he could lower himself between her parted thighs. He pressed the maid's knees wider apart, opening the wet folds of her cunt for his attentions.

He blew a waft of air across the succulent flesh, and the lovers smiled at the involuntary arching of the maid's hips as she responded to the fluttering coolness. He bent until his mouth was just touching the split pouch of her sex. The girl's hips surged again as he tickled the softness, just touching the oval split where the lips of her sex swelled and parted with her excitement.

Helene, not to be left out, traced the whorls of her maid's ear with the tip of her tongue while one hand caressed the hardening peaks of Jenni's breasts. 'He's going to make you spend, you know that, don't you, Jenni?' The whispered words brought another gasp from the girl as she felt Jonathan's tongue delicately teasing the folds of her body, and she gasped again as his fingers parted her, opening the way so his tongue could return, slithering and teasing over her sex, making her heave and twist in delight. 'That's better, isn't it?' the woman coaxed. 'Can you feel him bringing you on. You can't stop it now, can you? Go on, ride his tongue, spend for me...'

Her fingers twisted the rigid nipples as the young maid's hips began their unstoppable surging rhythm, trying to force Jonathan's mouth harder against her body to increase the pleasures driving her to a peak of excitement.

Jonathan's powerful hands held her legs apart to their widest extent. He was in control, restraining her thrusting hips, building her anguish as he held her down against the surging sensations his tongue was drawing from her. He began to focus on the nub of Jenni's cleft, flicking it rapidly with the very tip of his tongue so that it stood proud, the direct masturbation finally too much for Jenni to take. Panting and crying, almost as though she were being beaten again, she tried in vain to break free of the arms and hands holding her down on the stool.

'Yes, yes, mistress,' she babbled. 'I'm there, yes, *yes!*' Her cries peaked as Jonathan continued to tease her clitoris, before lifting his head and sitting back on his haunches, his chin and lips glistening with the juices of her orgasm.

Helene, sighing with satisfaction, moved lazily around Jenni's body, enjoying the sight of her maid's heaving attempts to recover her breath. She leaned across to kiss Jonathan, savouring the sharp tang of Jenni's body as she licked her moisture from his face. Her hand caressed the thick length of his penis, now curving up so hard that the polished crown tapped against his flat belly with each movement. 'Your turn now, my love.' She ran her hands back down across the warmth of Jenni's stomach, turning to smile at the glazed eyes and gasping mouth below her. 'I will ride her too and let her tongue please me again.'

Suiting action to words Helene straddled the bench, facing Jenni's feet. 'Come now, Jenni, before Jonathan takes you to your pleasure again, show me last night's skills once more.' She bent her knees until the wet lips of her cunt nuzzled her maid's face.

'M-m-m-m...' was all the supine maid managed before the delicious warmth of her mistress's flesh pressed against her nose and mouth, and Helene wriggled in delight as she felt her maid's tongue probing into her vagina.

Jonathan, eyes fixed on Helene's blissful expression, saw her bite her lip in sudden ecstasy, as Jenni started to lap and tease her mistress properly. He inched forward, sliding the engorged head of his penis between the glistening folds of Jenni's sex.

Still unbearably sensitive from her climax, Jenni bucked at the first sliding contact. Helene's gasp echoed her maid's as Jenni's cry of surprise added another twist of delight to the sensations she was feeling.

'Now, my darling, now,' Jonathan urged as he hooked his arms under Jenni's knees, lifting and spreading her body to press the smooth head of his penis into the soft, wet opening. She surged again on the wet leather, her cries muffled by her mistress's body as the bulbous tip popped through the stretched ring and she felt Jonathan's shaft filling her.

'Yes, yes!' came the echoing wail from above as Jenni blubbered against Helene's sex, driving the woman on to her climax as she did. Jonathan rocked slowly to and fro, each stroke drawing back until the polished helmet just rested between the wet, pink lips... then driving forward, deeper and deeper with each long thrust. Helene clawed at his chest in frantic excitement, bending to force Jenni's lips against the nub of her clitoris. 'Go on, Jonathan, go on! She's coming again, I can feel it! Faster, *faster!*'

Helene rode Jenni's face, rocking as the spasms of ecstasy convulsed her body. Between her thighs the young maid was also riding her own orgasm, the second within minutes, as the relentless fucking drove her to another shuddering release.

The twin sensations of Jenni's climax and the maid's screams vibrating against her cunt were too much for Helene to take as Jonathan continued to fuck the maid, intent only on achieving his own release. His iron control broke and he began to piston into her with animated thrusts, shouting in release as the hot jets erupted deep within her. Driven on by the deep penetration, Jenni shuddered her way to a third orgasm before flopping like a limp rag doll on the damp leather stool.

Helene got to her feet and languidly embraced Jonathan. 'Thank you, that was glorious,' she whispered wearily, then pulled him across the room until they could both fall, exhausted, onto the soft covers of the bed. 'I think Jenni will remember her lessons in future.' She kissed her lover, fondling the wet softness of his penis, feeling it begin to stir in her hand. 'But I do hope she hasn't tired you out...'

CHAPTER 19
Sex and Survival

Dawn broke to reveal nothing but the heaving lines of a heavy swell. The canoe had been swept completely out of sight of land. Clutching the sodden remains of her dress, Elizabeth tried to sit up, but the increased rocking panicked her into a huddle at the bottom of the canoe. Only one broken paddle, she thought ruefully. What could she do with only one broken paddle? Even if she knew which way to row, with one ineffectual paddle she'd probably just go round in circles.

Suddenly the events of the past few days, the betrayal by Sir Roger, Kemal's punishment, her escape and now this, were all too much. Elizabeth Aston curled up in the frail security of the canoe's hull and wept. Eventually the sobbing eased, though, and despite being terrified, wet and cold, she slept.

The storm reached her a few hours later.

The wind had been rising steadily, and by noon it was clear to Elizabeth that she was fully in its path. The canoe's motion was sickening, twisting and surging over the great ocean rollers. Bailing out the water was a futile exercise as the canoe slowly became waterlogged, then one frightening lurch and it was all over, the canoe capsized. Elizabeth found herself threshing wildly in the water as the next curling wave drove her down. Blind determination for survival drove her, gasping and spluttering, back to the surface. She managed to tear the cotton shift just enough to free herself from the waterlogged material, which threatened to drag her down. She was utterly exhausted and almost on the verge of giving up when a rigid shape showed for a moment as she rose on the crest of a wave. When it appeared again as the next wave lifted her she realised it was the hull of the canoe, upside down but still afloat. Threshing madly she struggled to cling on to the rounded shape as it surged and lifted in the rollers. With one last effort she was just able to heave herself half out of the water, sprawling across the smooth curve, gasping for air and desperately hanging on.

Elizabeth lay semiconscious through the long night, barely aware of the storm's force gradually easing. It was the comfort of the sun on her shoulders that woke her, and looking round through eyes blurred by salt she saw that the hostile seas had been replace by a languid swell. With extreme care she was able to move, to straddle the upturned hull so she could sit up and take her first proper look around.

To her utter amazement she found the canoe was drifting barely a hundred yards off a tree-fringed coastline, and before she had time to think she slipped back into the water, striking out for the shore heedless of exhaustion. Away from the relative security of the hull the distance seemed endless. Elizabeth once more sank beneath the water, almost willing to give up the unequal struggle. But her toes stubbed into sand and she pushed furiously against the undertow of the surf. Thrusting her head clear of the waves she took a deep breath, fighting for a foothold until, at long last, she was able to keep her balance and stand upright. Staggering out of the sea and up the beach she collapsed in the shade of an overhanging palm.

Stiff, her skin raw from salt and exposure and aching with the cramps of exhaustion, she looked around. Behind her an innocent blue ocean rolled and broke along the palm-fringed shore. Before her a line of palms and thick forest presented an impenetrable green barrier.

There was no sigh of human life at all. From her raging thirst and dry skin she knew she had to find fresh water, even before food. She scanned as far as she could up and down the shoreline. To her left a group of rocks and a taller mass of trees offered hope of a stream, so gathering her strength she struggled through the fine white sand towards the trees.

To her amazement and against all real hope, there was indeed a stream, which proved her salvation. With spirits daring to rise Elizabeth waded up it into the humid shade of the forest for some way before it opened out into a small pool. Gratefully she sipped fresh water from the fall at the far end before throwing herself in, soaking away the clinging salt from her hair and body. The tattered remains of her lacy drawers were discarded on a rock, and any thoughts of how she might clothe herself were ignored as she rejoiced her miraculous good fortune, shrieking and splashing like an excitable child, exalting in the delight of survival, soothed by the fresh, clear water.

Clean and restored to some semblance of her usual self, Elizabeth sat on a rock combing her fingers through her long fair hair trying, more or less successfully, to remove the worst of the tangles. She had given up the idea of trying to wear the tattered drawers for the present.

Feeling hungry but rejuvenated, she looked around. Muted to a background roar by the thick vegetation, she could hear the persistent thunder of the surf, and deciding that as the beach offered only heat and insects, she would explore upstream a little more. As long as it was possible to make progress, she thought.

Determined not to give in to her fear of this unknown and probably hostile land, Elizabeth kept hold of the useless remnants of her drawers whilst wading cautiously to the other end of the pool. A scramble up the rocks brought her to a large clearing and a second pool but, more importantly, she saw the edge of a distinct trail leading away from the water into the forest, and she was about to wade across to the start of the trail when she heard the voices.

Frightened by the prospect of discovery and suddenly aware of her nakedness, she moved back into the thick vegetation so she could kneel unseen and watch whoever might be coming to the pool.

First into view was a tall black woman. She ran forward with flowing grace, stopping on the edge of the pool and turning to look back up the trail. Apart from a waist string that held a small, brightly beaded apron over her sex, she was naked. Her ebony skin glowed in the shafts of sunlight. Her breasts were sharply pointed, her figure perfect - broad shoulders, slim waist and long muscular legs. The full curve of her bottom was emphasised by the string of her waistband and another running down from it and disappearing in the deep valley between her buttocks.

Elizabeth's candid inspection of the girl was interrupted by the arrival of her companion. Taller and impressively muscled, apart from a band high up round one arm and a small breechcloth, he too was naked. His ebony skin, like the girl's, gleamed with a faint sheen of sweat.

Elizabeth could see the girl was teasing him and that the clearing was the end of some game or chase they had been enjoying. He moved forward into the dappled shade and then tugged the cord free from her waist. Quickly dipping her body and spreading her knees she helped him remove the little cache-sex that had protected her genitals. The man, and Elizabeth, gazed intently at the strong curve of her mound and the darker patch of hair at the junction of her thighs.

Naked and giggling, the girl cupped the man's breechcloth in obvious invitation before turning away and running a few steps. With a quick movement he slipped off his own garment. Elizabeth, trying to crouch even lower in the bushes, choked back a gasp as she saw the massive size of his erection curving up to a swollen, purple helmet. The girl licked her lips in anticipation, smiling broadly as she saw her lover's obvious readiness, but she was still feeling playful. As he reached for her she darted away to the edge of the pool.

Shouting something to her in their own language, the man raced after her, their bodies obscured by the spray as they chased each other through the shallows. Slowly the water settled and Elizabeth could see the couple again. They'd stopped almost directly in front of her, the man behind the girl, his hands around her front so he could slide his fingers across her pointed breasts and play with her nipples. From the girl's gentle rocking Elizabeth knew she was rubbing the thick shaft of his erection in the cleft of her buttocks.

More words passed quietly between them and the girl freed herself, moving forward so she could sink down, her knees spread apart. Looking back and smiling deliberately she lowered her upper body, her breasts grazing the ground and the full curves of her bottom arched in invitation. Elizabeth stared with rising excitement and amazement as she saw the vivid pink flesh gleaming with moisture as the girl reached back, parting her labia, deliberately displaying herself for her lover's attentions.

Elizabeth's hand slipped between her thighs, stroking herself in response to the girl's blatant invitation. Her fingers caressed the slippery folds as she teased that one special spot. Eyes fixed on the clearing, Elizabeth rubbed one finger against her clit, teeth clamped on her lower lip to stifle any cries as her excitement increased.

The man responded to the girl's erotic invitation. Wading forward, he knelt close behind her, obviously deciding to do a little teasing of his own. Despite her urging, he stroked his smooth helmet very slowly across the girl's sex lips. The slick friction was too much for her and she twisted, trying to force her body onto the sturdy shaft, her eyes closed in ecstasy as she took the shaft deeper with each rocking thrust of their hips. Once fully embedded the man's thrusts became longer and deeper, the watching girl able to see the slick length of his cock moving in and out with a regular rhythm that was driving the girl steadily to a peak. Moaning beneath him she was trying to arch her back even more, seeking an extra inch of penetration from the rod impaling her so deeply. In the bushes Elizabeth was on the brink herself, desperately trying to ride the spasms of her own orgasm as well as stifling the gasping cries as her finger made her come and come again.

The girl was crying out in ecstasy at each stroke. Suddenly he pumped furiously, jolting her forward as he erupted deep within her body. Her cries rose to a wail of bliss and she threshed frantically as her own orgasm claimed her. They remained locked for a few moments before falling forward, gasping and whispering in their shared joy.

It was only as the breathing of all three - the two lovers and their secret observer - began to return to normal that Elizabeth made her mistake. Feeling a sudden cramp she tried to move, only to catch a thorn across the curve of one breast. The pain and the cramp knocked her off balance and before she could do anything she crashed forward to land in a sprawling tangle of tanned limbs just beside the entwined couple.

Flopping winded onto her back, Elizabeth looked at the lovers who were frozen in shock at the sudden disturbance and appearance of a naked white woman apparently from nowhere. The man was first to react, throwing himself astride her body, one hand pinning her head down by the hair, the other clubbed and raised ready to strike. Elizabeth closed her eyes and waited for the blow to fall...

But when nothing happened she peered from beneath squinted lids to see the girl holding back his arm and whispering fiercely at him. She was gesturing towards the ocean, telling him that Elizabeth must have come from there. Gradually his tension relaxed until both he and Elizabeth became aware of the position he was in. His strong thighs were clamped across her belly and the soft length of his penis lay in a curve, the head just nudging the valley between her breasts. Elizabeth was suddenly very aware of the heat and tang of his body, too, feeling the movement on her ribs as his cock began to thicken once again.

He moved aside and the two of them studied the strange new arrival in close detail. They looked in wonder, running their hands through the tangled golden waterfall of Elizabeth's hair. They inspected her hands, turning them over so they could check both sides, before comparing them to their own dark skin and lighter palms. Seeing that the first shock of the unexpected encounter was wearing off, Elizabeth knelt up, returning their enquiring gazes as calmly as she could manage.

Not having any idea what to say she contented herself with pointing at her body and saying, 'E-liz-a-beth,' clearly and slowly.

The girl was quicker to grasp her meaning, pointing to herself and the man in turn and saying, 'N'tala, N'gozhi...'

They all tried out the sounds of their names and the first hesitant smiles broke out between them. Elizabeth, using various signs and much pointing, managed to convey the idea that she had come from the sea in the storm and was now lost and alone.

Then, blushing with deep embarrassment, she tried to make apologies for spying on their lovemaking, but neither seemed in the least put out, and N'tala even laughed as Elizabeth belatedly began to try and shield her own breasts and sex from N'gozhi's increasingly appreciative gaze. She gently moved the young blonde's arms away so she could gently caress each pink tip for herself, then taking Elizabeth's hand, she placed it on the hard buds of her own dark nipples.

After caressing both of Elizabeth's breasts for a few minutes, N'tala lifted them, making a comment to N'gozhi as she displayed the evidence of Elizabeth's excitement. Giggling, she clasped his shaft, stroking slowly up and down, and as his erection began to stir again she smiled at the reaction she'd provoked, using her other hand to reach between Elizabeth's parted thighs.

The white girl gasped as the black fingers discovered the revealing wetness of her recent orgasm. N'tala laughed again, showing the glistening tips of her fingers to N'gozhi, who grinned back at this evidence of their new acquaintance's arousal. Now the girl's movements became more deliberate, sliding her fingers deeper so that the blonde girl bit her lip and mewed softly at the delightful feelings being stroked from her willing body.

Without thinking she reached forward and very hesitantly touched the warm flesh of N'gozhi's manhood, feeling it begin to thicken and stiffen even more as he responded to the stimulation he was seeing and feeling. Keeping her fingers buried deep in Elizabeth's body, N'tala shuffled round to kneel behind her so that Elizabeth could lean back against her breasts, shuffling her knees apart and offering her own firm breasts for attention from N'tala's other hand, pushing her hips forward, opening and offering herself to N'gozhi.

At first N'tala seemed reluctant to allow her expert masturbation to be interrupted, but once N'gozhi knelt between the English girl's parted knees she withdrew her soaking fingers from Elizabeth's body. Very gently N'tala used her wet fingers to fondle and coat her lover's rigid penis with the moisture of Elizabeth's arousal, before carefully inserting the smooth helmet into the golden body spread open before them.

They both watched excitedly as Elizabeth's eyes opened wide, feeling that delicious stretching as she took the large purple head a little at a time. She surged with excitement as the rim slipped into the entrance of her body and her inner muscles clenched round him.

N'tala opened Elizabeth's labia wider so the trembling young blonde could look down and watch the slow impalement she wanted so badly. N'gozhi pushed forward and N'tala did the same, and between them Elizabeth was forced to sink down the thick, gnarled length of his erection.

The blonde Englishwoman's wail of delight echoed in the trees as she felt the intense, sliding stimulation building, pushing her slowly towards yet another climax. But N'tala was in no mood to let her new friend relax and enjoy her lover at that pace, so she carefully began to toy with the little hood of flesh at the summit of her cleft, flicking and teasing the English girl's clitoris.

'Oh yes,' moaned the blonde girl as she twisted in the sandwich between the two toned black bodies. 'Don't stop, please don't stop,' she urged desperately. 'I'm coming... yes, I'm coming!'

The babbling may have been in a foreign language but the sounds and the wild involuntary movements told their own story. N'tala smiled broadly and increased her efforts as she felt Elizabeth begin to spend in frantic bursts. Using all her skills she kept the white girl writhing and pleading for long minutes as her lover continued to thrust into her shuddering body. Finally N'gozhi reached his climax too and both girls felt the contractions and short stabbing movements as he growled and copiously discharged again.

CHAPTER 20
Captured!

After a few minutes of rest, N'tala urged Elizabeth to her feet. Pointing to the sky and miming both walking and sleeping, she managed to explain to Elizabeth that they must leave now if they were to get back to the village before nightfall. There was also some underlying worry in N'tala's gestures telling Elizabeth that she needed to be both watchful and careful on the journey.

It was only seeing N'tala retying her little apron that reminded Elizabeth of her own nakedness. She found the tattered, nearly dry drawers and slipped them on, ignoring the tears and split seams that undid most of her efforts at modesty.

N'gozhi, who had disappeared down the path, returned carrying a short spear with a leaf-shaped blade, and a small oval shield covered in some kind of animal skin. His face was set in an anxious frown and every gesture emphasised the need for haste. He set off rapidly along the narrow trail, and following as best she could, the soles of her feet still not accustomed to being without shoes, she was able to keep up with N'tala as they trotted along, carefully avoiding the thorns and scratching lianas looping from the tall trees.

After twenty minutes or so the forest thinned, giving way to a sea of grass interspersed with clumps of thorny trees and strange conical mounds. The leaf litter and soft earth changed to a path of hard red clay, uncomfortably hot under the remorseless blaze of the midday sun. Elizabeth began to regret the loss of her slippers as her feet became steadily more painful.

Then, without warning, they were plunged into horror.

N'gozhi had stopped at a fork in the trail and was looking anxiously towards a thick plume of black smoke rising in the distance, and there was no warning - just a vicious swish, a heavy thud and N'gozhi crashed back onto the ground, unconscious.

Elizabeth and N'tala screamed in terror, N'tala throwing herself forward over his motionless body. Quicker than Elizabeth to assess the danger she was scrabbling in the dust beside her lover, trying to wrench the short spear from his hand.

She was too late; yells and whoops erupted all round them as a group of warriors in full wardress charged from the cover of the long grass. One swung a polished wooden club, knocking N'tala senseless in the dust beside N'gozhi, while two others pounced on the screaming figure of Elizabeth. She raked her nails down the face of one and then a club caught the side of her head and, like N'tala, she crashed into a heap on the dusty red earth.

Consciousness returned slowly, and uncomfortably. Pounding pain and a jerking motion jarring into Elizabeth's belly and breasts brought her round, and she realised she was being carried over the shoulder of one of their attackers. The pounding in her head and abdomen was because the whole group was trotting along the track in double file, heading towards the rising pillar of smoke that N'gozhi had seen before being struck down by the raiding party.

Elizabeth's arms had been tied in front of her so her fingers hovered above the ground as she bounced on the warrior's back. A sideways glance showed N'tala being carried in the same way. The raiding party consisted of about twenty men, all tall and muscled with short hair. Most had raised scars on their chests and arms as well as stripes of coloured clay daubed across their chests and faces.

There was some brief chatter as they discovered Elizabeth was conscious, but all they did was increase the pace so that the jostling became worse. The ride was intensely uncomfortable as her breasts ground against her captor's back and every breath was snatched from her lungs by the hard shoulder she was slung across. At last they entered a clearing, there was a shouted order, the men halted and the two bound and helpless figures were dumped onto the dusty ground.

Dazed but thankful just to be able to catch her breath, Elizabeth struggled up until she was kneeling on all fours, and from the corner of her eye she saw N'tala struggling into the same position.

Before she could do anything else, she saw that N'tala had pushed her hands even further forward and was pressing her face into the dirt in some kind of sign of respect. Elizabeth looked up to see a group of four men towering above her. All were powerfully built but, unlike the warriors, each wore a short cape of animal skin and two of them had beads, necklaces and ornaments around their necks, waists and arms. Elizabeth shuddered in terror at the sight of the bones and teeth comprising the grim trinkets; there were also nameless pieces of wrinkled skin and leather pouches dangling from their beaded belts. They both held a thin wand about four feet long in one hand, and a thin switch in the other. The other two, younger and without the awful ornaments, carried vicious clubs set with sharp white spikes.

One of the leaders barked a command and Elizabeth screamed as a warrior struck her across her bottom with the shaft of his spear. A second vicious stroke followed, with unspoken commands for Elizabeth to adopt the same position as N'tala. Dreading a third stroke across her tender rump she quickly bowed forward, pressing her cheek against the warm, red earth.

Some kind of heated exchange went on between the four leaders before both girls were pulled to their feet, and the two older men wearing the dismal decorations walked to them. The ties around their wrists were cut and their arms held, then suddenly twisted up and back against the joint, forcing the girls up on agonising tiptoe, lifting and offering their breasts towards the two sinister central figures. Then the final indignity came as another warrior sliced away the flimsy coverings from the loins of the two helpless girls.

N'tala was the first to be inspected. Fingers probed and pushed into her mouth and her jaw was held wide so that both the old men - Elizabeth could see now they were both wrinkled with age - could explore her tongues and teeth. Next they inquisitively pinched the firm flesh of her breasts, the taller of the two spitting on his fingers and working a nipple between finger and thumb. He leered as he watched the glistening tip thicken and jut even harder under his manipulations. The others gathered round more closely, a keen interest in their eyes as he twisted the tender peak so that N'tala squirmed against the guards' hold. Tiring of his game, he flicked the swollen teat and reached into her groin with those same wet fingers.

Elizabeth could see N'tala was squeezing her thighs together, crossing her legs to deny him access as he snapped at her. Barking a command at the two guards he took a step back, then lifting the grey switch he slashed it hard across her breasts. She shrieked in pain as Elizabeth saw a dark line appear across the polished ebony flesh.

Another slashing cut and this time N'tala danced in agony, her face raised to the hot blue sky as the vicious implement cut across both nipples. The guards struggled to hold N'tala still for the whipping to continue, but the old man smiled as he waited for her to settle. He did not whip her again immediately. First, he ran one fingertip along the second of the two weals, making N'tala wriggle and squeal as his nail agitated the line of pain. Then, sniggering at her reaction, he stepped back so he could bring a third slicing cut across those tensely quivering globes.

With N'tala dancing from toe to toe in agony, the guards dragged her legs apart and held her wide by brute force. The evil, wizened figure probed and fondled her prominent labia. Her twists and cries of protest continued as his fingers worked deeper, but a few minutes more and the girl's cries began to change and the witchdoctor cackled, talking excitedly with the others as they watched the way she was beginning to thrust her hips onto the expert fingers buried deep in her vagina.

The steady masturbation continued until N'tala was on the brink of coming. Immediately he pulled his fingers from her, leaving her whimpering and jerking in frustration. He sniffed his fingers, now glistening and coated with the juices of her body, holding them out so all could see the evidence of her arousal. Then another swift order and she was hustled to one side.

Their inspection of Elizabeth's mouth was almost perfunctory, as they all wanted to touch and feel her long blonde hair. One of them scrabbled at her scalp to see if the colour was the same throughout.

The witchdoctor took his time running his nails over the smooth curves of each breast. They seemed transfixed as each white line changed to deeper pink. His nails scraped more heavily, covering her breasts in shallow scratches. The torment continued and Elizabeth bit her lip as her nipples became firmer despite her terror and the threat of the tribesmen gathered around her.

'No, please no,' she pleaded. 'Leave me alone.'

The scratching stopped and his fingers, now held like fleshy pincers, reached out to grip both nipples, and her shameful gasp was more pleasure than pain as he rolled the peaks as he had done to N'tala.

'I won't let you touch me,' she told the man determinedly, clenching her thighs together, but the guards were ready for her. She felt her arms being wrenched back even further, then agony as the thin switch cut a line along the tender undersides of her breasts. Another line scored parallel to the first as she screamed and struggled in the grip of the two strong guards.

There was a pause, Elizabeth fought to catch her breath then cried out as she was arched back even further, thrusting the delicate tips of her breasts towards the four leaders in front of her.

Thwick!

The switch sliced a thin line of fire right across her nipples, the pink nubs compressing under the impact. Elizabeth almost fainted as her shrieks filled the clearing, and she didn't even feel the calloused feet of the guards forcing her into a wide stance; all she could deal with was the scalding pain across her breasts and the throbbing in her nipples.

She ignored the fingers parting her sex lips but, as the witchdoctor knew, they were gradually tormenting her body, the scalding pain in her breasts seeming to stoke another fire deep inside her body. Elizabeth knew she was becoming wetter, and she could feel herself being opened wider as first one, then two, then three fingers slid deep into her vagina.

'Oh no, I don't want to, please... oh yes, go on,' she babbled, bending her knees and thrusting her hips desperate to try and sink those crafty fingers even further inside. Laughing in evil delight at his skill, the elderly man again pulled his hand away and displayed the gleaming wetness on his fingers to the others. All jabbered enthusiastically as Elizabeth tried to bring herself to the peak she needed.

The two witchdoctors consulted in low voices and then said something to the others. Immediately both girls were dragged off to a small compound surrounded by a thorn fence. Their hands were bound and their legs hobbled with a length of rawhide so they could only take short steps. Finally strong leather collars were buckled loosely around their necks. They were dark with use and age, and one of the guards had another three tucked into his waist belt, ready for use if needed. Once secured they were both pushed through the gap in the encircling fence and more thorn bushes were moved across to close it.

Clinging to each other and trying to ignore the stinging pain in their breasts, the two girls studied the five or six girls already inside. N'tala threw herself at one of them and began to hug her as best she could with her wrists bound. The others gathered around Elizabeth, gabbling and touching her hair. Then unexpectedly, one of them said, 'Ingleesh?'

Elizabeth almost collapsed in shock. 'Who said that?' she gasped. 'Are you English too? I got into trouble at sea. What's happening? Why are we here?'

A petite girl with long black hair and copper-coloured skin moved forward. Elizabeth saw that she, like all of them, was quite naked apart from the hobble and the leather collar. Her pert breasts were unmarked but, as she moved, Elizabeth saw the remains of many stripes crisscrossing her buttocks.

'I am Amana,' she said shyly. 'I have little English, but what the mission fathers taught me. They were pale, like you.'

'Oh, thank God,' Elizabeth sighed. 'But why are we here, what are they going to do with us?'

'This is the Mamaweyo's doing.' Amana saw Elizabeth's baffled look. 'Mamaweyo, the Lion of Asane, the ruler of this land. This village was burned because the headman did not send the tribute he demanded. The king's warriors and the Seekers of the Dead came and killed them. Those two,' she nodded to where N'tala and another girl were talking quietly, 'will go to the king.' She paused and looked at the females in the little compound. 'We are from other villages they have visited, all of us chosen for king's pleasure.' She looked at Elizabeth curiously. 'Did the Seekers not test your body?'

Elizabeth shuddered at the memory of the mauling fingers, then turned so that the dying sunlight threw the three parallel weals across her breasts into sharp relief. 'I did not do as they wanted, so one of them did this...'

'That is Watanga, chief among the Seekers. Fear him and keep from his sight if you can.' She moved a little so Elizabeth could see the lines striping her bottom. 'I too fought when they took me, but what use my feeble strength against Mamaweyo's warriors?' She shivered. 'If stories they tell are true, these marks are nothing to what happen when we see the king. But what of you, why you here?'

Elizabeth told her story as simply as she could, even though such things as ships and cities were outside Amana's experience. The African night fell swiftly as she talked and eventually the girls fell into an uneasy sleep. Elizabeth kept waking as roars and grunting calls broke the stillness, and occasionally, on the side of the compound away from the guard fire of the warriors, there was movement in the dry grass as though something large but unseen was prowling in the darkness.

Elizabeth huddled closer to Amana, trying not to think about the morning.

CHAPTER 21
Tribute for the King

Shouts and the scrape of the thorn bushes being dragged away woke them at dawn. Herded outside they stood, blinking and stretching, as the raiding band prepared to move off. Unceremoniously pushed into a line, each girl's ankle hobble was removed and a short tether fastened from a loop at the back of the neck collar down to the bound hands of the girl behind. The whole line had to move as one or everyone risked being choked or tripped as the ropes dragged and pulled at the stiff collars.

With shouted commands from the Seekers, accompanied by a rain of blows from their canes, the line moved off up the trail, away from the burned village and the coast on which Elizabeth had been cast ashore. For everyone the first hour was the worst as the line jerked and stumbled while the two new slaves got the rhythm of the march established.

Once everyone was settled the pace increased and, to Elizabeth's amazement, some of the girl's began to sing a kind of low chant. She was even more surprised when some of the guards joined in but quickly discovered that the chanting actually helped keep everyone in rhythmic step. Softly, she began to mimic the sounds she was hearing as they moved at a gentle trot through the unending grasslands.

This became the pattern of the next few days. Early starts and regular pauses for meals and personal needs, but always the pounding pace as the group headed back to the king's kraal. Elizabeth rapidly learned that she had to keep iron control of her own body, for there was no chance for a break or a rest at any other time. One early lesson of the penalty for disobedience was warning enough.

It came when one of the other girls, who had drunk too much at the last halt, tried to pause to relieve herself. Immediately the line was broken and she was held spread-eagled on the ground while the older of the Seekers, the one who Amana had called Watanga, slowly and carefully thrashed her bottom with his switch. By the tenth stroke the girl's buttocks were laced with thin welts and she was struggling against the four men holding her down. Completely ignoring the anguished wails, Watanga gave her ten further strokes before she was released, and Elizabeth saw the damp patch on the ground where she had wet herself during the pain of the whipping.

All the other girls had been forced to watch, and afterwards Watanga walked slowly along the line, gently waving the grey switch close to their faces. The lesson completed, the sobbing girl was forced back into the line, the ropes refastened and the coffle of slave girls moved off once again.

Elizabeth's whole world was confined to the yellow walls of the tall grass and the jiggling buttocks and sweat-beaded back of the girl in front of her.

The eighth day brought a change in the routine. Throughout the morning they had been passing small compounds and groups of huts, the track steadily widening until it was now a wide road of beaten earth. Elizabeth noticed small groups of people standing aside, partly turned away from them as the raiding party trotted past; ordinary people making sure they did not impede the progress of Mamaweyo's guards. For the first time the midday halt was ignored and the party trotted on until they turned into a very large compound on the edge of the track. Among the huts and store sheds there was a stone-lined pool fed by a small stream. The line of girls staggered to a halt while the guards walked along removing everyone's bonds, but leaving the leather collars in place.

More orders were shouted, and Amana whispered, 'They want us to bathe and clean ourselves. They wish to make show as we enter king's kraal.'

Taking the hint, Elizabeth joined the others in the clear fresh water, revelling in the chance to get the caking dust from her body, and to remove the worst of the tangles and grime from her hair. As she enjoyed the refreshing experience she noticed how the journey had firmed and defined her body. Her skin had tanned to a deep gold and her figure was now much more clearly defined, especially the toned muscles of her legs. She was also aware that the sculpting of her body made her breasts even fuller and firmer.

Another shouted order brought them all out of the water, bodies glistening with clear droplets, and for the first time Elizabeth realised just how beautiful the other girls were in their different ways. Clearly the raiding party had not only been carrying out the king's vengeance, they had also been selecting new stock for his pleasure. Elizabeth shivered, feeling the stirrings of fresh fear as she wondered what form that pleasure might take.

N'tala and Amana solved the problem of her tangled hair. A piece of thorn twig served as a rudimentary comb and with that her long blonde hair was rapidly restored to relative glossy order. Elizabeth ruefully noticed that the sun had taken its toll there as well, the deep golden hues now bleached almost white in places.

Two of the guards ordered some of the girls to hand round small containers of palm oil. The rest began to smooth it into their newly washed skin, helping each other to ensure that no part of their bodies was left without a moisturising coating. Elizabeth followed the actions of the others, revelling in the sensuous feel of her oily hands slithering across her revitalised flesh.

Their gentle reverie was interrupted by more shouted commands, and the girls jostled quickly back into a line. With guards around them once more, and the Seekers leading the way, the whole party trotted onto the road again. To their delight they were left unbound, and for the first time Elizabeth was able to move freely without the neck trace hobbling her stride.

The journey was only a few miles and gradually she started to make out the white walls and roofs of what looked like a small city. Getting closer they crossed a stone bridge, the road surface changing to stone blocks as they approached the high mud walls, glaring in the afternoon sun. Crowds thronged round them but, for all the chatter and excitement, the party was again given a respectfully wide passage. The road cleared before them, leading to huge wooden gates.

Their eyes accustomed to the bright daylight, Elizabeth and the others found it difficult to see in the sudden darkness as they trotted under the gateway arch, before emerging into a noisy maze of streets and alleyways. Trotting deeper and deeper into the city, the column eventually arrived in an open space in front of a second wall, also pierced by a high gateway. The square was filled with people, all of whom seemed to be concentrating on a platform on one side of it. The Seekers began calling out, using their switches to clear a path through the crowd so the group could reach the second gateway. The throng moved reluctantly aside and as they passed, the girls looked up to see what was happening on the high wooden platform beside them.

Two solid uprights of aged dark wood, each about ten feet high and set about six feet apart, rose from the platform. Heavy iron staples were driven into the wood at intervals and an equally solid crossbar joined the two stout posts at the top. Like the posts, the crossbar was studded with more of the heavy iron staples, the purpose of which was clear from the position of the heavily muscled figure splayed between them. The young man's ankles were stretched wide, lashed to the staples at the base of each pillar. His bound hands had been dragged above his head and his whole body held in an inverted 'Y' by the rope leading from his wrists to the central metal loop on the crossbar.

He was completely naked, his long penis curving downwards, the heavy sac of his testicles swaying gently against his thighs as he writhed in his bonds.

Guards and officials were standing quietly at the back of the platform, but like all the others, Elizabeth only had eyes for the large figure in a white loincloth standing behind the pinioned man.

Amana had been listening to comments from the watching masses, and whispered in Elizabeth's ear. 'This the justice of the king,' she said carefully. 'That man raise his fist to one of the Seekers. Now he being flogged as punishment.'

'Are they going to kill him?'

'No, he receive fifty strokes and be left hanging there till dawn.'

Just as they got to the platform the huge figure of the torturer raised his long black whip and sent the tail cutting across the man's back with a flat *thwack!* The punishment had obviously been going on for some time, because the man was biting his lip to keep silent, his back and buttocks already laced with crimson. Elizabeth could see his clenched teeth and staring eyes as his body jerked under the searing agony of the cut.

Forced to move on, they heard another *thwack!* and caught the reflex jerk of his hips. Amana, looking back, said calmly, 'He will be screaming in ten strokes more. That whip is elephant hide. His back be raw by end of punishment.'

'But that could kill him,' Elizabeth said, her stomach churning with revulsion. 'You said the king was being merciful.' She whitened, hearing another *thwack!* that brought the first agonised groan from the figure on the platform.

'The king did not sentence him to death,' Amana said simply. 'If beating kills him then is matter for the gods. The sentence lighter than he expect for such offence.' Amana seemed completely unmoved by the young man's fate. As they walked into the shadow of the gateway a roar from the crowd greeted the first harrowing scream from him.

The sounds of the baying crowd died away as the gateway opened out into a wide courtyard set with palms and pools of water. The majority of the guards had left them before they entered the palace proper, and now two Seekers began to divide the girls into groups. Most were sent away with the remainder of the guards but Elizabeth, N'tala and Amana were kept to one side. One of the Seekers began to talk quickly to Amana and N'tala. Elizabeth couldn't follow what was going on but he appeared to be giving them instructions. Finally he stopped and Amana began to explain to Elizabeth.

'You be taken to the king because you have skin and hair like the sun,' she explained in her broken English. 'They think he will want you to be one his special women, but I to warn you that you must do your best to please him. N'tala and I also chosen. We go with you to explain ways and customs so you not cause offence to the king.' Amana stopped and looked at the ground. 'Please be very careful, we are in danger every moment. Be specially careful of the king's daughters.'

Before she could explain further the Seekers interrupted with more commands, obviously feeling that Amana had been given enough time. The three girls were hurried along an open corridor, down some steps and through an archway into another part of the palace. Here the walls were plain and the floor laid with small clay tiles. There were more and more guards. Once, when they passed a heavily guarded archway, Amana whispered, 'That leads to women's quarters, forbidden to all but us, the half-men and the king.'

The long corridor turned, ending in another arch, this one ornately decorated and carved. The small group stopped and Elizabeth could see they were at the entrance to a large open hall with a high peaked roof. Stools, cushions and benches were set down against each wall. Small groups stood around chatting quietly, but all eyes were watching the procession, especially the bronzed figure with the golden hair, as they walked slowly across the cool floor of beaten earth. Watanga pointed with his staff of office, giving a barked command as he did so. The two girls immediately fell flat on the floor, and although Elizabeth was slow to react she followed their lead as soon as she realised what was happening.

One of the two Seekers of the Dead crawled up to the low dais at the end of the room and, still looking at the floor, began to speak. Elizabeth, peeking with one eye, got her first sight of Mamaweyo, King of Asane, Lord of the Endless Grass and Ruler of the Sky.

The king was a vast figure. His oiled and bloated body was clad in a gold-embroidered loincloth, a single leopard skin draped over his back, the head resting, teeth bared, across his right shoulder. Necklaces of animal teeth and gold set with coloured stones hung around his neck. In his right hand he held a spear with a golden blade, while his left clutched a clay drinking bowl. His throne was a wide stool of black wood, inlaid with silver and covered with two lion skins. The backrest was formed from two enormous elephant tusks that curved up to form a narrow arch behind him.

Watanga finished speaking and used his staff to wave the girls forward. Slowly they shuffled closer, still kneeling. Then there was another barked command and Amana whispered, 'Stand up... but keep eyes on floor.'

CHAPTER 22
In the Hands of Mamaweyo's Daughters

The three of them stood naked before the king.

Elizabeth saw that Mamaweyo was not alone. Curled at his feet were two young women, both had smooth, light brown skin that was almost matt in texture. They were full figured; with heavy breasts and a languorous expression as though they had just awoken, or were sated from making love. They were almost naked, apart from silver bangles at wrists and ankles and a silver cord around the waist holding a tiny triangle of beaded cloth over their sex. Both girls looked up at the king, stretched and studied the three prisoners with an unhealthy intensity. The king must have given them some signal because they slid off the platform and slowly began to prowl round the three captives. There was an air of increasing menace as the girls circled them, Elizabeth knew without any explanation that these two sinister figures were the daughters Amana had warned about.

They stopped their stealthy pacing behind N'tala, and then standing close on either side, they edged her forward until she was right in front of the dais. Elizabeth's breathing deepened as they ran their hands over her muscular body, posing her in a number of different positions so they could tease any area of her flesh. Her breasts were stroked for long moments before each girl gently took a nipple in her mouth, licking and sucking on the nubs until they stood out like pegs from the broad aureoles. Satisfied with her involuntary reaction, the daughters cupped the swollen peaks, offering them to the king. He nodded inscrutably.

N'tala's legs were parted, the lips of her sex held open for his inspection. Fingers probed deep inside her and, once again, the evidence of her quick arousal was offered to him. Then N'tala was turned and bent over so that her buttocks could be spread while one of the girls carefully sank first one, then two fingers into her anus before gently working them to and fro. Not to be outdone, the other girl reached below her companion so she could continue to tease the girl's labia, sliding her own fingers into the slick depths of N'tala's vagina. The double invasion was too much for N'tala to resist. She began to gasp and tremble in response. Elizabeth could see the girls knew exactly what they were doing and were finding their own pleasure in tormenting their new victim, moaning and panting between them.

They exchanged a few quick words before posing her before the king. Pressure on her shoulders and urging hands on her thighs positioned the girl until she was kneeling upright with her knees parted. He leaned forward, watching every movement as his two tormentors worked another quarry to a peak of pleasure for his entertainment. With the girl positioned as they wanted, one of the daughters stood close behind N'tala and very gently pulled her hands above her head, straightening her arms so that her breasts lifted, their peaks pointed towards the king. With N'tala held wide and open, the other girl crouched down, sucking her erect nipples once again.

After only a few more minutes N'tala was panting and beginning to move her hips uncontrollably, the girl on the floor fondling her open sex. The steady thrusting movements became harder as the girl urged N'tala towards her climax.

The second daughter then led Amana to stand before the throne. Like Elizabeth, Amana was already aroused and transfixed by the erotic display being forced from N'tala. The second of the king's daughters stood close behind her and nudged her feet apart until Amana was standing in a wide straddle. Then she fondled Amana's rigid nipples, while her other gently closed around the plump lips of her sex. Amana, fully aware that she too was going to be forced to a climax for the king's benefit, moved her hands back so she could stroke the shaven mound of the girl masturbating her with expert fingers.

The first daughter was relentlessly pushing N'tala to even greater peaks of pleasure when her sibling slipped a wet finger into the deep slot of Amana's cunt, and began to swirl it round the slick button of her clitoris. The sister on the floor, hearing the first gasping cries from Amana, looked up and once more smiled conspiratorially at her partner, licking her lips as she did.

Working together, the two timed their efforts so that the cries mingled, helping to build the passion in each of the girls being tormented by their skilful manipulations.

A sudden flurry of pounding thrusts was enough to send N'tala into a shaking orgasm as she cried, jerking on the fingers impaling her so deeply, and her cries encouraged the movements of the second daughter; her strumming masturbation soon bringing Amana to a similar release.

Both the captives were simply left to collapse on the floor in front of the throne. The two sisters pressed against each other, smiling in satisfaction. They exchanged a long kiss, looked at the king, then down at the two young women lying on the floor.

Then they turned, and like stalking cats, padded softly to where Elizabeth was standing alone. Close to, she could smell the sharp tang and sexual odour of their bodies and see the sheen of sweat on their dark skin. She shivered, knowing instinctively that the show had been for her arousal, and the king's daughters were now intent on wringing a similar response from her own trembling body.

Their full breasts swayed as they circled closely around her. Elizabeth felt the peaks of their nipples brushing her each time they pressed closer. Then hands held her and she was urged forward until she stood before the throne.

This time Elizabeth's golden hair was the first thing to be reverently stroked. She was bent forward from the waist and she smelt a scent of oil and the tang of male excitement as the king's fingers combed her golden strands. After what seemed like an age she was eased upright again, and fingers moved her hands behind her back so the two daughters could concentrate on her proud breasts.

Elizabeth shivered in delight as oiled fingers squeezed the tender globes, gradually working up until each girl was using one hand to cup the soft weight while her fingers milked and rolled the sensitive tip. She gasped, lost in the pleasure of her tormentors' hands.

In the grip of such intense stimulation she reached blindly for the girls' breasts, repaying each teasing stimulus in kind. She could feel their nipples hardening at her touch, excited in turn as they increased their efforts in response.

It was the girls who broke away first, anxious to move on to their intended target and not letting Elizabeth distract them from their goal. Unlike N'tala, Elizabeth was to be left standing, although her feet were pushed as wide apart as she could manage. By now she was grateful to put her arms around the shoulders of the girl on either side to hold herself upright. She trembled, feeling the lips of her sex being parted so that the king was able to see the soft inner folds. Clever fingers slowly began to tease across the sensitive flesh and she could feel herself becoming wetter and wetter as they toyed with her.

One raised her fingers to Elizabeth's mouth, and knowing what was wanted - and what she now wanted so badly - the blonde began to suck them, tasting the tang of N'tala's juices whilst helping to prepare them to be thrust into her own body.

The other girl continued to explore her body, concentrating on Elizabeth's anus and using her fingers to tease into the dark rosette.

Her sister removed her wet fingers from Elizabeth's mouth and sank to her knees, twisting her fingers into the succulent opening of Elizabeth's vagina. She worked her hand deeper and deeper, listening to the rising moans from the young blonde at the new stretching fullness in her cunt. Suddenly Elizabeth wailed, her mouth wide in astonishment at the rush of feeling as the heel of the girl's hand slipped through the opening of her body, the mouth of her vagina closing like a velvet vice on the slim wrist. With her captive fully impaled, the girl slowly moved her arm, her fingers stroking the delicate flesh deep inside Elizabeth's body.

'Oh yes, that's wonderful, yes, *yes!*' Elizabeth babbled frantically, and not to be outdone, the second daughter slipped one finger deep into her bottom and slowly began to move it in and out, carefully matching the rhythm of her sister's movements.

Elizabeth was near delirium, riding the two hands as earnestly as possible, trying to press herself even deeper onto them. In unison the girls reached up to torment a jutting nipple, increasing the pleasure-flood drowning the young blonde. Her own hands clawed at the girls on either side, her hips writhing in a lewd display of total abandon before the throne.

Mamaweyo was gazing at the show being induced from the white girl by his two favourite tormentors. All round the great hall in the soft dimness, others of the court were also watching, gripped with obvious excitement and anticipation as they heard Elizabeth's cries taking on a stronger note as she stormed towards her orgasm.

'I'm coming...!' she wailed, riding towards the peak of her second climax before she'd even come down from the first.

Far from London and polite society, Elizabeth Ashton entertained the Great Lion of Asane, as she rode the impaling hands of two African girls to a second shattering orgasm in the dim grandeur of the great hall of the king's palace.

CHAPTER 23
The King's Pleasure

All three girls lay on the floor, slowly recovering from the attentions of the king's two tormentors. Watanga, Chief among the Seekers of the Dead, once more knelt before him. A few muttered words and he turned, standing upright and raising his staff of office in a signal to the guards at the back of the hall. Still dazed from the force of her orgasm, Elizabeth was only dimly aware of a group of palace servants, all clad in identical white loincloths, carrying a large object into the open space before the throne. Placing it carefully and always moving so as never to turn their back on the king, the men bowed low before padding silently backwards into the shadows.

Watanga barked another command, bringing Amana and N'tala to their feet immediately, their heads bowed low in respect. He pointed at Elizabeth and the two girls helped the young blonde to her feet. 'The king will take you now, be strong, remember he is only a man,' whispered Amana, as they held the frightened white girl between them, facing the throne of Mamaweyo.

The daughters were once more crouched at his feet, their hands now busy under the leopard skin covering his groin, clever fingers stimulating his genitals.

He smiled at his blonde captive, eyes smouldering with lust, and then said something to the chief Seeker. Watanga bowed and glared at the two native girls, then his staff pointed first to Elizabeth, then at the object placed in the middle of the floor, and Amana and N'tala pulled Elizabeth gently towards the sinister black frame. Their friend might be the centre of attention, but they were expected to control her as the king took his pleasure with the newest addition to his harem.

The frame looked like half a large barrel mounted on four short legs, the dark wood clearly old and immensely strong. Elizabeth shuddered in anticipation of how it might be used as she saw that the end wasn't flat, but hollowed. There was also a rounded ridge on the upper rim, a ridge that flared into a blunt horn on either side. As the girls urged her closer to the curving end, she was able to see there were two more stubby projections, like handles or footrests, jutting from each side.

'You must lie forward, over the top,' Amana said, pushing the blonde into the deep curve of the barrel's end. Elizabeth shivered uncontrollably, suddenly recalling her birching at Helene's hands across that frame with the same kind of rounded pegs jutting from each side. The apparatus was clearly a whipping frame, and they were going to stretch her across it.

'No, I can't,' Elizabeth whispered desperately. 'Please, don't let them hit me. Amana, don't do this to me.'

Amana shook her head, pushing her forward in response to the angry commands from Watanga.

'Help me, please someone, please help me,' wailed Elizabeth, terrified by the memory of the caning her breasts received the last time she'd defied the witchdoctor's orders. But shivering with mounting fear, she knew she had to acquiesce and let the two girls pull her arms forward, stretching her torso over the frame until her toes were only just touching the floor, her hips nestling firmly between the two horn-like projections on the top rim.

The two girls readjusted their hold on her wrists, dragging her arms forward and down, squashing the English girl's breasts and belly hard against the wooden surface.

The king lumbered to his feet, and everyone in the hall sank to their knees, including the two girls holding Elizabeth.

The only two people to remain on their feet were Mamaweyo's daughters, who stepped forward to prepare her further, each girl bending a leg up around the side of the barrel, then without giving her any time to resist, hooking her knees over the stubby projections.

Elizabeth found herself locked against the frame and completely helpless, her buttocks parted so the moist furrow of her sex was exposed. The horns on the barrel rim prevented her hips from moving forward and the stubby projections held her legs immobile because of the natural tension of her body.

The daughters knelt beside Elizabeth's flanks as the king prepared to take his pleasure from his newest possession. Beneath the leopard skin and the heavy curve of his belly, his large penis was now fully erect. Sensing their master was ready, the two girls concentrated on guiding the head of his penis to Elizabeth's vulnerable sex. Once lodged in place they used their fingers to spread her buttocks even wider so he could look down to watch as he slowly impaled the beautiful, quivering blonde on the knotty shaft of his cock.

Her arms still held by her two new friends and the daughters caressing her thighs and buttocks, Elizabeth was panting with a mixture of discomfort and simmering passion as the king thrust in and out of her, and despite her anguish, she felt her body shamefully responding yet again.

Mamaweyo dug his fingers into her tanned hips as he moved faster and faster, intent on his own climax. There was a pause, a bellow of satisfaction, and he arched back in triumph, his shaft embedded to the root in Elizabeth's heaving body. Around the hall murmurs of approval could be heard as the king publicly demonstrated his virility, and

Elizabeth was sobbing helplessly as his ejaculation triggered her own release, leaving her gasping and exhausted, slumped across the cunning apparatus.

The king withdrew his glistening penis and turned away, and supported by his daughters, shuffled back to flop down on his throne. One of the girls knelt between his legs, using her mouth to lick and cleanse his manhood, holding his softening penis gently in her hand as she did so. Completely ignoring the girl's ministrations, the king growled some orders to Watanga.

Obviously annoyed at not being allowed to continue with Elizabeth's sexual humiliation, Watanga signalled for Amana and N'tala to help the drained girl off her uncomfortable perch. They eased her up before unhooking her knees, then acting upon Amana's whispered advice they knelt again before Mamaweyo's throne.

CHAPTER 24
The House of Women

The king, yawning, waved them away, and it was Watanga who hissed instructions at them. Following Amana's lead, they crawled backwards until they were able to stand up at the arched entrance to the hall. Still quivering at some imagined slight, Watanga stalked down the long corridors to the entrance of the women's quarters they'd passed earlier, the girls struggling to keep up. He hammered on the heavy wooden door with his staff, ordering the three inside immediately it opened, and then slammed it shut behind them.

'I am Sosu.'

The girls whirled round to see a tall figure standing in the curtained archway leading from the antechamber they were in. 'Keeper of the Women, I command here and you will obey me in all things.' He was dressed in a flowing white robe with a gold belt and a gold chain of office lying on his broad chest. He also had a slim ivory switch hanging from his belt. 'The king is pleased to take you into the House of Women.'

He studied the girls with a look of distain on his face. 'You were wise enough to provide our king with some small diversion, but be warned; there are other diversions that are not so easily dispensed. The path is narrow. Step to the side and you will find that Mamaweyo's pleasures can be terrible indeed. Now come with me.'

He turned and led them through the arch into an enclosed courtyard, and ominously there was a wooden platform in the centre, smaller and lower than the one outside the palace, but still with a pair of uprights set in the middle. The three females looked apprehensively at it as they passed, but no one said anything.

Through another arch and they found themselves in a series of rooms with sleeping platforms covered in rugs and large cushions. Here they were also met by a crowd of other women and girls, all wearing long skirts or gauze trousers but all naked to the waist. They crowded around the newcomers, chattering like a flock of birds. Sosu shouted a single command and silence fell.

'Take notice of what I say,' Sosu announced. 'Here you see Amana, N'tala and Elitbet.' Elizabeth recognised the mangling of her name. 'They are favoured by the king. He has taken Elitbet for his own this afternoon.' From the gasps, Elizabeth was aware that these women thought she had been highly honoured by the king's attentions.

Sosu looked at two of them. 'N'shema, N'zosa,' he said, 'see that your new guests have somewhere to sleep tonight. Tomorrow you will see they are cleansed and prepared as is proper. You will bring them to me by the rest time.'

The selected women made deep bows to Sosu as he swept out, and instantly the three newcomers were submerged in a press of bodies. Although they were clearly excited by each of them, it was Elizabeth's colouring that attracted the attention. Her hair was stroked and pulled and she found herself fending off countless inquisitive hands that simply wanted to feel her.

Eventually the girls assigned to look after the three newcomers were able to persuade the others to leave them alone.

Food and drink was provided and the five of them sat in a circle exchanging information. Elizabeth's story took longest because so much had to be explained through Amana and N'tala. In the gaps, whilst awaiting a translation, Elizabeth was able to study their two new companions. N'shema was slim, very dark with long black hair and dark eyes fringed with long black lashes. Her waist was tiny, and although her breasts were quite small her nipples were prominent.

N'zosa was very different. About Amana's height, she was lighter skinned with a sensuously curvy figure and large, full breasts. Elizabeth was also able to see, through the transparent gauze of their loose trousers, that neither of them had any trace of pubic hair and their sex lips were clearly visible.

Amana was obviously attracted to N'zosa, and made sure she sat close beside her. When everyone had relaxed and the first rush of questions and explanations were out of the way, Elizabeth noticed Amana's arm had encircled the slim waist of her new friend.

N'shema was also aware of the closeness of the two girls and, when they finally began to make the sleeping arrangements for the night, she let N'zosa lead Amana away into another area. Seeing Elizabeth looking after them she smiled and beckoned with her forefinger.

With Amana out of the way, the two black girls settled down beside Elizabeth. N'tala had already explained to N'shema how they met. Elizabeth began to relax, and despite her continuing parlous predicaments, she felt an unexpected feeling of companionship and security.

CHAPTER 25
A Lesson for the House of Women

Bright shafts of sunlight woke Elizabeth from a dreamless sleep. Stretching, one hand touched the smoothness of another body. She sat up. N'tala and N'shema were still asleep and curled around each other among the cushions, but the English girl's movements were enough to wake them and they too stretched luxuriously in the warm glow of the rising sun.

N'tala ran one hand down her body, lazily caressing her breasts before stroking the dark shadow in the delta of her thighs, her glance catching Elizabeth watching. She deliberately edged her legs apart then licked one finger and very slowly slid it between her prominent labia, watching Elizabeth's reaction carefully, and seeing the young blonde's immediate flush of excitement and embarrassment, N'tala smiled, making a quiet comment to N'shema who was observing the scene between the two girls.

N'shema pulled N'tala's finger away from her body, and with her eyes firmly fixed on Elizabeth she put it in her own mouth, sucking gently on the fragrant tip. Elizabeth felt herself redden even more, feeling her wetness at such an erotic display. N'tala read the signs correctly, and rolling playfully across the cushions she knelt at Elizabeth's side, her hands gently urging the young blonde's thighs apart.

Leaning back on her elbows, Elizabeth parted her knees so that her sex opened to N'tala's eager gaze. N'tala stroked the open petals, then the tormenting masturbation became more insistent, N'tala smiled at Elizabeth's involuntary little thrusting movements, signalling her growing arousal.

Knowing the blonde was ready to come, N'tala slid two fingers into the warm heat of her vagina. With every delicate movement she waited for the breathless cries and little spasms to tell her that she'd found that special place within her young friend's body, and Elizabeth's mouth opened in a gasp of pleasure as she was caressed to ecstasy.

Impatient at just watching her friend's slow pleasuring of the young blonde, and careful not to disturb her concentration, N'shema edged behind Elizabeth so she could reach round between her straddled thighs to part the oily lips even more. She waited until N'tala's fingers made Elizabeth gasp again in bliss, then used the middle finger of her other hand to flicker gently across the top of the English girl's exposed clitoris.

Between the two of them Elizabeth was lost in a storm of delight, her breath rasping in her throat as she panted and whimpered, tipping over the edge, riding her orgasm in a series of cries and wordless sounds.

Elizabeth opened her eyes and drew a shuddering breath before flopping against N'shema as she slowly recovered. She eased N'tala's fingers from her body and lifted them to her lips. 'Oh, thank you,' she sighed. 'Now it's my turn, I think...'

But any chance of further dalliance was cut short as Amana and N'zosa returned. Something was obviously wrong and a heated discussion took place between the four in their native tongue, Amana trying to bring Elizabeth up-to-date in bursts.

'We must all go to the bathing room... One other girl is to be punished this morning and we are ordered to watch... Sosa has ordered all must be ready by third hour... There be no time if we delay longer.' Elizabeth tried to gather her wits, knowing that any delay from her could bring retribution on them all. Holding N'tala's hand, she got unsteadily to her feet.

The five girls made their way deeper into the complex of rooms until they reached a pool of water fed from a nearby spring. They washed quickly, a deep drumbeat starting to pulse through the building. Elizabeth was then dragged from the water as a small bundle was thrust into her hands. 'Put these on, it is commanded,' Amana told her.

It was a pair of the baggy trousers all the other females wore. Made of the finest and sheerest cotton they were quite transparent, apart from a triangular front panel of heavier cloth, with a simple drawstring at the waist and ankle.

Everyone was moving steadily back into the women's quarters, some still busily tying and tidying their hair as they walked. One of them smiled at Elizabeth, she said something, reached into her waistband and then offered a small length of braid. Elizabeth realised it was to tie her hair back, so she smiled, nodding her head in thanks. She had only just finished pulling her hair into an attractive ponytail when they reached the place they'd passed last night; the ominous platform and low bar set between the wooden posts.

Sosa was standing on the platform, watching the girls gathering silently. Other guards stood motionless by the archway. Edging through the throng Elizabeth stood next to Amana, and they had reached the edge of the platform just as Sosa began haranguing them all in an excitable rant in his native tongue. As the diatribe went on it was obvious he was working himself into an acute pitch of anger and agitation. Elizabeth, unable to understand the words but well able to appreciate the performance, wondered if it was all for show, or whether he would lose control completely. After about ten minutes, apparently in mid-sentence, Sosa stopped abruptly, turned and stepped down from the platform.

'We not worthy to be here, he say,' whispered Amana. 'One of us insulted the king and will be punished. He say we lucky that king is merciful; we all to watch the lesson that be given. He go to bring the guilty one out.'

'What did she do?' Elizabeth asked timorously.

'She caught with one of king's warriors, without permission. He was touching her body. She belong to the king and is one of his special women, so second offence is greater.'

'What's happened to the man?'

'He dead; the guards kill him immediately they discovered.'

Elizabeth saw Sosa returning, and behind him two more guards dragging a young woman by her upper arms. She was completely naked, sweat gleaming on the glossy copper skin, and her breasts swayed as she was pulled unceremoniously up onto the platform.

The guards, holding one of her wrists each, held the girl ready for the punishment to come. A hush fell as two more figures stepped up onto the platform - it was the king's gloating daughters. They circled the girl held between the guards, the silver bangles on their wrists chinking as they prowled, getting closer and closer.

A quiet command from one of the two and the guards pushed the girl forward, pressing her towards the wooden bar, but another sharper command from the same daughter stopped them.

The girl was dragged to the other side of the bar and held again, her buttocks pressing into the smooth wooden rail. The guards kicked her feet apart, spreading her stance until each ankle was against an upright. Then her tormentors knelt, each with a leather thong, each taking her time lashing an ankle to a wooden post.

Sosa swept his eyes across the females crowded before him. This time the words were measured, and Elizabeth saw a mixture of cruel anticipation and shock on the faces around her. With Sosa looking she did not ask Amana to translate.

Sosa held up a little bundle of polished sticks, asking the girl a question. She moaned, lifting her face to the clear blue sky and shaking it desperately from side to side. Sosu repeated the question, jerking the sticks towards her again.

Amana's lips brushed her ear. 'She choose the strength of punishment for herself; the parts of her body defiled by the man's touch will be beaten with ten strokes, then as

108

reminder, she be forced to reach her pleasure. Now she must choose a stick. Each has coloured bands, the number of bands show how many times the punishment be repeated. Once or twice if she lucky, ten or more if not. If she do not choose Mamaweyo's daughters choose for her.'

One hand had been freed for the accused to pull out a stick, and it clattered to the planked floor before anyone could see the coloured bands. Sosu bent, studied it for a moment and then held it up, six blue bands encircling it.

'The choice is made, let it be done.' Sosu turned and left the platform as the guard seized the trembling girl's wrist again, and Elizabeth knew they were going to beat her breasts; going to punish her for someone else's crime. It was so unfair, so barbaric. She shuddered, remembering her own agony on the Seat of Correction all those weeks ago. 'What will they beat her with?' she asked.

'She lucky, the daughters will use an *itmana* - a strap, this long,' she held her hands about two feet apart. 'It hurts, but will not cut the skin, even here,' Amana touched her nipple. 'That the mercy of the king, there are other things they use.' She shuddered. 'They could cut her to pieces if they wish. Even so, it be terrible for her.'

The two guards stretched and arched her torso back, offering the firmness of her breasts, crowned with dark aureoles and nipples, more fully to the cruel and expert attentions of Mamaweyo's daughters.

One of them clapped her hands and another girl appeared, carrying a roll of cloth. Handing it to the daughter she quickly left the scene again, clearly keen to get out of the way. The cloth was shown to the pinioned girl, and then her tormentor gripped the end of the object concealed within the folds, letting the cloth drop to the platform.

There was a collective murmur of anticipation and dread as the onlookers saw the implement of punishment. From Amana's description Elizabeth had been expecting a strap, but this was different. A wooden handle was attached to a flat piece of thick black leather, which was pierced with an intricate pattern of small holes.

Another quiet command and the guards braced the girl again, turning her arms to push her breasts even further forward, ignoring the head shaking of their prisoner.

The punisher swung the leather blade, swatting the girl's breasts with a harsh *thwap!* There was a low chorus from the gathered onlookers as they counted the stroke and the girl jerked, feeling the full effects of that first fiery assault.

'The holes make it worse, like little teeth biting,' Amana whispered. 'I know, my father used to beat us with strap like that. She manage first ten, I think,' Amana shook her head, 'but next time they strike the same places again and again.'

Elizabeth shuddered, as she understood the full horror of the girl's punishment. Amana was right, the first ten strokes might be bearable, but then five more sets of ten would be slowly applied to flesh already on fire from the previous strokes. She would never endure it.

Thwap!

The fifth stroke slapped against the underside of the girl's breasts, and the next stroke after that was also swung in from below, the flexible blade curling to swat the tender undersides of each breast, making them quiver with the force of the impact. Each stroke was accompanied by a sobbing wail of pain and the girl was in constant motion, squirming against the hold of the guards.

The unoccupied daughter knelt between the girl's outstretched legs, watching her sister avidly, running her hands up the length of each limb, stroking the rigid muscles, letting her fingers trace the junction of each thigh, probing into the cleft of the girl's buttocks where they pressed against the bar.

Thwap!

The seventh stroke sliced across the lower half of each dark summit, but the wails and the accompanying dance of torment were cut off abruptly as the eighth stroke fell across her nipples, the girl arching even further back, straining uselessly as she voiced her shrill song of agony to the sky.

CHAPTER 26
A Bitter Twist of Fate

The kneeling daughter concentrated on the girl's succulent sex as the whipping reached its inevitable conclusion. As the final two blows whipped across the hard black nipples, she fingered her victim's cunt, pressing and squeezing the delicate tissues, spreading her juices in a glistening coating on her skin.

Her sister placed the leather strap on the platform and ordered the guards to allow the girl to straighten up. Her breasts flushed with an angry hue, the girl writhed to a different kind of stimulation as the expert fingers slithered between her labia, stroking and fondling. But the girl's pleasure was not to be painless, for the second of Mamaweyo's devilish daughters cupped and squeezed the tormented breasts she had cruelly beaten only moments before. The girl writhed and sobbed, and Elizabeth could see sweat dripping from her body as she tried desperately to avoid the unbearable attention to skin already made too tender to touch by the hot kiss of the leather tongue.

Feeding off each other's actions, the daughters of Mamaweyo took the girl to the brink of delirium, teasing and stimulating until she lost all control. The kneeling daughter was licking her sex, carefully probing deep into the girl's vagina, clever fingers coaxing forth her victim's explosion of release, and when it came her cries were nothing but a gibbering gabble as she collapsed against the restraining arms of the guards.

An eerie silence fell across the compound, broken only by the girl's rasping breaths. Elizabeth was beginning to appreciate the full horror of the king's punishment, for now the girl faced the same ordeal five more times. But it could have been even worse. What if she'd chosen a stick with ten or more rings on it? Elizabeth shuddered at the thought.

A single wavering sob brought everyone's attention back to the platform. The daughters were changing places and the new tormentor was whispering in the girl's ear. She was using the rounded leather tip of the blade to trace idle circles around the nipple of each breast, watching as the dark nubs roused and thickened at the leather's touch. Then another piteous cry rang out as the girl was braced back again, her breasts again offered to the blazing kiss of the leather tongue.

So close to the front of the platform, Elizabeth could clearly see the constant movement of the girl's breasts as her fearful trembling made them quiver uncontrollably.

Splat!

No warning, no time to prepare; the cruel leather strap landed with a hissing slap across the upper swell of the girl's breasts, striking exactly where the first stroke had kissed her flesh previously.

'She'll never manage another ten, let alone forty,' Elizabeth whispered to Amana.

'She has no choice,' Amana replied. 'Even the pleasuring will become a torment when they play next time with her.' She looked at the ground, speaking furtively. 'Be warned, the daughters and the guards watch all of us. If anyone turn away they will be punished too. They would enjoy it if next victim be you.'

The girl had endured three more strokes when the interruption came. They all became aware that there was the noise of shouting and the clash of metal in the distance. As they listened there was the sharp popping of musket fire, too, and there was a general panic.

The daughters of Mamaweyo stared in alarm, threw down the leather blade and fled from the platform to be followed seconds later by the two guards. In the courtyard the females milled around, no one taking charge, so Elizabeth clambered onto the platform where the sobbing girl had fallen to her knees, crying with frustration because she couldn't free her ankles from their leather ties. Elizabeth grabbed a viciously hooked knife, dropped by one of the guards, which lay a little way from the bar. Two sawing strokes and the leather thongs parted, the girl instantly rolling into a ball, crying, trying to cradle her breasts and soothe the pain of the flogging.

Elizabeth shouted down to Amana. 'Be quick, it's an attack of some kind. Get the others. We must find out what's going on. We could be in more danger from the attackers than from the king. Especially if they see us as the spoils of victory!'

Amana gathered N'tala and N'gozhi, explaining in a torrent what Elizabeth had said. Then the four of them started to force their way through the seething mass of panicking women and guards, following Elizabeth's lead as she ran through the quarters, along the corridors towards the back of the great hall.

Amana stopped, lifting her head and sniffing the air. 'Smoke,' she warned. 'I smell smoke. They have fired the roof to drive us out!' Above the cries and calls of fighting, the girls could now hear the rustling roar as dry grass thatch blazed. Elizabeth scanned the long corridor, searching desperately for a way out.

This time it was N'gozhi who took the lead, winding rapidly through a maze of small rooms, across some open compounds and through ornate hallways until they reached the tall outer wall. Opening the heavy iron gate they found a scene of fury and devastation. Milling hordes of warriors were battling in a bloody melee, and to one side the wooden gates that had guarded the entrance to the palace lay in ruins, while all around women and children wandered in helpless confusion.

Elizabeth grabbed some lengths of cloth from a nearby hut, signalling to the others that they should wrap themselves a little more modestly before any of the attackers found them. Clothed, and at least partially disguised, the four crept through the noise and confusion, their only aim to get clear of the palace so they could stop and think about what to do next.

They were nearly clear of the huts clustered on the edge of the settlement when their luck ran out. A group of men stepped into the red dust of the roadway, spears lowered and shields held ready. The girls turned back, only to find another group now barring the route behind them. There was a shouted command and one of the men thrust his spear in an aggressive, stabbing motion, and the command was repeated. N'tala said something to the others and Amana whispered to Elizabeth. 'He tell us to take robes off.'

The girls complied, knowing they had no chance of sensible resistance. An excited and appreciative babble of conversation rose as the beautiful bodies of the four girls were revealed. Confident and relaxed the men swaggered forward, very much in charge, and Elizabeth felt a growing anger. She had endured and survived so much, and just when they were so nearly free...

She was about to lose her temper spectacularly when a small group of white-robed figures rode up, their horses nervous with the noise and the scent of fresh blood. Long muskets pointed at the girls as the horsemen circled them, then one let the corner of his robe fall away from where it had been masking his face.

'Miss Ashton,' he said, 'I am delighted to see you safe and well after all. I think we have some unfinished business together, don't we?'

Elizabeth froze in shock as she heard the words. Very slowly she raised her eyes, and looked up into the cruel face of Prince Kemal. 'No, not you... it can't be,' she gasped. Blackness and despair enveloped her, and Elizabeth Ashton slumped unconscious onto the red earth.

Thanks for reading!

CHIMERA